The White Lie

The White Lie

William Le Queux

MINT EDITIONS

The White Lie was first published in 1914.

This edition published by Mint Editions 2021.

ISBN 9781513280899 | E-ISBN 9781513285917

Published by Mint Editions®

 MINT
EDITIONS
minteditionbooks.com

Publishing Director: Jennifer Newens
Design & Production: Rachel Lopez Metzger
Project Manager: Micaela Clark
Typesetting: Westchester Publishing Services

Contents

I

Is Mainly Mysterious

A woman—perhaps?"

"Who knows! Poor Dick Harborne was certainly a man of secrets, and of many adventures."

"Well, it certainly is a most mysterious affair. You, my dear Barclay, appear to be the last person to have spoken to him."

"Apparently I was," replied Lieutenant Noel Barclay, of the Naval Flying Corps, a tall, slim, good-looking, clean-shaven man in aviator's garb, and wearing a thick woollen muffler and a brown leather cap with rolls at the ears, as he walked one August afternoon up the village street of Mundesley-on-Sea, in Norfolk, a quaint, old-world street swept by the fresh breeze of the North Sea. "Yesterday I flew over here from Yarmouth to see the cable-laying, and met Dick in the post-office. I hadn't seen him for a couple of years. We were shipmates in the *Antrim* before he retired from the service and went abroad."

"Came into money, I suppose?" remarked his companion, Francis Goring, a long-legged, middle-aged man, who, in a suit of well-worn tweeds, presented the ideal type of the English landowner, as indeed he was—owner of Keswick Hall, a fine place a few miles distant, and a Justice of the Peace for the county of Norfolk.

"No," replied the aviator, unwinding his woollen scarf. "That's just it. I don't think he came into money. He simply retired, and next we heard was that he was living a wandering, adventurous life on the Continent. I ran up against him in town once or twice, and he always seemed amazingly prosperous. Yet there was some sort of a mystery about him—of that I have always felt certain."

"That's interesting," declared the man at his side. "Anything suspicious—eh?"

"Well, I hardly know. Only, one night as I was walking from the Empire along to the Rag, I passed a man very seedy and down-at-heel. He recognised me in an instant, and hurried on towards Piccadilly Circus. It was Dick—of that I'm absolutely convinced. I had a cocktail with him in the club next day, but he never referred to the incident."

"If he had retired from the Navy, then what was his business, do you suppose?"

"Haven't the slightest idea," Barclay replied. "I met him here with a motor-bike late yesterday afternoon. We had a drink together across at the Grand, against the sea, and I left him just after five o'clock. I had the hydroplane out and went up from opposite the coastguard station," he said, pointing to the small, well-kept grass plot on the left, where stood the flagstaff and the white cottages of the coastguard. "He watched me get up, and then, I suppose, he started off on his bike for Norwich. What happened afterwards is entirely shrouded in mystery. He was seen to pass through the market-place of North Walsham, five miles away, and an hour and a quarter later he was found, only three miles farther on, at a lonely spot near the junction of the Norwich road and that leading up to Worstead Station, between Westwick and Fairstead. A carter found him lying in a ditch at the roadside, stabbed in the throat, while his motor-cycle was missing!"

"From the papers this morning it appears that your friend has been about this neighbourhood a good deal of late. For what reason nobody knows. He's been living sometimes at the Royal at Norwich and the King's Head at Beccles for the past month or so, they say."

"He told me so himself. He promised to come over to me at the air-station at Yarmouth to-morrow and lunch with me, poor fellow."

"I wonder what really happened?"

"Ah, I wonder!" remarked the slim, well-set-up, flying officer. "A mere tramp doesn't kill a fellow of Dick Harborne's hard stamp in order to rob him of his cycle."

"No. There's something much more behind the tragedy, without a doubt," declared the local Justice of the Peace. "Let's hope something will come out at the inquest. Personally, I'm inclined to think that it's an act of revenge. Most probably a woman is at the bottom of it."

Barclay shook his head. He did not incline to that opinion.

"I wonder with what motive he cycled so constantly over to this neighbourhood from Norwich or Beccles?" exclaimed Goring. "What could have been the attraction? There must have been one, for this is an out-of-the-world place."

"Your theory is a woman. Mine isn't," declared the lieutenant, bluntly, offering his friend a cigarette and lighting one himself. "No, depend upon it, poor old Dick was a man of mystery. Many strange rumours were afloat concerning him. Yet, after all, he was a real fine fellow, and as smart an officer as ever trod a quarter-deck. He was a splendid linguist, and had fine prospects, for he has an uncle an admiral on the National Defence Committee. Yet he chucked it all and became a cosmopolitan wanderer, and—if there be any truth in the gossip I've heard—an adventurer."

"An outsider—eh?"

"Well—no, not exactly. Dick Harborne was a gentleman, therefore he could never have been an outsider," replied the naval officer quickly. "By adventurer I mean that he led a strange, unconventional life. He was met by men who knew him in all sorts of out-of-the-world corners of Europe, where he spent the greater part of his time idling at *cafés* and in a section of society which was not altogether reputable."

"And you say he was not an adventurer?" remarked the staid British landowner—one of a class perhaps the most conservative and narrow-minded in all the world.

"My dear fellow, travel broadens a man's mind," exclaimed the naval officer. "A man may be a cosmopolitan without being an adventurer. Dick Harborne, though there were so many sinister whispers concerning him, was a gentleman—a shrewd, deep-thinking, patriotic Englishman. And his death is a mystery—one which I intend to solve. I've come over here again to-day to find out what I can."

"Well," exclaimed Goring, "I for one am hardly satisfied with his recent career. While he was in the Navy and afloat—gunnery-lieutenant of one of His Majesty's first-class cruisers—there appears to have been nothing against his personal character. Only after his retirement these curious rumours arose."

"True, and nobody has fathomed the mystery of his late life," admitted Barclay, drawing hard at his cigarette and examining the lighted end. "I've heard of him being seen in Cairo, Assouan, Monte Carlo, Aix, Berlin, Rome—all over the Continent, and in Egypt he seems to have travelled, and with much more means at his disposal than ever he had in the ward-room."

"There are strange mysteries in some men's lives, my dear Barclay. Harborne was a man of secrets without a doubt. Some of those secrets may come out at the inquest."

"I doubt it. Poor Dick!" he sighed. "He's dead—killed by an unknown hand, and his secret, whatever it was, has, I believe, gone to the grave with him. Perhaps, after all, it is best."

"The police are very busy, I understand."

"Oh, of course! The Norfolk Constabulary will be very active over it all, but I somehow have an intuition that the crime was one of no ordinary character. Dick must have dismounted to speak to his assailant. If he had been overthrown his machine would most probably have been damaged. The assassin wanted the motor-cycle intact to get away upon. Besides," he added, "the victim took over an hour to cover the three miles between North Walsham and the spot where he was found. Something unusual must have occurred in that time."

"Well, it can only be left to the police to investigate," replied the tall, country squire, thrusting his hands into his jacket pockets.

"They won't discover much—depend upon it," remarked the naval officer, who, as he strolled at his friend's side, presented the ideal type of the keen, British naval officer. "Dick has been the victim of a very carefully-prepared plot. That is my firm belief. I've been making some inquiries at the Grand Hotel, and learn that Dick came over from Norwich on his motor-cycle at nine o'clock yesterday morning for some purpose, and idled about Mundesley and the neighbourhood all the day. The head-waiter at the hotel knew him, for he had often lunched there. But yesterday he evidently came here with some fixed purpose, for he seemed to be eagerly expecting somebody, and at last, a little before two o'clock, a young lady arrived by the motor-bus from Cromer. They describe her as a neat, dark-haired, good-looking young person, rather well-dressed—and evidently a summer visitor. The pair walked about the village, and then went down to the beach and sat upon deck-chairs to chat. They returned to the hotel at half-past three and had tea together, *tête-à-tête*, in a small sitting-room. The waiter tells me that once, when he went in, suddenly, she was standing up, apparently urging him to act in opposition to his own inclinations. Her attitude, he says, was one of unusual force, it being evident that Dick was very reluctant to give some promise she was endeavouring to extract from him. She left again by the motor-bus for Cromer just after four."

"Ah! There you are! The woman!" exclaimed the owner of Keswick Hall, with a smile. "I thought as much."

"I don't think she had anything to do with the affair," said Barclay. "The police this morning obtained a detailed description of her—just as I have done—and they are now searching for her in Cromer, Runton, and Sheringham, believing her to be staying somewhere along this coast. She was dressed in a pale blue kit of a distinctly seaside cut, so the police are hoping to find her. Perhaps she doesn't yet know of the tragic fate that has befallen poor Dick."

"I wonder who the girl can be? No doubt she'd be able to make a very interesting statement—if they could only discover her."

"I think she left Cromer last night," Noel Barclay suggested to his companion.

"She would, if she were in any way implicated. Perhaps she has already gone!"

"No, I don't agree. I believe she is still in ignorance."

"What, I wonder, was the motive for their meeting here—in this quiet, out-of-the-world little place?" asked Goring. "If he wanted to see her, he might have motored to wherever she was staying, and not have brought her over here in a motor-bus. No, it was a secret meeting—that's my opinion—and, as it was secret, it probably had some connection with the tragedy which afterwards occurred."

The two men were now close to the "Gap," or steep, inclined cart-road which ran down to the sands. On their right, a little way from the road, stood a small, shed-like building where the rocket life-saving apparatus of the Board of Trade was housed. In front, the roadway, and indeed all down the "Gap" and across the sands to where the waves lapped the shore, had been recently opened, for upon the previous day the shore end of the new German telegraph-cable connecting England with Nordeney had been laid. At that moment, while the cable-ship, on its return across the North Sea, was hourly paying out the cable, a German telegraph engineer was seated within the rocket-station, constantly making tests upon the submerged line between the shore and the ship.

Up from the trench beside the rocket-house came the cable— black, coiled, and snake-like, about three inches in thickness—its end disappearing within the small building.

"Been inside to-day?" asked Goring, just as they were passing.

"No. Let's see how they are progressing," the other said; and both turned into the little gate and asked permission to enter where the tests were being made.

Herr Strantz, the German engineer, a dark-haired, round-faced, middle-aged man, came forward, and, recognising the pair as visitors of the previous day, greeted them warmly in rather imperfect English, and bowed them into where, ranged on a long table, the whole length of the left-hand wall, stood a great quantity of mysterious-looking electrical appliances with a tangle of connecting wires, while below the tables stood a row of fully fifty large batteries, such as are used in telegraph work.

On the table, amid that bewildering assortment of queer-looking instruments, all scrupulously clean and highly polished, were two small brass lamps burning behind a long, narrow strip of transparent celluloid whereon was marked a minute gauge. On the edge of the table, before these lamps, was a switch, with black ebonite handle.

As the two Englishmen entered, the German's eyes caught the small, round brass clock and noted that it was time to make the test—every five minutes, night and day, while the cable was in process of completion.

Therefore, without further word to his visitors, he carefully pulled over the long ebonite handle of the switch, and, at the same instant, a tiny spot of bright light showed upon the transparent gauge.

This the engineer examined to see its exact place upon the clearly-defined line, afterwards noting it in his book in cryptic figures, and then carefully switching off again, when the tell-tale light disappeared.

"Well?" asked Barclay. "How are you getting along? Not quite so much excitement in this place as yesterday—eh?"

"No," laughed the engineer. "Der people here never see a shore-end floated to land wiz bojes (buoys) before. Dey have already buried der line in der trench, as you see. Ach! Your English workmen are far smarter than ours, I confess," he added, with a pleasant accent.

"Is it being laid all right?" the airman asked.

"Ja, ja. Very good work. Der weather, he could not be better. We have laid just over one hundert mile in twenty-four hours. Gut—eh?"

As he spoke the Morse-sounder at the end of the green baize-covered table started clicking calling him.

In a moment his expert hand was upon the key, tapping a response.

The ship tapped rapidly, and then the engineer made an enquiry, and received a prompt reply.

Then tapped out the short-long-short-long and short, which meant "finish," when, turning to the pair, he said:

"Dey hope to get it am Ufer (ashore) at daybreak to-morrow. By noon there will be another through line between Berlin and London."

Lieutenant Barclay was silent. A sudden thought crossed his mind. At Bacton, a couple of miles farther down the coast, the two existing cables went out to the German shore. But this additional line would prove of immense value if ever the army of the great War Lord attempted an invasion of our island.

As a well-known naval aviator, and as chief of the whole chain of air-stations along the East Coast, the lieutenant's mind was naturally ever set upon the possibility of projected invasion, and of an adequate defence. That a danger really existed had at last been tardily admitted by the Government, and now with our Navy redistributed and centred in the North Sea, our destroyer-flotillas exercising nightly, and the establishment of the wireless at Felixstowe, Caister, Cleethorpes, Scarborough, and Hunstanton, as well as the construction of naval air-stations, with their aeroplanes and hydroplanes from the Nore up to Cromarty we were at last on the alert for any emergency.

When would *"Der Tag"* ("The Day")—as it was toasted every evening in the military messes of the German Empire—dawn? Aye, when? Who could say?

II

Concerns a Pretty Stranger

A short, puffy, red-faced man in grey flannels went past.

It was Sir Hubert Atherton, of Overstrand—that little place declared to be the richest village in all England—and Francis Goring, recognising him, bade a hurried farewell to his naval friend, and with a hasty word of thanks to the German, went out.

The naval airman and the German were left alone.

Again the round-faced cable engineer pulled over the double-throw switch, examined the tiny point of light upon the gauge, and registered its exact position.

"You remember, Herr Strantz, the gentleman who accompanied me here yesterday," exclaimed Barclay, when the engineer had finished writing up his technical log.

"Certainly. Der gentleman who was a motor-cyclist?"

"Yes. He was found on the road last evening, murdered."

"Zo!" gasped the German, staring at his visitor. "Killed!"

"Yes; stabbed to death fifteen miles from here, and his motor-cycle was missing. It is a mystery."

"Astounding!" exclaimed Herr Strantz. "He took tea mit a lady over at the hotel. I saw them there when I went off duty at half-past three o'clock."

"I know. The police are now searching for that lady."

"Dey will not have much difficulty in finding her, I suppose—hein?" the engineer replied. "I myself know her by sight."

"You know her!" cried the Englishman. "Why, I thought you only arrived here from Germany two days ago. Where have you met her?"

"In Bremen, at the Krone Hotel, about three months ago. She call herself Fräulein Montague, and vos awaiting her mother who vos on her way from New York."

"Did she recognise you?"

"I think not. I never spoke to her in the hotel. She was always a very reserved but very shrewd young lady," replied Herr Otto Strantz, slowly but grammatically. "I was surprised to meet her again."

"Montague!" the airman repeated. "Do you know her Christian name?"

"Jean Montague," was the German's response as he busied himself carefully screwing down one of the terminals of an instrument.

Noel Barclay made a quick note of the name in a tiny memorandum-book which he always carried in his flying-jacket.

He offered the German one of his cigarettes—an excellent brand smoked in most of the ward-rooms of His Majesty's Navy—and then endeavoured to obtain some further information concerning his dead shipmate's visitor.

But Herr Strantz, whose sole attention seemed centred upon the shore-end of the new cable which was so soon to form yet another direct link between Berlin and London, was in ignorance of anything connected with the mysterious young person.

The statement that Harborne—the motor-cyclist who had spoken the German language so well when he had accompanied the pretty young girl the day before to watch the testing—was dead, seemed to cause the cable-engineer considerable reflection. He said nothing, but a close observer would have noticed that the report of the murder had had a distinct effect upon him. He was in possession of some fact, and this, as a stranger on that coast, and a foreigner to boot, it was not, after all, very difficult to hide.

Noel, however, did not notice it. His mind was chiefly occupied in considering the best and most diplomatic means by which the missing lady, who lived in Bremen as Miss Montague, could be traced.

The two men smoked their cigarettes; Strantz pulling over the switch every five minutes—always to the very tick of the round brass clock—examining the tiny point of light which resulted, and carefully registering the exact amount of current and the position of the ship engaged in paying out the black, insulated line into the bed of the German Ocean.

While Noel watched he also wondered whether, in the near future, that very cable across the sea would be used by England's enemy for the purposes of her destruction. True, we had our new wireless stations all along the coast, and at other places inland at Ipswich, Chelmsford, and elsewhere, yet if what was feared really came to pass, all those, together with the shore-ends of the cables, would be seized by advance parties of Germans already upon British soil—picked men, soldiers all, who were already living to-day in readiness upon the East Coast of England as hotel-servants, clerks or workers in other trades. Our shrewd, business-like friends across the grey, misty sea would take care to strike a blow on our shores by the wrecking of bridges, the disabling of railways, the destruction of telegraphs, and the like, simultaneous with their frantic dash upon our shore. Germany never does anything by halves, nor does she leave anything to chance.

Herr Strantz, having finished some calculations, and having tapped out a message to the ship, raised his head, and with a smile upon his broad, clean-shaven face, said, with his broad German accent:

"Ech! You are an officer. I suppose that, if the truth were told, England hardly welcomes another cable laid by Germany—hein?"

"Well," laughed the airman, pushing his big, round goggles higher upon his brow, "we sometimes wonder when your people are really coming."

"Who knows?" asked the other, smiling and elevating his shoulders. "Never—perhaps."

"Ah! Many there are in England who still regard invasion by the Kaiser's army as a bogey," Noel Barclay remarked. "But surely it is not impossible, or why should the British authorities suddenly awaken to the peril of the air?"

"All is possible to Germany—when the time is ripe. That is my private opinion as a Deutscher, and as one who has an opportunity of observing," the other frankly responded.

"I quite agree," was Noel's reply. "Dreams of ten years ago are to-day accomplished facts. Aeroplanes cross the Channel and the Alps, and fly from country to country in disregard of diplomatic frontiers, while your German airships—unfortunate as they may be—have actually crossed to us here, and returned without us being any the wiser. Had they been hostile they could have destroyed whole cities in a single night!"

"And your ever-watchful coastguards who actually saw them were disbelieved," the German laughed.

"Yes. I admit the air is conquered by your people—and Great Britain is now no longer an island. Wireless messages can be transmitted five thousand miles to-day, and who knows that it may not be possible to-morrow, by directing similar electric rays, to blow up explosives wherever they may be concealed—in the magazines of battleships or in land forts?"

"Ach, yes!" agreed the engineer. "Ten years ago war between England and Germany was more improbable than it is to-day, for each day, I fear, brings us nearer to hostilities—which we, in Germany, know to be inevitable."

WILLIAM LE QUEUX

"And when that day dawns we shall have to exert every force, every nerve, every muscle, if we are to repel you," remarked Noel, his clear-cut face unusually dark and serious.

"I fear that you will, sir," was the other's quiet response. "Individually we want to be friends mit England, but you, as a British officer, know quite well that one day the powder magazine will explode and there must be der war. It will be forced suddenly and swiftly upon the Kaiser and upon the people."

"Yes," sighed the naval airman. "So all we can now do is to remain good friends as long as ever we can—eh? Forewarned is forearmed."

"Exactly; but," added the German, "I trust the openness of my remarks has given you no offence, sir. If it has, then I beg you to accept my most sincere apologies. You are an officer and serve your country. I, too, am an officer of reserve and serve mine."

"Surely no apologies are needed, my dear Herr Strantz," laughed the lieutenant, extending his hand frankly. "We have both exchanged our opinions. In most I agree with you, although, of course, I naturally believe in England's invincible power on the sea."

"That is but natural, my dear lieutenant. You are English," was the engineer's response, and while he turned again to pull over the testing-switch and bent to examine the point of light, Noel was puzzled as to his exact meaning.

Presently Noel Barclay, shaking Herr Strantz's hand, humorously expressed a hope that they might never find themselves enemies, and that the cable might be successfully completed and inaugurated on the morrow; strode out into the village street, and down the "Gap" to that wide expanse of golden sands where a big Post Office gang were busily at work covering up the long black cable lying in its trench.

The engineer of the General Post Office who was in charge, recognising the airman, wished him good afternoon; but his thoughts were centred upon the mysterious death of the man about whom so many queer rumours had been afloat.

Rumours! Ah, how well he recollected one of them—a rumour that had gone around the Service—namely that he had retired with the money earned by selling to a foreign power a certain secret concerning "plotting." For that reason, it was said, he had lived so constantly abroad. Though the offence had never been brought home to him by the Admiralty, yet the rumour had never been contradicted. Mud thrown, alas! always sticks.

Was it true, or was it a lie? his friend was wondering, as he stood looking out upon that calm blue summer sea, bathed in the warm light of that August afternoon, the sea in the deep bed of which lay the new link connecting Berlin with London.

What could Dick Harborne have been doing, motoring so constantly about that rural, out-of-the-world corner of England, that delightful little strip of the open Norfolk coast so aptly termed Poppyland? That he was not there as a summer visitor was quite certain. He had his headquarters in Norwich, twenty miles away, and his constant journeys over the roads between the Norfolk capital and the sea were certainly not without some definite motive.

That Strantz should have recognised Harborne's fair companion was also remarkable. What could she have been doing in Bremen? he wondered.

Noel Barclay looked around him anxiously. The wind, which had risen for the past couple of hours while he had been in Mundesley, was now dropping. With the sunset he would have a nice flight back to the hangars standing on the shore beyond Yarmouth. The "old bus," as the fine Bleriot monoplane was affectionately termed by the four flying-officers at the air station, had been running like a clock. Indeed he had flown her from Eastchurch two days previously, and intended, on the morrow, to make a flight to inspect the station up at Scarborough.

He lit another cigarette and sat down upon a boat to think, the white surf rolling almost to his feet.

During the time the naval aviator had been watching the testing of the cable, a tall, broad-shouldered, well-dressed, clean-shaven, broad-browed young man in a drab tweed golf suit and cap, a man whose great, dark, deep-set eyes wore a keen, intense look, and whose countenance was one which once seen would be easily remembered, lounged into the Old Ship Hotel. He was accompanied by a pretty, dark-haired girl in a summer gown of cream serge and wearing a neat little hat of pale blue silk. The girl's skirt displayed small, well-shaped ankles, yet her shoes were stout and serviceable, and there was a cheapness about her dress and an independent air which stamped her as a girl accustomed to earn her own living.

Both were foreigners—French, apparently, for they spoke that language together. His clothes were English, evidently from a smart tailor, and he wore them with that easy nonchalance of the English golfer, while his pretty, dark-eyed companion, although her gown was of cheap material, it was nevertheless cut well, and both in figure and in gait she had all the *chic* of the true Parisienne.

"Yes, dearest," the young man exclaimed in French, as he rose and looked out into the village street, "this is a very interesting little place, I believe. We will have a stroll along the *plage* and see it after our tea. How quiet, how charming it is, after London—eh?"

"Ah! I always love the country, Ralph," was her reply in English, and as she sat composedly in her chair, after walking from Overstrand, where they had been to see that lonely, crumbling old church tower which the late Clement Scott has called "the Garden of Sleep," she gave him a look which was unmistakable—a look of true, passionate affection.

Indeed, upon her finger, now that she had removed her glove, was a diamond engagement ring, an ornament which meant so very much to her—as it does to all girls in all stations of life who are beloved.

The man turned from the window, his big, deep-set eyes upon her, and, bending, kissed her fondly. But the expression upon his hard, aquiline face as he turned away was a strange, unusual one, though, perhaps unfortunately for her, she was unable to see it. The look was not one of love—nay, rather of world-weariness and of deep anxiety.

"I wish my holiday was not yet at an end, Ralph," she sighed, wistfully, after a brief pause. "But father is inexorable, and says he must get back to business, while, as you know, I am due back at the Maison Collette on Monday morning. I've already had three days longer than the other girls—three delightful sunny days."

"Yes," sighed the young man. "I suppose, dearest, you will be compelled to go back for a time to your *modes* and your hat-making and your workroom friends. But only until November—until you become my wife." He spoke English with only a slight trace of accent.

"Ah! What supreme happiness!" cried the girl, in ecstasy, again speaking in French, as he bent until his lips touched hers. "I will remain patient, Ralph, till then, even though all the girls may envy me. They are all English, and just because I happen to be French, they are never too friendly."

The young man was silent for a few moments; then he sprang from her side as the waiter entered with the tea.

After he had swallowed a cup of tea he suddenly exclaimed in perfect French:

"Ah! I quite forgot, dearest. I wonder if you would excuse me if I leave you here for ten minutes or so? I want to send a telegram."

"*Certainement*," she laughed happily. "I shall be quite all right, Ralph. There are papers here to amuse me."

"Very well," he said; "I won't be a minute longer than possible," and, taking up his cap, he went out and closed the door behind him.

It was then about half-past five o'clock.

But the instant he had gone she sprang to her feet. Her face changed. A haunted, wild look shone in her dark, terrified eyes, and she stood rigid, her hands clenched, her face pale to the lips.

"*Dieu!*" she whispered aloud, to herself, startled at the sound of her own voice, and staring straight before her. "I was a fool—a great fool to return here to-day! Someone may recognise me, though it was to the other hotel I went with M. Harborne. Ah! No, I cannot—I dare not go down on the beach," she went on in French. "I must get away from this accursed place as soon as ever Ralph returns. What if he is suspected? Besides, the police may be looking for me, as it must now be known that I was here with him in Mundesley yesterday. Ah, yes! I was a fool to dare to return like this, even in different clothes. As soon as Ralph comes back I must feign serious illness, and he will take me back to Cromer, and on to London to-morrow. What evil fate it was that he should bring me here—here, to the one place on all the earth that I desired never again in my life to see!"

And the girl sank back inertly into the horsehair arm-chair in the old-fashioned room, and sat, white-faced and breathlessly anxious, staring straight before her.

Meanwhile Ralph Ansell—who, although actually a Frenchman, bore an English name—walked quickly up the village street and out upon the high road towards Parton. From time to time he turned, as though he feared that he might be followed, but there being nobody in the vicinity, he suddenly, when about half a mile from the village, struggled through a hedge into a grass-field where, in the corner, sheltered from the wind, stood Noel Barclay's naval monoplane, with its star-like Gnome engine and wide planes of pale yellow.

The spot was a lonely one. Before him stretched a wide heath covered with gorse, and the Norfolk Broads beyond. Nobody was nigh.

Bending, he crept swiftly along the high hedge, until he reached the machine. His attitude was that of an evil-doer. From his pocket he produced a small bolt of wood painted to resemble steel. He advanced to the left wing-spar of the monoplane and, apparently possessing expert knowledge of the point where it was the most vulnerable, he swiftly drew out a split pin, removed a small steel bolt at the end of the main-stay cable, and replaced it with the imitation bolt.

The dastardly, murderous action was only the work of a couple of minutes, when, placing the bolt in his pocket, he crept back again beneath the hedge, and ten minutes later reached the Old Ship unnoticed, having taken a certain route with which he seemed well acquainted.

As he approached the hotel he came face to face with Noel Barclay, who, cigarette in mouth, strode at an easy pace along the road towards the spot where he had left his machine. He passed the young foreigner without recognition. The man in the golf suit was a mere summer visitor, and to his knowledge he had never seen him before. Unsuspicious of what had been done, he went forward, eager to rise in the air again and return to his headquarters.

But when he had passed Ralph Ansell turned and, glancing covertly after him, an evil expression upon his strong, clean-shaven face, muttered a fierce imprecation in French beneath his breath.

The officer, however, strolled forward in ignorance of the stranger's sinister glance or his malediction, while the foreigner, with a crafty smile of triumph, entered the hotel, to find, to his alarm, that Jean had been taken very unwell.

In a moment he expressed the greatest consternation, and at once rang and ordered a cab in which to drive her back to Cromer.

A quarter of an hour later Jean Libert—whose feigned illness had now almost passed—was seated happily at her lover's side, slowly ascending the hill on the cliff-road leading towards Cromer, when, of a sudden, a loud whirr was heard in the air behind them.

"Why, look, there is an aeroplane!" cried the girl, enthusiastically, turning and watching with interest the naval monoplane rising beyond the village they had just left.

The driver pulled up, and the pair stood up in the vehicle to watch the splendid ascent of the dauntless aviator, who rose against the clear sky in a wide spiral higher and higher, twice passing over their heads, until he had reached an altitude of fully eight hundred feet. Then, after a final circle, he turned and made straight towards the yellow declining sun, speeding evenly and swiftly in the direction of Great Yarmouth.

Next second a loud, shrill shriek escaped the girl as she covered her face with her hands to shut out the appalling sight which met her gaze.

The machine, flying so beautifully, had, of a sudden, collapsed as though she had broken her wing, which rose at right angles, and then the machine, out of control, pitched forward and, nose first, fell straight to the ground like a stone.

III

Describes Two Inquiries

The fatal accident to Lieutenant Noel Barclay caused a wave of sympathy throughout the country.

As a daring and experienced aviator he was well known. He had assisted in the foundation of the Naval Flying School at Eastchurch, and had been the first aviator to fly from land and greet the King on the occasion of a great review off Weymouth. Many splendid feats of airmanship had he accomplished, flying from Paris to London on three occasions, and going far out to sea and back, scouting on one or other of the Government hydroplanes.

Several important inventions were to his credit, and it had been due to his genius that certain of the aircraft had been fitted with wireless apparatus and experiments carried out with success. He had done excellent service during the naval manoeuvres of the previous year, and his name had been written large in the annals of aviation.

But alas! the public had one morning opened their daily papers to find a tragic picture of his wrecked machine, and beneath was printed the news of his fatal fall from a distance of eight hundred feet.

The inquest had been held at the Old Ship Hotel at Mundesley, the day after the accident, and, in addition to representatives of the Admiralty, a number of aviation experts who had examined the wreckage had been present.

The inquiry was a searching one, for an important London newspaper had hinted that, owing to the parsimonious policy of the Admiralty, certain of their aeroplanes were not of the same stability as those owned by private individuals. Hence the authorities at Whitehall had set themselves to refute such damaging allegations.

To that quiet little fishing village had come some of the greatest aviation experts, world-famous pilots, and representatives of that select body whose dictum in all aviation is law—the Royal Aero Club. And all were there with one object—to decide as to the reason of the sudden collapse of the naval Bleriot.

The coroner sat in a stuffy little room, the windows of which were open. Nevertheless, with the place crowded the atmosphere was oppressively hot.

The inquiry was long and tedious, for after evidence had been given as to the lieutenant's departure, and eyewitnesses had described his fall, there came a quantity of highly technical evidence put forward by the Admiralty with the object of proving that the machine had been in a perfectly satisfactory condition. The Gnome engine was of 80 horse-power, the monoplane had been thoroughly overhauled only four days previously, and the flights which Barclay had made in her from Eastchurch proved that there had been no defect which could have been detected.

Curious it was that that inquiry was being held in the same hotel where Ralph Ansell and Jean Libert had taken their tea.

One man alone knew the terrible truth—the man who, on that fatal evening, had crept under the hedge unseen, and substituted the small steel bolt with one of wood with such an expert, unerring hand—the man who had stood up in the cab and calmly watched the awful result of his evil handiwork without the slightest sign of pity or remorse.

He had hurled Noel Barclay to his death with as little compunction as he would have crushed a fly. And yet little Jean, with the neat figure and great, dark eyes, in her innocence and ignorance, loved him so dearly and so well. She never dreamed the truth, and therefore he was her ideal, while she was his affianced wife.

In that small, over-crowded room, clean-shaven experts stood up one after the other, each expressing a different theory as to the cause of the accident.

When poor Barclay had been found, the engine was lying upon his chest, his neck was broken, his face battered out of all recognition, and both arms were broken. So utterly wrecked was the machine that it presented the appearance of a mass of splintered wood, tangled wires, and torn strips of fabric flapping in the wind.

All had been examined carefully, piece by piece, after the mangled remains of the unfortunate pilot had been extricated. The bolt was missing and search failed to find it. A quantity of evidence was forthcoming, and many theories advanced, the conclusion arrived at being that the left wing collapsed owing to undue strain, and the machine, instantly out of control, fell to earth.

There was but one verdict which the twelve honest men of Mundesley could return.

Expert evidence agreed that the quick-release at the end of one of the stay-wires was faulty. The steel bolt holding the main-stay cable and secured by a split-pin could not be found. It had evidently broken and fallen out, so that the left wing, being thus unsupported, had collapsed in mid-air.

And in face of these facts the jury returned a verdict of "Accidental death."

This the public read next morning in their newspapers, together with expressions of deep sympathy and declarations that the air was, as yet, unconquered.

On the same day as the inquest was held upon the body of Lieutenant Barclay, a coroner's inquiry was held at the little market-town of North Walsham, which, though inland, is the relay for the telegraph-cables diverging to Northern Europe, into the discovery on the highway of the body of the motor-cyclist, Mr. Richard Harborne.

Held in a schoolroom near the railway station, public and witnesses sat upon the school benches, while the coroner occupied the headmaster's desk.

Again there was an array of witnesses, but from the first the crowd at the back of the room scented mystery.

A carter of the village of Worstead, speaking in his broad Norfolk brogue, described how he had discovered the body and had come into North Walsham and told a constable.

"I was a coomin' into North Walsham wi' a load o' hay what I'd got from Mr. Summers, o' Stalham, when just after I turned into the Norwich road I saw sawmthin' a-lyin' in the ditch," he said slowly, while the grey-haired deputy-coroner carefully wrote down his words.

"Well?" asked the official, looking up at the witness.

"Well, sir, I found it was 'im," the man replied.

"Who?"

"The gentleman what war killed."

"The deceased, you mean," said the coroner.

"Yes, sir. I went over and found 'im a-lyin' face downwards," was the reply. "I thought 'e wor drunk at first, but when I see blood on the road I knowed there'd been sawmthin' up. So I went over to 'im."

"In what position was the body when you discovered it?" the coroner asked.

"'E wor a-lyin' with 'is feet in the water an' 'is 'ead in the brambles like."

"As if he had fallen there?"

"No, sir. As if 'e'd been thrown into the side o' the road. There was blood—a lot of it all alon' the road."

"What did you do?"

"Well, I pulled 'im out, and saw a nasty cut in 'is throat. So I drove on to North Walsham and saw Mr. Bennet."

"Anything else?"

"No, sir, nawthin' else."

"Any juryman wish to ask a question?" inquired the coroner, looking across at the twelve local taxpayers.

The foreman, a stout farmer, said:

"I'd like, sir, to ask the witness if the gentleman was dead when he pulled him out of the ditch."

"Dead as mutton," was the witness's prompt reply.

"You think he was dead? He may not have been," the coroner remarked.

"Well, I put my 'and on 'is 'eart an' it didn't beat, sir."

"Very well," said the official holding the inquiry, "that will do."

Superintendent Bennet, of the Norfolk Constabulary, stationed at North Walsham, gave evidence regarding the discovery. He described how the previous witness had called at the police-station, and how they went out in a light trap on the Norwich road together.

"I found deceased lying on the grass on the left side of the road close to a telegraph post," he said, while a tall, grey-faced, well-dressed man of forty-five, of a somewhat military appearance, who was seated at the back of the room, leaned forward attentively to catch every word. "The thorn bushes beside the ditch were broken down by the body apparently being cast there. It was getting dusk when I arrived on the spot, but I could clearly see traces of blood for about forty feet from the ditch forward in the direction of Norwich."

"Then the body must have been carried back from the spot where the blow was struck?"

"It was dragged back. A shower had fallen in the afternoon, and there were distinct marks on the damp road where the heels of the deceased had scraped along, and also the footmarks of the murderer."

At these words those present in court held their breath.

"Have you taken any action in regard to those footmarks?"

"I have not, sir. But the detectives from Norwich have," answered the officer.

"Could you see the track of deceased's motor-cycle?"

"Quite plainly. The deceased apparently dismounted close to the spot where the first trace of blood appeared, for there were marks of a struggle. The gentleman must have been struck down and promptly flung into the ditch, after which his assailant mounted the cycle and rode off."

"Towards Norwich?"

"Yes, sir—in that direction."

The grey-faced man at the back of the room was now all attention. Upon his countenance was a curious, intense look. The coroner noticed him, and became puzzled, even suspicious. Nobody knew the man or why he was present. Yet to him the death of Richard Harborne was, without a doubt, of the very greatest concern.

More than once the coroner looked suddenly up from writing the depositions, regarding him with covert glances. Though he had all the appearance of a gentleman, yet there was about him a strange, almost imperceptible air of the adventurer. A close observer would have noticed that his clothes bore the cut of a foreign tailor—French or Italian—and his boots were too long and pointed to be English. His well-kept, white hands were the hands of a foreigner, long and pointed, with nails trimmed to points, and upon his left wrist, concealed by his round shirt-cuff secured by solitaires in place of links, he wore a gold bangle which inside bore an inscription.

At times his grey, hard face was impassive and sphinx-like, yet to the narrative of how Richard Harborne was discovered he listened with a rapt attention it was impossible to conceal.

Yes, the coroner himself decided that there was an air of mystery surrounding the stranger, and resolved to tell the police at the conclusion of the inquiry.

Superintendent Bennet, in answer to further questions put by the coroner, said:

"At Gordon's Farm, to which we carried the body, I searched the dead man's pockets. From the Foreign Office passport I found, I learned the name of the gentleman, and from some letters addressed to him at the King's Head, at Beccles, I was soon able to ascertain by telephone that he had been stopping there for some little time. Most of the letters were private ones, but two of them were enclosed in double envelopes, and written on plain paper without any address or any signature. They were written in the dots and dashes of the Morse alphabet. A post-office telegraphist has seen them, and says that the letters are a jumble and form no words, therefore they must be secret correspondence in code."

And he handed the two letters in question to the coroner, who examined them with considerable curiosity, while the stranger at the back of the court folded his arms suddenly and looked entirely unconcerned.

"I also found this," the superintendent went on, handing a piece of tracing linen to the coroner. "As far as I can make out, it is a tracing of some plan or other. But its actual significance I have been unable to determine."

The coroner spread it out upon his writing-pad and looked at it with a puzzled expression.

"Anything else?" he inquired.

"Yes, sir; this," and the officer produced the torn half of a man's visiting-card.

"This is apparently part of one of the deceased's own cards," the coroner remarked, holding it before him, while the court saw that it had been torn across obliquely, leaving a jagged edge.

"He seems to have signed his name across the front of it, too, before it was torn," he added.

"The piece of card was carefully preserved in the inside pocket of his wallet," the inspector said. "On the back, sir, you will see it is numbered '213 G.'"

The coroner turned it over and saw on the back the number and letter as the police-officer had stated.

"There are three others, almost exactly similar," the inspector went on, producing them carefully from an envelope. "They are numbered '103 F,' '91 I,' and '321 G.'"

"Curious," remarked the coroner, taking them. "Very curious indeed. They are all signed across, yet only half the card is preserved. They have some secret significance without a doubt."

He glanced across at the stranger, but the face of the latter betrayed no sign of further interest. Indeed, just at that moment, when the whole court was on the tenterhooks of curiosity he looked as though bored by the entire procedure.

"The deceased carried a Smith-Wesson hammerless revolver fully loaded," the officer added; "but he was so suddenly attacked, it seems, that he had no time to draw it."

The detectives from Norwich who had the case in hand were not called to give evidence, for obvious reasons, but Dr. Dennan, of North Walsham, whom the police called, a short, white-haired, business-like little man, stepped forward, was sworn, and deposed that when he saw the body at Gordon's Farm, deceased had been dead nearly two hours.

"He was struck in the throat by some thin, sharp instrument—a deep wound. The artery was severed, and death must have occurred within a few minutes," he said. "Probably deceased could not speak. He certainly could not have uttered a cry. The blade of the instrument was, I should judge, only about half an inch wide, extremely keen, and tapered to a fine point. Whoever struck the blow was, I am inclined to think, possessed of some surgical knowledge. With Doctor Taylor, I made a post-mortem yesterday and found everything normal. There were some scratches and abrasions on the hands and face, but those were no doubt due to the deceased having been flung into the brambles."

Again the grey-faced stranger craned his thin neck, listening to every word as it fell from the doctor's lips.

And again the coroner noticed him—and wondered.

IV

DESCRIBES A TORN CARD

The Norfolk Mystery," as it was termed by the sensational journalists and Press-photographers, was but a nine days' wonder, as, indeed, is every modern murder mystery.

It provided material for the sensational section of the Press for a full week; a hundred theories were advanced, and the police started out upon a dozen or more false scents, but all to no purpose. Therefore the public curiosity quickly died down, and within ten days or so the affair was forgotten amid the hundred and one other "sensations" of crime and politics, of war rumours, and financial booms, which hourly follow upon each other's heels and which combine to make up the strenuous unrest of our daily life.

And so was the fatal accident to the naval aviator quickly forgotten by the public.

Many readers of these present lines no doubt saw reports of both affairs in the papers, but few, I expect, will recollect the actual facts, or if they do, they little dream of the remarkable romance of life of which those two unexplained tragedies formed the prologue.

On the night when the coroner's jury returned in the case of Richard Harborne a verdict of "Wilful murder by some person unknown," a girl sat in her small, plainly-furnished bedroom on the top floor of a house in New Oxford Street, in London, holding the evening paper in her thin, nerveless fingers.

It was Jean Libert.

She had been reading an account of the evidence given at the inquest, devouring it eagerly, with pale face and bated breath. And as she read her chest rose and fell quickly, her dark eyes were filled with horror, and her lips were ashen grey. The light had faded from her pretty face, her cheeks were sunken, her face haggard and drawn, and about her mouth were hard lines, an expression of bitter grief, remorse, despair.

A quarter of an hour ago, while in the small, cheap French restaurant below, kept by her father—a long, narrow place with red-plush seats along the white walls and small tables set before them—an urchin had passed, selling the "extra special." On the contents bill he carried in front of him were the words, in bold type: "Norfolk Mystery—Verdict."

She had rushed out into the street, bought a paper, and hastily concealing it, had ascended to her room, and there locked herself in.

Then she sank upon her bed and read it. Three times had she carefully read every word, for the report was a rather full one. Afterwards she sat, the paper still in her white hand, staring straight at the old mahogany chest of drawers before her.

"Poor Dick!" she murmured. "Ah! Heaven! Who could have done it? Why—why was he killed on that evening? If he had not gone to Mundesley to meet me he would not have lost his life. And yet—"

She paused, startled at the sound of her own voice, so nervous had she now become.

She glanced at the mirror, and started at sight of her own white, drawn countenance.

She placed both hands upon her eyes, as though striving to recall something, and in that position she remained, bent and pensive, for some moments.

Her lips moved at last.

"I wonder," she exclaimed, very faintly, speaking to herself, "I wonder whether Ralph will ever know that I met Dick? Ah! yes," she sighed; "I was foolish—mad—to dare to go to Mundesley that afternoon. If only I could have foreseen the consequence of our secret meeting—ah! if only I had known what I know now!"

Again she was silent, her face pale, with a fixed, intense look, when at last she rose, unlocked one of the small top drawers of the chest, and, taking the drawer entirely out, extracted something that had been concealed beneath it.

She held it in her hand. There were two halves of one of Dick Harborne's visiting-cards—signed and torn across in a similar manner to those pieces which had been handed for the coroner's inspection. Each half bore a number on its back, while on the front, as she placed them together, was Harborne's name, both printed and written.

For a long time she had her eyes fixed upon it. Her brows narrowed, and in her eyes showed a distinct expression of terror.

"Yes," she whispered; "I was a fool—a great fool to have dared so much—to have listened, and to have consented to go across to Bremen. But no one knows, except Dick—and he, alas!—he's dead! Therefore who can possibly know?—no one."

She held the halves of the torn card between her fingers for some moments, looking at them. Then, sighing deeply, she rose with sudden impulse and, crossing the room, took up a box of matches. Striking one, she applied it to the corners of the half cards and held the latter until the blue flame crept upwards and consumed them.

Then she cast them from her into the grate.

It was the end of her romance with that man who had been struck that cowardly blow in secret—Richard Harborne.

She stood gazing upon the tiny piece of tinder in the fender, immovable as a statue. Her dark brows slowly narrowed, her white, even teeth were set, her small hands clenched, as, beneath her breath, she uttered a fierce vow—a hard, bitter vow of vengeance.

Before her arose the vision of her good-looking lover, the man with the dark, intense eyes—Ralph Ansell. And then the memory of the dead Dick Harborne instantly faded from her mind.

Her romance with Dick had been but a passing fancy. She had never really loved him. Indeed, he had never spoken to her of love. Yet he had fascinated her, and in his presence she had found herself impelled by his charm and his easy-going cosmopolitanism, so that she had listened to him and obeyed, even against her own will.

She recollected vividly that adventurous journey to Bremen—recalled it all as some half-forgotten, misty dream. She could feel now the crisp crackling of those Bank of England notes which she had carried secreted in her cheap little dressing-case with its electro-plated fittings. She remembered, too, the face of the stranger, the fat, sandy-haired German, whom she had met by appointment upon a flat country road a mile distant from the city towards Ottersberg—how he had given her, as credential, one of those pieces of visiting-card, together with a bulky letter, and how, in return, she had handed him the English bank-notes.

Then there was the mysterious packet she had subsequently given to Dick, when she had met him one evening and dined with him at the Trocadero. Then he had thanked her, and declared his great indebtedness.

From that night, until the day of the tragedy, she had not seen him. Indeed, she had made up her mind never to do so. Yet he had persuaded her to meet him at Mundesley, and she had consented, even though she knew what risk of detection by Ralph she must run.

Was it possible that Ralph knew?

The thought held her breathless.

Ralph Ansell loved her. He had sworn many times that no other man should love her. What if Dick's death had been due to Ralph's fierce jealousy!

The very suspicion staggered her.

Again she sank upon her little white bed, gripping the coverlet in her nervous fingers and burying her face in the pillow.

She examined her own heart, analysing her feelings as only a woman can analyse them.

Yes. She loved Ralph Ansell—loved him sincerely and well. Eighteen months ago he had casually entered the little restaurant one evening and ordered some supper from Pierre, the shabby, bald-headed waiter, who had been for so many years in her father's service. At that moment Jean—who was employed in the daytime at the Maison Collette, the well-known milliners in Conduit Street—happened to be in the cash-desk of her father's little establishment where one-and-sixpenny four-course luncheons and two-shilling six-course dinners were served.

From behind the brass grille she had gazed out upon the lonely, good-looking, well-dressed young fellow whom she saw was very nervous and agitated. Their eyes met, when he had instantly become calm, and had smiled at her.

He came the next night and the next, with eyes only for her, until he summed up courage to speak to her, with the result that they had become acquainted.

A young man of French birth, though his father had been an American domiciled in Paris, he was possessed of independent means, and lived in a cosy little bachelor flat half-way up Shaftesbury Avenue on the right-hand side. Far more French than English, in spite of his English name, he quickly introduced himself into the good graces of Jean's father—the short, dapper old *restaurateur*, Louis Libert, a Provençal from the remote little town of Aix, a Frenchman whom many years' residence in London had failed to anglicise.

For nearly twenty years old Louis Libert had kept the Restaurant Provence, in Oxford Street, yet Mme. Libert, on account of the English climate, had preferred to live with her mother in Paris, and for fully half the period had had her daughter Jean with her. In consequence, Jean, though she spoke English well, was, nevertheless, a true Parisienne.

Since her mother's death, four years previously, she had lived in London, and was at present engaged as modiste at the Maison Collette, where many of the "creations" of that world-famous house were due to her own artistic taste and originality.

At first, her father had looked askance at the well-dressed young stranger who so constantly had dinner or supper at the restaurant, but ere long, in consequence of secret inquiries he had made of the hall porter of the flats in Shaftesbury Avenue, he had accepted the young man, and had even been gratified by the proposal of marriage which Ralph had placed before him.

Thus the pair had become engaged, the wedding being fixed to take place in the middle of November. Even as Jean stood there, a faint tap was heard at the door, and the maid-of-all-work announced:

"Mr. Ansell is downstairs, miss."

Jean responded, and after washing her hands and patting her hair before the glass, put on her hat and descended to the rather dingy, old-fashioned drawing-room over the shop, where stood her lover alone at the open window, looking down upon the traffic in the broad, brilliantly-lit London thoroughfare.

Very neat and dainty she looked in her well-cut, dark skirt, and blouse of white crêpe de Chine, which she wore with a distinctly foreign *chic*, and as she entered, her pretty face was bright and happy: different, indeed, to the heavy, troubled expression upon it ten minutes before.

"Ah, Ralph!" she cried, in warm welcome, as she sprang into his ready arms, and he bent till his lips touched hers. "You are earlier than you expected," she added in French. "I hardly thought you would be able to get back from the country in time to-night."

"Well, you see, dearest, I made an effort, and here I am," replied the young man with the strong, clean-shaven features and the large, round, penetrating eyes. "I've been travelling ever since three o'clock, and it's now nearly ten."

Though he, too, spoke in French, his appearance was very English. No one would have taken him for anything else but an honest, upright, thorough-going young Englishman. He was of that strong, manly, well-set-up type, the kind of level-headed, steady young man, with whom no father would hesitate to entrust his daughter's future. As he stood in his smart, blue serge suit with well-ironed trousers, and a fine diamond in his cravat, holding her in his arms and kissing her fondly, he looked the true lover, and assuredly their hearts beat in unison.

Jean Libert loved him with a great, all-consuming affection, a blind passion which obliterated any defects which she might have observed, and which endowed him in her eyes with all the qualities of a hero of romance.

They were, indeed, a handsome pair. Her dark head was resting upon his shoulder, while his strong right arm was about her slim waist.

Since her return, three days ago, from her summer holiday by the sea at Cromer they had not met. That morning, being Monday, she had resumed her daily labours in the big, long workroom of the Jewish firm who traded under the name of the Maison Collette, and she had, as is usual with girls, related to her friends many of the incidents of what she declared to be "a ripping holiday."

As she stood with her white hand tenderly upon his shoulder, looking lovingly into his eyes, she was describing her return to business, and how she regretted that the long summer seaside days were no more, whereupon he said, cheerfully, in English:

"Never mind, darling; November will soon come, and you will then have no further need to go to business. You will be mine. Shall we go out for a walk?" he suggested, noticing that she already had her hat on.

To his suggestion she willingly assented, and, raising her full, red lips to his, she kissed him, and then they descended to the restaurant below, empty at that hour save for the seedy old waiter, Pierre, and her father, an elderly, grey, sad-looking man, whose business in later years had, alas! sadly declined on account of the many restaurants which had sprung up along Oxford Street during the past ten years. He had seen better times, but nowadays it was always a hard struggle to make both ends meet, to pay the landlord and to live.

Ralph and old Libert exchanged greetings in French, and then, with Jean upon his arm, young Ansell stepped out into Oxford Street.

The August night was dry, warm, and starlit. Few people were about as they strolled along, chatting and laughing merrily. Before the theatres discharge their chattering crowds, the main thoroughfares of central London are usually quiet and half-deserted, and as the pair walked in the direction of Regent Street, Jean's heart beat gladly with supreme satisfaction that at last Ralph had returned to London.

November! Far off seemed that day of all days in her life when she would be Ralph's bride.

Upon her finger was the engagement ring he had given her, one set with diamonds of such fine quality that old Libert had wondered. Indeed, a jeweller, whose habit it was to take his luncheon there each day, had noticed it upon Jean's finger, and had valued it roughly at a hundred pounds. Therefore Ralph could certainly not be badly off!

They had turned the corner into Regent Street, but were too engrossed in each other's conversation to notice that, in passing, a tall, grey-faced man, who wore a crush-hat, with a black coat over his evening clothes, had suddenly recognised Ansell.

For a few steps he strode on with apparent unconcern, then he paused and, having gazed for several moments after them still walking with linked arms, unconscious of being remarked, he turned on his heel, crossed the road, and strolled in the direction they were walking.

The watcher was the same grey-faced, keen-looking stranger who, earlier that day, had sat in the country schoolroom at North Walsham listening to the evidence given before the coroner concerning the mystery of the Norwich Road.

His thin lips curled in a smile—a smile of bitter triumph—as he went on with crafty footsteps behind the pair, watching them from across the road.

V

Secrets of State

T he right honourable the Earl of Bracondale, His Majesty's Principal Secretary of State for Foreign Affairs, crossed his big, business-like library at Bracondale Hall, near Torquay, and stood upon the Turkey hearthrug ready to receive his visitor.

Beneath the red-shaded lamplight he presented a handsome picture, a tall, well-built man of refined elegance, upon whom the cares of State weighed rather heavily. His age was about forty-three, though, in his well-cut evening clothes, he looked much younger; yet his face undoubtedly denoted strength and cleverness, a sharpened intellect ever on the alert to outwit foreign diplomacy, while the lines across his brow betokened deep thought and frequent nights of sleeplessness.

To Great Britain's Foreign Minister is entrusted the care of her good relations with both friends and enemies abroad, and surely no member of the Cabinet occupies such a position of grave responsibilities, for a false step upon his part, the revelation of a secret policy, of an unfriendly attitude maintained injudiciously, may at any moment cause the spark in the powder magazine of Europe.

To preserve peace, and yet be in a position to dictate to the Powers is what a British Foreign Minister must do, a task the magnitude and difficulty of which in these days can very easily be understood.

With his hands behind his back, his dark brow slightly contracted, his eyes were fixed blankly upon the big, littered writing-table before him; he was thinking deeply.

In profile his features were clean-cut, his forehead high and above the average intelligence; his hair, though a trifle scanty on top, was as yet untinged by grey, while he wore the ends of his carefully-trimmed moustache upturned, which gave him a slightly French appearance.

In his youthful days, long before he had succeeded to the title, he had been honorary attaché at the Embassy in Rome, and afterwards in Paris, to which was attributable the rather Continental style in which he wore both hair and moustache.

He drew his hand wearily across his brow, for ever since dinner he had never left his writing-table, so busy had he been with the great pile of documents which had been brought that afternoon by special messenger from the Foreign Office.

Suddenly Jenner, the grave old butler who had been fifty years in the service of his family, opened the door and announced:

"Mr. Darnborough, m'lord."

"Halloa, Darnborough!" cried the earl cheerily, as his visitor entered. "Where have you sprung from at this time of night?"

"From London," replied the other. "I wanted to see you urgently, so I ran down."

And the two men shook hands.

That the visitor was no stranger to the house was apparent, for, without invitation, he sank into an arm-chair, stretched out his legs, and looked very gravely up into the face of the Cabinet Minister before him.

He was dressed in a dark brown suit, and was none other than the grey-faced stranger who, four days before, had sat in the schoolroom at North Walsham and had aroused the curiosity of the coroner.

"Well, Darnborough, what's the matter?" asked the Earl, passing his visitor the cigar-box. "I can see there's trouble by your face. What's the latest problem—eh?"

The visitor selected a cigar, turned it over in his fingers critically, and then, rising suddenly, bit off the end viciously and crossed to the electric lighter near the fireplace.

"Well," he answered, "there are several things. First, we know why poor Harborne was killed."

"Good," replied his lordship. "You Secret Service men always get to know all there is to know. You're marvellous! Have you told them at Scotland Yard?"

"No, and I don't mean to," replied Hugh Darnborough, the chief of the British Secret Service, the clever, ingenious man whose fingers were upon the pulse of each of the Great Powers, and whose trusty agents were in every European capital. Long ago he had held a commission in the Tenth Hussars, but had resigned it to join the Secret Service, just as Dick Harborne had resigned from the Navy to become a cosmopolitan, and to be dubbed an adventurer by those in ignorance. That had been years ago, and now he held the position of being the most trusted man in any Government department, the confidant of each member of the Cabinet, and even of the Sovereign himself, who frequently received him in private audience.

"You have reasons for not telling them at Scotland Yard—eh?" asked the Foreign Minister.

"Strong ones," replied the other, pulling hard at his cigar. "A woman who, I have ascertained, was on one occasion very useful to us, would be dragged into it—perhaps incriminated. And you know we are never anxious to court publicity."

"Ah! A woman—eh?"

"Yes; a young, and rather pretty, woman."

"And you've come all the way from London, and got here at eleven o'clock at night, to tell me this?"

"I have something else—of greater gravity."

"Well, let's hear the worst," said the Earl with a sigh. "Every day brings its troubles. Look yonder!" and he pointed to the table. "Those are despatches from all the Embassies. The eternal Balkan trouble seems threatening to break out, unless we take strong action. Bulgaria is mobilising again, and Turkey is protesting."

"There has been a leakage from the Admiralty. How, I cannot explain. A copy of the secret report upon our last naval manoeuvres is in the hands of our friends in the Wilhelmstrasse."

"What?" cried the Earl, starting, his face pale with alarm.

"I repeat that the report is known in Germany—every word of it!"

"And our weakness is thereby revealed?"

"The exact position is known."

"But the confidential report has not yet come through to me!"

"And yet it has somehow leaked out from Whitehall," Darnborough replied, drily.

"A full and drastic inquiry must be ordered. I will telephone at once to the First Lord."

"He already knows. I saw him this afternoon," was the quiet reply of the head of the Secret Service, a man whose coolness in great crises was always remarkable. When danger threatened he was always far more cool and collected than when all was plain sailing.

"But what are the main features of the report? Tell me, Darnborough. You always know everything."

"The chief points of the secret report reached me from one of my agents in Berlin this morning. It was brought over by messenger," replied the Earl's visitor, seating himself and puffing thoughtfully at his cigar. "You will recollect that two fleets were engaged in the North Sea, Blue being the British Fleet, and Red representing the German."

"How foolish of the Admiralty not to have issued a report for public consumption. They ought to have done so long ago, and issued the confidential report afterwards—as was done two years ago," interrupted His Majesty's Minister.

"Yes, that is what should have been done," the other assented. "It is useless to tell the world the truth when national defence is in question. But to resume. Blue's commander was given two hundred and thirty ships to Red's one hundred and seventeen, or nearly two to one. Blue had twenty-eight battleships and battle-cruisers to Red's eighteen, or fifty-five per cent. more."

"An advantage far greater than we should possess in actual war, unless every British fighting ship was brought home from the Mediterranean."

"Exactly. War was declared on June 18th—earlier than is usual—and six days later a truce was suddenly ordered from Whitehall. War was resumed three days afterwards, but was stopped suddenly four days later."

"Well, and what did really happen? I mean, what facts have our friends in Berlin got hold of?" asked the Earl, with the greatest interest.

"Proofs undeniable that, under our present arrangements for home defence, a serious raid must entail a vital blow at the heart of the Empire," he replied slowly.

"How?" asked Lord Bracondale sharply.

"Because the enemy, notwithstanding all our efforts at defence, our destroyers, our scouting hydroplanes, and our look-outs along the coast, raided the Humber, landing thirty-six thousand men, and, on the following day, made raids on the Wear, Blyth, and Sunderland, putting twenty-four thousand men ashore. Thus, four of the most important ports and bases on the East Coast were captured within two days, together with the wireless stations at Cleethorpes, Hunstanton, and Caister, and sixty thousand men were ashore. Moreover, the supposed enemy inflicted very heavy losses upon us without sustaining any disasters, and, further, they sent a strong force of cruisers into the Atlantic to prey upon British trade."

"Bad," sighed the Earl, the corners of his mouth hardening. "Very bad, Darnborough. It is to be hoped that the Press won't get wind of this!"

The ubiquitous Chief of the Secret Service shrugged his shoulders.

"It may leak out to the Opposition journals, just as it has already leaked out to the Wilhelmstrasse. If the Admiralty had not ordered a sudden cessation of hostilities the enemy's admiral would next have been heard of in such a position that a panic would have been caused throughout the country. As it was, the enemy's submarines of the D and E classes, which were sent away to hunt on their own, established a reign of terror, getting to the entrance of Cromarty Harbour, which was our base, and torpedoing the ships which were guarding the Fleet inside. They also torpedoed the Dreadnoughts *St. Vincent* and *Collingwood*, while another section of the enemy's submarines inflicted very heavy loss on the British Fleet in the North Sea and seized the wireless at Cleethorpes."

The Earl was silent for a long time, thoughtfully stroking his moustache.

"But all this betrays our weakness to Germany!" he exclaimed at last. "It is astounding—incredible!"

"But it is, nevertheless, true," remarked Darnborough. "The security of the country is in gravest danger. Why, only a few days ago the Post Office allowed Germany to lay another cable across the North Sea from Mundesley, in Norfolk, to the Island of Nordeney."

"Mundesley?" repeated the Earl. "Why, that was where poor Harborne went on the day he lost his life."

"Yes. He had been in that neighbourhood for some time—upon a secret mission, poor fellow!—a mission which he had not lived to fulfil."

A silence fell between the two men.

"The situation is, I see, one of the utmost gravity. Steps must be taken at once to reassure the public in case rumours should be published regarding the truth. The Opposition will certainly not spare the Government the facts, and must, if disclosed, give an impetus to the campaign for universal service, which would be very inconvenient to us at the present time. And more than that—Germany now actually knows the rottenness of our defences!"

"That, unfortunately, is the case."

The Earl of Bracondale bit his under lip. A Cabinet Council had been summoned for the next afternoon, and he must place the true situation before it. All the clever diplomacy he had exercised with the Powers during the past five years had now been nullified, and England stood exposed in all her vulnerability. The inflated bubble of the strong, invincible British Navy had been pricked and burst.

Black days had, alas! fallen upon our nation, and a grave peril hourly threatened. Germany had hitherto hesitated to attack England because of the uncertainty regarding our true strength. Our land defences were known to Germany, even to the most minute detail, all reported accurately and methodically by the enemy's spies living amongst us. But our naval secrets had all been well preserved, so that the British Fleet had always been regarded as able to repel invasion and make reprisals.

Now, however, its failure to prevent an armed raid was known to our friends across the North Sea, and most certainly they would seek to take advantage of the valuable knowledge they had gained.

Suddenly the Earl, turning to where Darnborough stood, exclaimed:

"You spoke of poor Harborne. He was a smart agent, I believe?"

"The best I ever had. He was clever, ingenious, utterly fearless, and devoted to the service. You will recollect how he obtained the accurate clauses of the secret Japanese treaty, and how he brought to us news of the secret French agreement over the Morocco question."

"I recollect," replied the Foreign Minister. "When he told me I would not believe it. Yet his information proved correct."

"Harborne's death is to be deeply regretted," Darnborough said. "I attended the inquest. Of course, to the public, the motive is a mystery."

"Not to you—eh, Darnborough?"

"No. If Richard Harborne had lived, Germany would never have learnt the truth regarding the recent naval manoeuvres," was the reply of the Chief of the Secret Service.

"You said something about a woman. Is she known?"

"No. I have suspicions that an indiscretion was committed—a grave indiscretion, which cost poor Harborne his life. Yet what is one man's life to his enemies when such a secret is at stake?"

"But who was the woman?"

"A friend of Harborne's. She had been, I believe, useful to him in certain negotiations regarding the purchase of copies of plans of the new Krupp aerial gun, and in several other matters."

"Any suspicion regarding her?" asked the Earl quickly.

"None. She is, of course, in ignorance of the truth, and probably unaware who killed the man with whom she was so friendly. I am endeavouring to trace her."

"Is she a lady?"

"No. A French milliner, I understand."

"A little romance of Harborne's which has ended fatally?"

"Yes—poor Harborne!" sighed the grey-faced man, in whose keeping were the secrets of the Empire, and who knew more of the political undercurrents of Europe than any other living person. "His loss is very great to us, for he was a fine specimen of the true-hearted, patriotic Englishman," he added, pulling hard at his cigar. "His place will be hard to fill—very hard."

"I know, Darnborough," remarked Lord Bracondale gravely. "To such a man the country ought to erect a monument, for he has laid down his life for his country. But, alas! our country recognises no heroes of the Secret Service!"

And as the Cabinet Minister spoke the telephone-bell rang. He crossed to his writing-table, took up the instrument, and responded to an urgent call from the House of Commons in London, where an important and heated debate regarding our foreign relations was in progress.

VI

The Safe-Breakers

The day had been hot and stifling in London—one of those blazing days when the tar on the roadway perfumes the air, the dry pavements reflect back the heat into one's face, and the straw-hatted Metropolis—or the portion of it that is still in town—gasps and longs for the country or the sea.

The warm weather was nearly at an end, and most holiday-makers were back again. London's workers had had their annual fortnight long ago, and had nearly forgotten it, and now only principals were away golfing, taking waters at Harrogate, Woodhall Spa, or in the Scotch hydros, or perhaps travelling on the Continent.

From the high-up windows in Shaftesbury Avenue, close to Piccadilly Circus, Ralph Ansell looked down upon the busy traffic of motor-buses, taxis, and cars, the dark-red after-glow shining full upon his keen, clean-shaven face.

He was already dressed to go out to dinner, and as he stood in his cosy bachelor rooms—a pleasant, artistic little place with soft crimson carpet, big, comfortable, leather arm-chairs, and a profusion of photographs, mostly of the fair sex, decorating mantelshelf and walls—his brows were narrowed and he blew big clouds of cigarette smoke from his lips.

Suddenly the door opened and a man, shorter and rather thick-set, also in evening clothes, entered. He was evidently French, and possessed neither the good looks nor the elegance of Ansell.

"Ah! my dear Adolphe!" Ralph cried in French, springing forward to welcome him. "I hardly expected you yet. Your train from Paris was not late—eh? Well, how goes it?"

"Infernally hard up—as usual," was his visitor's reply, as he tossed his black overcoat on to the couch, flung his soft felt hat after it, and then sank into a chair. "Why all this emergency—eh?"

The man who spoke was of low type, with black, rather curly hair, sharp, shrewd eyes like his friend's, ears that lay slightly away from his head, and a large, rather loose, clean-shaven mouth. Between his eyes were three straight lines, for his brow wore a constant look of care and anxiety. He did not possess that careless, easy, gentlemanly air of Ansell, but was of a coarser and commoner French type, the type one meets every day in the Montmartre, which was, indeed, the home of Adolphe Carlier.

Ansell walked to the door, opened it as if to ascertain there was no eavesdropper, and, closing and locking it, returned to his friend's side.

"I sent for you, my dear friend, because I want you," he said, in a low voice, gazing straight at him.

"Anything good?" asked the other, stretching out his legs and placing his clasped hands behind his head wearily.

"Yes, an easy job. The usual game."

"A jeweller's?"

Ansell nodded in the affirmative.

"Where?"

"Not far from here."

"Much stuff?"

"A lot of good stones."

"And the safe?"

"Easy enough with the jet," Ansell answered. "You've brought over all the things, I suppose?"

"Yes. But it was infernally risky. I was afraid the Customs might open them at Charing Cross," Carlier replied.

"You never need fear. They never open anything here. This is not like Calais or Boulogne."

"I shan't take them back."

"You won't require to, my dear Adolphe," laughed Ansell, who, though in London he posed as a young man of means, was well known in a certain criminal set in Paris as "The American," because of his daring exploits in burglary and robbery with violence.

A year before, this exemplary young man, together with Adolphe Carlier, known as "*Fil-en-Quatre*," or "The Eel," had been members of the famous Bonnemain gang, to whose credit stood some of the greatest and most daring jewel robberies in France. For several years the police had tried to bring their crimes home to them, but without avail, until the great robbery at Louis Verrier's, in the Rue des Petit-Champs, when a clerk in the employ of the well-known diamond dealer was shot dead by Paul Bonnemain. The latter was arrested, tried for murder, and executed, the gang being afterwards broken up.

The malefactors had numbered eight, six of whom, including Bonnemain himself, had been arrested, the only ones escaping being

Carlier, who had fled to Bordeaux, where he had worked at the docks till the affair had blown over, while Ansell, whose *dossier* showed a very bad record, had sought refuge in England.

The pair had not met since the memorable evening nine months before, when Ansell had been sitting in the Grand Café, and Carlier had slipped in to warn him that the police had arrested Bonnemain and the rest, and had already been to his lodgings. Two hours later, without baggage or any encumbrance, he had reached Melun in a hired motor-car, and had thence left it at midnight for Lyons, after which he doubled his tracks and travelled by way of Cherbourg across to Southampton, while Carlier had, on that same night, fled to Orleans.

Part of the proceeds of the robbery at the diamond merchants had been divided up by the gang prior to Bonnemain's arrest—or rather the fifty thousand francs advanced by the Jew broker from Amsterdam to whom they always sold their booty. Therefore both men had been possessed of funds. Like others of their profession, they made large gains, but spent freely, and were continually short of money. Old Bonnemain, however, had brought burglary to a fine art, and from the proceeds of each *coup* he used to keep back a certain amount out of which to assist the needy among his accomplices.

Ansell, in addition, had a second source of revenue, inasmuch as he was on friendly terms with a certain Belgian Baron, who, though living in affluence in Paris, was nevertheless a high official of the German Secret Service. It was, indeed, his habit to undertake for the Baron certain disagreeable little duties which he did not care to perform himself, and for such services he was usually highly paid. Hence, when he fled to London, it was not long before a German secret agent called upon him and put before him a certain proposal, the acceptance of which had resulted in the death of Dick Harborne.

The young adventurer threw himself into the arm-chair opposite to where Adolphe Carlier was seated, and in the twilight unfolded his scheme for a *coup* at a well-known jeweller's in Bond Street, at which he was already a customer and had thoroughly surveyed the premises.

"I expected that you had some new scheme in hand," Carlier said at last, in French, after listening attentively to the details of the proposition, every one of which had been most carefully thought out by the pupil of the notorious Bonnemain. "On arrival this afternoon I put up at the Charing Cross Hotel—so as to be handy if we have to get out quickly."

"Good. Probably we shall be compelled to move pretty slick," Ansell said, in English. Then, after a few moments' pause, he added: "Do you know, my dear Adolphe, I have some news for you."

"News?"

"Yes. I'm going to be married in November."

"Married!" echoed Carlier, staring at his friend. "Who's the lucky girl?"

"She's French; lives here in London; smart, sweet—a perfect peach," was his answer. "She'll be a lot of use to us in future."

Carlier was silent for a few moments.

"Does she know anything?" he asked in a low, serious voice.

"Nothing."

"What will she say when she knows?"

"What can she say?" asked Ansell, with a grin.

"She's not one of us, I suppose?"

"One of us? Why, no, my dear fellow. I'll introduce you to-morrow. You must dine with us—dine before we go out and do the job. But she must not suspect anything—you understand?"

"Of course," replied the young Frenchman. "I'll be delighted to meet her, Ralph, but—but I'm thinking it is rather dangerous for you to marry an honourable girl."

"What?" cried the other, angry in an instant. "Do you insinuate that I'm not worthy to have a decent, well-brought-up girl for a wife?"

"Ah! you misunderstand me, *mon vieux*. I insinuate nothing," replied Carlier. "I scent danger, that is all. She may turn from you when—well—when she knows what we really are."

Ansell's mouth hardened.

"When she knows she'll have to grin and bear it," was the answer.

"She might give us away."

"No, she won't do that, I can assure you. The little fool loves me too well."

"Is that the way you speak of her?"

"Every girl who loves a man blindly is, in my estimation, a fool."

"Then your estimation of woman is far poorer than I believed, Ralph," responded Carlier. "If a girl loves a man truly and well, as apparently this young lady loves you, then surely she ought not to be sneered at. We have, all of us, loved at one time or other in our lives."

"You're always a sentimental fool where women are concerned, Adolphe," laughed his companion.

"I may be," answered the other. "And I can assure you that I would never dare to marry while leading the life I do."

"And what better life can you ever hope to lead, pray? Do we not get excitement, adventure, money, pleasure—everything that makes life worth living? Neither you nor I could ever settle down to the humdrum existence of so-called respectability. But are these people who pose as being so highly respectable really any more honest than we are? No, my dear friend. The sharks on the Bourse and the sharp men of business are just as dishonest. They are thieves like ourselves under a more euphonious name."

Carlier smiled at his friend's philosophy. Yet he was thinking of the future of the girl with whom he was, as yet, unacquainted—the girl who had chosen to link her life with that of the merry, careless, but unscrupulous young fellow before him. They were bosom friends, it was true, yet he knew, alas! how utterly callous Ralph Ansell was where women were concerned, and he recollected certain ugly rumours he had heard, even in their own undesirable circle.

They spoke of Jean again, and Ralph told him her name.

"We will dine there to-morrow night," he added. "Then we will come on here, and go forth to Bond Street at half-past eleven. I've watched the police for the past week, and know their exact beat. Better bring round the things you've brought from Paris in a taxi to-morrow morning."

The "things" referred to were an oxy-acetylene gas-jet, and a number of the latest inventions of burglarious tools—indeed, all the equipment of the expert safe-breaker.

That night the pair went forth and dined at the Café Royal in Regent Street, and afterwards went to the Palace Theatre, finishing up at a night club in Wardour Street. Then, on the following morning, Carlier returned, bringing with him the heavy but unsuspicious-looking travelling trunk he had conveyed from Paris.

In the evening Ralph and he went to the Provence Restaurant, but, to their disappointment, Jean was not there. She had been home, but had left half an hour later to go to Balham to visit one of her fellow-assistants at the Maison Collette who was dangerously ill. She had taken with her some fruit and flowers.

Annoyed at her absence, Ralph had suggested the Trocadero for dinner.

"It's better than in this wretched little hole," he added to Carlier, in an undertone. "And we'll want a good dinner before we get to business," he added, with a sinister grin.

So they had wished old Libert a merry *bon soir*, and were driven in a taxi along to the Trocadero grill-room, where, amid the clatter of plates, the chatter, and the accompanying orchestra, they found themselves in their own element.

At half-past ten they ascended to Ansell's flat, and each had a stiff brandy-and-soda and a cigar.

Both men were expert thieves, therefore it was not surprising that, by half-past two o'clock next morning, wearing cotton gloves and dark spectacles to hide the glare from the jet, they stood together before the great safe at the back of Matheson and Wilson's, the well-known jewellers, and while Ansell put up his hand and cleared shelf after shelf of magnificent ornaments, Adolphe expertly packed them away into the small black canvas bag he held open.

Those were breathless, exciting moments. The jet had done its work. It had gone through the hardened steel plates like a knife through butter, and the door, believed to be burglar-proof, stood open, displaying wonderful diamond tiaras in cases, ropes of pearls and paper packets containing uncut gems worth a huge amount.

The haul was a magnificent one, and though they had not yet succeeded in getting clear, both men were gloating over their booty—a triumphant satisfaction that no burglar can repress.

The scene was a weird one. The glaring light thrown by the jet had been extinguished, but the steel still glowed with heat, and Ansell blistered his fingers when they had accidentally touched the edge. The only light now was a small electric torch which threw direct rays in a small zone. But of a sudden, both men heard a noise—the distinct footsteps of a man crossing the shop!

They straightened their backs, and, for a second, looked at each other in alarm.

Next instant a big, burly night-watchman dashed in upon them, crying:

"What do you fellows want 'ere—eh?"

"Nothing. Take that!" replied Ansell, as he raised his hand and dashed something into the man's face.

But too late. The man raised his revolver and fired.

Though the bullet went wide, the report was deafening in that small inner room, and both intruders knew that the alarm was raised. Not a second was to be lost. The police-constable on duty outside would hear it!

Without hesitation, Ralph Ansell raised his arm and instantly fired, point blank, at the man defending the property of his master.

A second report rang out, and the unfortunate night-watchman fell back into the darkness. There was a sound of muffled footsteps.

Then all was silence.

VII

The Downward Path

A year had gone by.

Since that memorable night when Ansell and Carlier had so narrowly escaped capture in Bond Street, and had been compelled to fly and leave their booty behind, things had gone badly with both of them.

With Bonnemain executed, and their other companions in penal servitude at Cayenne, a cloud of misfortune seemed to have settled upon them.

Of the tragedy on the Norwich road no more had been heard. The police had relinquished their inquiries, the affair had been placed upon the long list of unsolved mysteries, and it had passed out of the public mind. Only to the British Cabinet had the matter caused great suspense and serious consideration, while it had cost the Earl of Bracondale, as Foreign Minister, the greatest efforts of the most delicate diplomacy to hold his own in defiance to the German intentions. For two whole months the Foreign Office had lived in daily expectation of sudden hostilities. In the Wilhelmstrasse the advisability of a raid upon our shores had been seriously discussed, and the War Council were nearly unanimous in favour of crossing swords with England.

Only by the clever and ingenious efforts of British secret agents in Berlin, who kept Darnborough informed of all in progress, was Lord Bracondale able to stem the tide and guide the ship of state into the smooth waters of peace.

And of all this the British public had remained in blissful ignorance. The reader of the morning paper was assured that never in this decade had the European outlook been so peaceful, and that our relations with our friends in Berlin were of the most cordial nature. Indeed, there was some talk of an *entente*.

The reader was, however, in ignorance that for weeks on end the British fleet had been kept in the vicinity of the North Sea, and that the destroyer flotillas were lying in the East Coast harbours with steam up, ready to proceed to sea at a moment's notice.

Nevertheless, the peril had passed once again, thanks to the firm, fearless attitude adopted by Lord Bracondale, and though the secret of England's weakness was known and freely commented upon in Government circles in Berlin, yet the clamorous demands of the war party were not acceded to. The British lion had shown his teeth, and Germany had again hesitated.

Ralph Ansell and Adolphe Carlier, after the failure of their plot to rob Matheson and Wilson's, in Bond Street, had fled next day to Belgium, and thence had returned to France.

Ralph had seen Jean for a few moments before his flight, explaining that his sudden departure was due to the death of his uncle, a landowner near Valence, in whose estate he was interested, and she, of course, believed him.

So cleverly, indeed, did he deceive her that it was not surprising that old Libert and his daughter should meet the young adventurer at the Hotel Terminus at Lyons one day in November, and that three days later Ralph and Jean were married at the Mairie. Then while the old *restaurateur* returned to London, the happy pair went South to Nice for their honeymoon.

While there Adolphe Carlier called one day at their hotel—a modest one near the station—and was introduced to Jean.

From the first moment they met, Adolphe's heart went forth to her in pity and sympathy. Though a thief bred and born, and the son of a man who had spent the greater part of his life in prison, Carlier was ever chivalrous, even considerate, towards a woman. He was coarser, and outwardly more brutal than Ralph Ansell, whose veneer of polish she, in her ignorance of life, found so attractive, yet at heart, though an expert burglar, and utterly unscrupulous towards his fellows, he was, nevertheless, always honourable towards a woman.

When their hands clasped and their eyes met upon their introduction, she instantly lowered hers, for, with a woman's intuition, she knew that in this companion of her husband's she had a true friend. And he, on his part, became filled with admiration of her great beauty, her wonderful eyes, and her soft, musical voice.

And he turned away, affecting unconcern, although in secret he sighed for her and for her future. She was far too good to be the wife of such a man as Ralph Ansell.

Months went on, and to Jean the mystery surrounding Ralph became more and more obscure.

At first they had lived quietly near Bordeaux, now and then receiving visits from Adolphe. On such occasions the two men would be closeted together for hours, talking confidentially in undertones. Then, two months after their marriage, came a telegram one day, stating that her father had died suddenly. Both went at once to London, only to find that poor old Libert had died deeply in debt. Indeed, there remained insufficient money to pay for the funeral.

Therefore, having seen her father buried at Highgate, Jean returned with Ralph to Paris, where they first took a small, cosy apartment of five rooms in the Austerlitz quarter; but as funds decreased, they were forced to economise and sink lower in the social scale—to the Montmartre.

To Jean, who had believed Ralph to be possessed of ample means, all this came as a gradual disillusionment. Her husband began quickly to neglect her, to spend his days in the *cafés*, often in Adolphe's company, while the men he brought to their rooms were, though well-dressed, of a very different class to those with whom she had been in the habit of associating in London.

But the girl never complained. She loved Ralph with a fond, silent passion, and even the poor circumstances in which already, after ten months of married life, she now found herself, did not trouble her so long as her husband treated her with consideration.

As regards Adolphe, she rather avoided than encouraged him. Her woman's keenness of observation showed her that he sympathised with her and admired her—in fact, that he was deeply in love with her, though he strenuously endeavoured not to betray his affection.

Thus, within a year of the tragic end of Dick Harborne, Jean found herself living in a second-floor flat in a secluded house in the Boulogne quarter, not far from the Seine, a poor, working-class neighbourhood. The rooms, four in number, were furnished in the usual cheap and gaudy French style, the floor of bare, varnished boards, save where strips of Japanese matting were placed.

On that warm August evening, Jean, in a plain, neatly-made black dress, with a little white collar of Swiss embroidery, and wearing a little apron of spotted print—for their circumstances did not permit the keeping of a "bonne"—was seated in her small living-room, sewing, and awaiting the return of her husband.

She had, alas! met with sad disillusionment. Instead of the happy, affluent circumstances which she had fondly imagined would be hers, she had found herself sinking lower and lower. Her parents were now both dead, and she had no one in whom to confide her suspicions or fears. Besides, day after day, Ralph went out in the morning after his *café-au-lait*, and only returned at eight o'clock to eat the dinner which she prepared—alas! often to grumble at it. Slowly—ah! so very slowly—the hideousness and mockery of her marriage was being forced upon her.

Gradually, as she sat at the open window waiting his coming, and annoyed because the evening meal which she had so carefully cooked was spoilt by his tardiness, the dusk faded and darkness crept on.

She felt stifled, and longed again for the fresh air of the country. Before her, as she sat with her hands idle in her lap, there arose memories of that warm afternoon when, in that charming little fishing village in England, she had met her good friend Richard Harborne, the man who that very same evening fell beneath an assassin's knife.

Her thoughts were stirred from the fact that, while out that morning, Mme. Garnier, from whom she purchased her vegetables daily, had given her a marguerite. This she wore in the breast of her gown, and its sight caused her to reflect that on that never-to-be-forgotten afternoon at Mundesley, when she had walked with Harborne, he, too, had given her a similar flower. Perfumes and flowers always stir our memories of the past!

She sat gazing out into the little moss-grown courtyard below, watching for Ralph's coming. That quarter of Paris was a poor one, inhabited mainly by artisans, yet the house was somewhat secluded, situated as it was in a big square courtyard away from the main thoroughfare. Because it was quiet, Ralph had taken it, and further, because Mme. Brouet, the *concierge*, a sharp-faced, middle-aged woman, wife of a cobbler, who habitually wore a small black knitted shawl, happened to be an acquaintance of his.

But, alas! the place was dismal enough. The outlook was upon a high, blank, dirty wall, while below, among the stones, grass and rank weeds grew everywhere.

The living room in which the girl sat was poor and comfortless, though she industriously kept the place clean. It was papered gaudily with broad stripes, while the furniture consisted of a cheap little walnut sideboard, upon which stood a photograph in a frame, a decanter, a china sugar-bowl, and some plates, while near it was a painted, movable cupboard on which stood a paraffin lamp with green cardboard shade, and a small fancy timepiece, which was out of order and had stopped.

In the centre of the room was a round table, upon which was a white cloth with blue border and places laid for two, and four rush-bottomed chairs placed upon the square of Japanese matting covering the centre of the room completed the picture.

Jean laid aside her needlework—mending one of Ralph's shirts—and sighed over the might-have-been.

"I wonder what it all means?" she asked herself aloud. "I wonder what mysterious business Ralph has so constantly with Adolphe? And why does Mme. Brouet inquire so anxiously after Ralph every day?"

For the past fortnight her husband, whose clothes had now become very shabby, had given her only a few francs each day, just sufficient with which to buy food. Hitherto he had taken her out for walks after dusk, and sometimes they had gone to a cinema or to one of the cheaper music-halls. But, alas! nowadays he never invited her to go with him. Usually he rose at noon, after smoking many cigarettes in bed, ate his luncheon, and went out, returning at any time between six and eight, ate his dinner, often sulkily, and then at nine Carlier would call for him, and the pair would be out till midnight.

She little guessed in what a queer, disreputable set the pair moved, and that her husband was known in the Montmartre as "The American." She was in ignorance, too, how Ralph, finding himself without funds, had gone to the Belgian Baron—the secret agent of Germany—and offered him further services, which had, however, been declined.

At first Ansell had been defiant and threatening, declaring that he would expose the Baron to the police as a foreign spy. But the stout, fair-moustached man who lived in the fine house standing in its own spacious grounds out at Neuilly, on the other side of the Bois de Boulogne, had merely smiled and invited him to carry out his threat.

"Do so, my friend," he laughed, "and you will quickly find yourself arrested and extradited to England charged with murder. So if you value your neck, it will, I think, be best for you to keep a still tongue. There is the door. *Bon soir.*"

And he had shown his visitor out.

At first Ansell, who took a walk alone in the Bois, vowed vengeance, but a few hours later, after reflecting upon the whole of the grim circumstances, had come to the conclusion that silence would be best.

Though he had endeavoured not to show it, he was already regretting deeply that he had married. Had he been in better circumstances, Jean might, he thought, have been induced to assist him in some of his swindling operations, just as the wives of other men he knew had done.

A woman can so often succeed where a man fails. But as he was almost without a sou, what could he do?

Truth to tell, both he and Carlier were in desperate straits.

Jean had been quick to notice the change in both men, but she had remained in patience, making no remark, though the whole circumstances puzzled her, and often she recollected how happy she had been at the Maison Collette when she had lived at home, and Ralph, so smart and gentlemanly, had called to see her each evening.

These and similar thoughts were passing through her mind, when suddenly she was recalled to her present surroundings by Ralph's sudden entrance.

"Halloa!" he cried roughly. "Dinner ready?"

"It has been ready more than an hour, dear," she replied, in French, jumping to her feet and passing at once into the tiny kitchen beyond.

VIII

Reveals the Grim Truth

Though Ralph Ansell's clean-shaven face was strong, and his eyes keen and searching, in the dress he wore he presented anything but the appearance of the gentleman he did when, twelve months before, he had lived in the cosy little bachelor flat in Shaftesbury Avenue.

His clothes were black, striped with grey, the coat edged with braid in the foreign manner, his neck was encircled by a soft collar tied with a loose, black cravat. His waistcoat was open, displaying his soft, white shirt and the leather belt around his waist, while on his head was a cloth cap with an unusually large peak.

He looked the true Parisian loafer, as indeed he was. Yet love is blind, and as yet Jean would believe nothing to his discredit, crushing out any suspicion that had arisen within her.

Having discarded his cap and tossed it across upon a chair, revealing his high, square forehead, he threw off his coat, and in his shirt-sleeves sat down at the table, exclaiming:

"Now, then, girl, I hope you've got something eatable to-night. I shall want something to keep me going before to-morrow morning."

"Why?" asked the girl, putting down the tureen of *pot-au-feu* and seating herself.

"I've got a little business on, that's all," he snapped, taking his soup, commencing it, and grumbling that it was badly made.

"I do my best, Ralph," she protested. "You know I've had no money for three days now."

"And if you had, the soup would be just the same," he declared. "You may be all very well to make hats, but you're no good as a man's wife. I've discovered that long ago. I—"

His words were interrupted by a loud rap at the door.

He started in alarm, but the next second sprang up and welcomed his visitor warmly.

"You, Adolphe, old fellow!" he cried. "Why, you gave me quite a start. Come in and have a bit of dinner. I want to talk to you. I was coming to find you as soon as I'd finished. Jean, another plate for Adolphe."

So the man who had entered laid his hard-felt hat on the sideboard, as was his habit, and sat down at the table in the chair that his friend had placed for him.

Then Ansell, having carefully closed the window, went back to the table and, bending towards his friend, said:

"Listen. I'm going to tell you something important. I've got a good thing on for us both to-night. You know the Baron's out at Neuilly? Well, to-night, it quite—"

"Hush, Ralph! Madame—" his companion cried, glancing at Jean, apprehensively.

"Oh, she may just as well know the truth at first as at last," laughed Ansell roughly. Then, turning to his wife, he exclaimed, with a sinister grin: "Perhaps, Jean, you may wonder how we live—how I have got my money in the past. Well, I may as well tell you, for one day you will surely discover our secret. We are burglars."

The girl started, staring blankly at her husband, and uttered a low scream.

"Burglars!" she gasped, astounded.

"Yes. And now you know the truth, take care that you never blab out a word to anyone, or, by Heaven, it will be the worse for you! If you say a word," he added, fiercely, with knit brows and glaring eyes, "if you let drop a hint to anybody, I'll break every bone in your body."

"Ralph!" she cried, starting up in horror. "Have you taken leave of your senses?"

"Enough!" protested Adolphe, angrily. "I won't stand by and hear such threats, Ralph."

"What, pray, is it to do with you?" asked Ansell, fiercely. "She's my wife, and I can speak to her. I can tell her what home-truths I like without your interference."

"I should have deemed it more prudent to have said nothing, Ralph," answered the other quietly.

Though Carlier was dressed also in a striped jacket and waistcoat and black trousers, he wore no collar, and looked even a greater blackguard than his friend.

His eyes met Jean's, and in them he saw an expression of silent thanks for taking her part.

Then she turned and, covering her face with her hands, burst into bitter, blinding tears, and disappeared into the little kitchen.

"Sit down," Ansell urged. "Now that little fool has gone, we can talk."

"You are a perfect idiot," declared the other, in disgust.

"That's my affair. She'll have to be brought to her senses and know the truth."

"It has upset her."

"I can't help that," he laughed. "She must get over it. If she wants fine dresses and a good time she must help us. And I mean that she shall before long. Look at Tavernier's wife."

"She is of a different type to madame."

"Rubbish!" he laughed. "Wait and see what I'll do. She'll be a valuable asset to us before long."

Adolphe leaned his elbows upon the table and shrugged his shoulders.

"*Bien!*" he said. "Let me hear the proposition."

"It is quite simple," the young adventurer said. "I know the interior of the Baron's house. There is a lot of good stuff there—some jewellery, too, and even enough table silver to make the job worth while. In his safe he keeps a lot of papers. If we could only get them they would fetch something in certain quarters—enough to make us both rich; but the worst of it is that we left our jet in London, and we cannot get it without." And he took a caporal from the packet before him and slowly lit it. Then he resumed, saying: "Now, I propose that we leave the safe out of the question, and go for the plate in the *salle-à-manger*. We have no tools for a really artistic job, so we must be content this time with the Baron's embroideries. His papers may come later—at least, that's my project. I've been out at Neuilly all day, and have had a good look around, and decided on the way we shall get in. It is perfectly easy—all save the watchdog. But a bit of doctored meat will do the trick. I got a little dose for him from old Père Lebrun on my way home," and from his pocket he produced a small bottle.

"Is the Baron at home?" asked his accomplice, to whom, of course, Ansell had never spoken about the failure of his plot for blackmail.

"Of course," was the reply. "But what does that matter? He'll be sound asleep, and to-morrow we shall be a couple of thousand francs the richer. It is childishly easy, my dear friend, I assure you."

"And if we meet the Baron, who, if all I hear be true, is an extremely shrewd person, what shall we do?"

"Well, if we meet anybody, we must act as we have always acted."

"Shoot, eh?"

Ansell nodded and grinned.

"We had bad luck in London, remember," said "The Eel."

"Yes; but it is easy out at Neuilly," the other declared. "I've been in the *salle-à-manger*, remember. Every bit of plate in use is solid silver. Much of it is kept in drawers in the room. Besides, there were a lot of knick-knacks about in the large *salon*. Levy will buy them in a moment. We are on a soft thing, I can assure you. I was an ass not to have thought of it long ago. Once the dog is silenced the rest is quite easy."

Caillet, who had only two francs in his pocket, reflected deeply. He was silent for fully three minutes, while his companion watched his face narrowly.

"When do you propose starting?"

"Say at eleven. We'll get your things from your place, and I'll take my flash-lamp, keys, and a few other necessaries."

"No, you'll not, Ralph!" cried Jean, as she rushed out from the kitchen, where behind the half-closed door she had been listening to the plot.

"Shut up, girl, will you?" her husband commanded roughly. "We want no woman's advice in our business."

And rising from his chair, he unlocked the drawer in the movable cupboard wherein he kept certain of his private belongings, and took therefrom a serviceable-looking revolver, which he examined and saw was fully loaded.

He also drew forth some skeleton keys, a burglar's jemmy in two sections, a pair of india-rubber gloves, a small, thin saw, and an electric pocket-lamp, all of which he carefully stowed away in his pockets.

The contents of that drawer were a startling revelation to Jean. He had always kept it locked, and she had often wondered what it contained.

Now that she knew she stood staggered.

She looked in horror at the revolver he held in his hand, and then with a sudden movement she flung herself upon him and grasped his arms, appealing to him for the sake of her love to desist from such an adventure.

Quick and passionate came the words, the full, fervent appeal of a woman deeply and honestly in love. But he heeded not either her tears or her words, and only cast her from him with a rough malediction, declaring her to be an encumbrance.

"But think!" she cried. "Now that I know what you are I am in deadly fear that—that one day they may come, Ralph, and take you away from me."

And she stood pale-faced and trembling before him.

"Ah, never fear, my girl," replied her husband. "They'll never have me. They've tried a good many times, haven't they Adolphe?" and he laughed defiantly. "The police! Zut! I do not fear them!" and he snapped his thin, long fingers in contempt.

"But one day, dear—one day they may be successful. And—and what should I do?"

"Do?" he asked. "Well, if I were put away I suppose you'd have to do as a good many other women have done."

She looked at him very straight in deep reproach, but uttered no word.

Disillusionment had fallen upon her, and utterly crushed her. Ralph—her Ralph—the man in whom all her love, all her thoughts, all her sympathies were centred, was a thief, and, further, he had cursed her as an encumbrance.

The poor girl drew her hand across her brow as though unable to actually realise the astounding facts. She was stunned by the hideous truth which had that evening been revealed. The blow had in an instant crushed all the light out of her life.

She now realised the reason of those many secret conferences with Carlier, and certain other rather disreputable-looking companions, jail-birds, without a doubt. She knew why he was sometimes absent all night, why he had stolen in, weary and worn, in the early hours of the morning, and why, on one occasion, he had remained in the house for two whole weeks and had never once gone out.

"Well, now you know the truth, girl, I hope you won't ask any more inquisitive questions," Ralph said, noticing how strangely she had stared at him. "Our business concerns nobody but ourselves—you understand?"

"Yes, I understand," she replied, slowly, in a strange, hard voice. "I understand, too, Ralph, that you no longer love me, or you would never have spoken to me as you have to-night."

And she burst into tears.

"Ralph, Ralph, this is too bad!" protested his friend. "You ought to have a little pity for poor madame—you really ought."

"I tell you I don't want any interference in my domestic affairs, so shut up, or you and I won't agree. Do you hear that—once and for all?" replied Ansell determinedly, thrusting his bony face into that of this companion.

The latter shrugged his shoulders, and merely remarked:

"Well, you surprise me greatly."

Of a sudden, however, Jean, with a quick movement, sprang towards her husband, who had already put on his coat and cap, and placed the revolver in his pocket preparatory to departing upon his midnight adventure. She seized him by both wrists and, throwing herself wildly upon her knees, begged and implored him not to go.

"For my sake, Ralph, don't go!" she urged. "Don't go! Give up the project! Work and lead an honest life, I beg of you."

"Honest life!" he laughed with a sneer. "Can you imagine me sitting in an office all day, adding up figures, or writing letters for some other thief with a brass plate on his office door? No, I'm not cut out for that, I assure you," he added.

"But for my sake, don't go," she urged again, his hands still in hers, for she held them firmly, and placed them to her lips.

His confession that he was a thief had fallen upon her, and for the first few moments had held her speechless, but now she had found tongue, and even though the disgraceful truth was out, her first thought was for his safety.

"You're a confounded little fool!" he declared, roughly. "Let me go. Come on, Adolphe! We haven't any use for women's tears."

And he twisted her hands roughly so that she was compelled to relinquish her hold.

He was leaving the room, but again she caught him, clinging to him resolutely, and beseeching him to heed her word.

This angered him. His face was pale, his eyes flashed quickly and, gripping her by the right hand, he raised his fist to strike her.

In a flash, however, Carlier, who stood with his hat on ready to depart, sprang in from behind, and gripped the brute's arm, shouting:

"No, you shall not strike her—not while I am present! Come away, you infernal coward!"

Jean gave vent to a hysterical shriek, and shook herself free, but ere she could realise what had actually happened, the two men, without further word, had left the room, her husband slamming the door after him with a fierce imprecation.

Then she stood alone, white-faced, terrified, heart-broken.

Ralph Ansell had at last shown himself in his true colours—a thief, a bully, a coward, and a blackguard.

And yet she had loved him until that hour—loved him with all the strength of her being—loved him as she had loved no other man in her whole life.

She had lived only for him, and she would have willingly died for him had he not raised his hand against her.

But she stood in the centre of that meagre little room, staring straight before her, her countenance white to the lips, her big, dark eyes fixed like one in a dream.

Poor Jean! Even then her brain was awhirl. She could scarcely realise the grim, terrible truth.

For a few moments she stood there motionless as a statue, then suddenly she staggered, reeled, and collapsed, inert and senseless, upon the floor.

IX

IN THE NIGHT

Not until several hours afterwards did Jean regain consciousness.

When slowly she opened her eyes and gazed wonderingly about the silent room, she found herself lying in a heap upon the floor, a terrible throbbing across her brow and a lump in her throat.

Gradually she recollected the horror of that half-hour before she had fainted, and slowly she raised herself and tottered to a chair.

Upon the table stood the empty bottle from which Ralph and Adolphe had drunk glass after glass of red wine, before going forth to commit the crime. There were the three empty plates, too; while on the top of the cupboard the cheap, evil-smelling lamp which Jean had lit on Ralph's arrival, was burning low, shedding a small zone of dim, yellow light.

"Gone!" she gasped aloud. "Oh, I can't believe it! Ralph—my own Ralph—a common thief! Impossible! impossible!" Then she sobbed, burying her pale face in both her hands in blank despair.

The horrible, bitter truth had been forced upon her, and she saw it in all its hideousness.

"He raised his hand to strike me down!" she murmured to herself. "He would have struck me, had it not been for Adolphe. Ah! yes," she sighed. "Adolphe knows—he knows the truth—of all I have suffered. Ralph is a thief, and—and the police will one day arrest him. He will be tried and punished, and I shall be left alone—alone!"

For a long time the despairing girl sat in her lonely room, bent and utterly crushed. Her thoughts were of the man she loved, and who, in return, had now revealed his contempt, even hatred. He had told her that she was but an encumbrance. He had not minced matters, but spoken openly and frankly, like the brute he was.

She was unaware that "The American" was well known in the Montmartre as a keen, unscrupulous man, against whom were so many charges. Next to Bonnemain himself, he had been the most daring and expert of all that dangerous gang.

How cleverly he had deceived her, however, she now knew. Her senses seemed benumbed, for the blow had rendered her, for the time, insensible.

A full hour went by.

The room was silent, save that from the courtyard below rose the drunken voice of a workman who lived in the ground-floor flat—the husband of the slatternly *concierge*—who had just returned.

The broken clock still pointed to the hour of four, therefore she had no idea of the time, but sat staring in front of her, like one in a dream.

Once or twice her breast slowly heaved and fell beneath her neat, black gown. Then at last she rose and, crossing to the cupboard with firm resolve, took out a small, ten-centime bottle of ink and an envelope.

Seating herself at the table, she took the pen in her trembling fingers, and with tears falling upon the paper, traced uneven words in French, as follows:

In spite of my love for you, Ralph, I cannot suffer longer. Certain hidden things in your life frighten me. Farewell. Forget me.

JEAN

Slowly she folded it, took off her wedding-ring, and placed it in the envelope, together with the letter. Afterwards she addressed it to her husband, and left it upon the table. Then slowly she rose with a hard, fixed look, and passed into the adjoining room, which was a bedroom.

She took a sad farewell of the few little treasures which she had brought from her own room in Oxford Street—knick-knacks, photographs, and the like—and, putting on her hat, passed back across the living-room, and then crept down the stairs and out—undiscovered and unheard by the ever-watchful old woman in the black, knitted shawl.

Without a glance back, she gained the broad, well-lit thoroughfare, and, turning to the left, went blindly and broken-hearted along in the direction of the Bois, out into the world, sad, despairing, and alone, heedless of where her steps led her, out into the unknown.

Meanwhile "The American" and "The Eel" were busy with their adventure.

To the left of the broad, main avenue, which, running through Neuilly-on-Seine, crosses the river to Courbevoie, lived the wealthy Baron de Rycker.

The house stood alone in a secluded spot, surrounded by its own spacious grounds, and hidden from the road by a high wall. In this was a big gate of ornamental iron, the top of which was gilded—a gate which the *concierge*, who lived in the lodge beside it, always kept locked.

But, through the gate, the house itself could not be seen, because plates of iron had been fixed half-way up, shutting out the view of house and well-kept grounds from the public view.

As Ralph was aware, the *concierge* was more than a mere lodge-keeper. He knew who were the Baron's friends, and admitted them without question, in whatever garb they might chance to be. But any inquisitive person, or stranger, never got within that gate, or if they attempted, they met with a warm reception from the fierce dog which constantly prowled about the grounds.

The two men arrived in Neuilly soon after eleven o'clock and, entering a *café* near the river, remained there smoking and drinking coffee, till midnight, when they went forth, treading lightly, for at "The Eel's" lodgings in the Rue Lapage, off the Boulevard de Clichy, they had both put on boots with india-rubber soles.

Passing the wall of the Baron's garden, they found all quiet and in darkness.

Then "The American" went back as far as the gate and threw a stone against the ironwork, with the result that the dog, which prowled there at night, barked furiously.

That was what Ralph Ansell desired.

Taking from his pocket a stone, to which was tied by cotton a piece of poisoned liver, he threw it over the gate and listened to it drop upon the gravel.

In a moment the dog, with natural curiosity, pounced upon it, and finding it to be a toothsome delicacy, could not resist it.

For another five minutes Ralph waited without making a sound.

Then he threw another stone against the iron sheeting of the gate.

The noise was loud. But there was no answering bark.

Then he crept back to where Adolphe lurked in the shadow.

A quarter of an hour later, both men were crouching before a long window which led out upon a well-kept lawn. They had scaled the wall, and crept across the grass without a sound.

The weather favoured them, for there was a slight west wind which, while catching the foliage of the trees, caused it to rustle and so conceal any slight noise they might make.

Ralph pressed the button of his electric lamp, and a small spot of light shone upon the glass. Then, with expert hand, he quickly smeared it with treacle, and afterwards, with a glazier's diamond, cut out a piece sufficient to allow him to insert his hand and turn the latch within.

A moment later, both men were inside the large, well-furnished *salle-à-manger*, treading noiselessly upon the thick Turkey carpet, though "The Eel," in entering, unfortunately stumbled, and in grabbing the door to prevent himself falling, cut his hand badly, even through the india-rubber gloves they both wore.

The pair lost no time in clearing the fine, carved sideboard of the quantity of valuable plate it contained. Then, led by Ralph, to whom the interior of the big house was well known, "The Eel" entered the cosy, luxuriously-furnished library, which was the private den of the chief secret agent of the German Empire.

It was not a large room. Its size was revealed to Adolphe by the flashing of his companion's lamp. Lined with books, and with a big, business-like writing-table placed in the window, it was a cosy place—a place with which many a spy of Germany was familiar and in which many a man had received a bundle of hundred-franc notes in return for information, or plans of France's armaments or defences.

From it a door led straight into the grounds, so that a visitor was not compelled to pass through the house in order to have a confidential chat with its owner, while in a farther corner of the garden was a door in the wall by which a side road might be gained.

Neither man spoke as they made a noiseless tour of the room. "The Eel" carried a capacious sack of black material, and into it thrust what knick-knacks seemed to be of value—several miniatures, a couple of gold snuff-boxes, a small box of Limoges enamel, and the like, while "The American" was busy with his skeleton keys at the drawers of the big writing-table.

Suddenly he beckoned to Adolphe, and the latter, as he approached, saw that he had succeeded in opening one of the small drawers. Within was a secret cavity known to the thief, for he had twice watched the German spy take money from it.

There was a spring at the back of the drawer, and as "The Eel" directed the rays of light inside, his companion fingered it, with the result that of a sudden a portion of the wood fell back and from within the other drew out a large bundle of French thousand-franc notes secured by an elastic band.

With a low whistle Ansell, with gloating eyes, slipped them into his breast pocket.

Then, diving his hand in again, he drew out several handsome bracelets set with diamonds and emeralds, two strings of matched pearls, a diamond and platinum pendant, a muff-chain set with diamonds, and a child's coral necklace—the jewellery belonging to the Baron's dead wife and his little daughter—which he kept concealed there—a relic of a long-past domestic happiness.

With scarce a glance at the valuables, the thief thrust them into his pocket.

Eagerly they cleared the secret space behind the back of the drawer. There were three other bank-notes lying loose, about twenty golden louis, two ruby rings, and lastly a safe-key, which Ralph held up in triumph, whispering:

"What about the Baron's secret correspondence—eh?"

"Where's the safe?" asked his companion.

"Upstairs—in his room, I expect. It is not here."

Then, leaving the drawer open, Ralph Ansell crossed the room and, opening his big clasp-knife, the blade of which was as sharp as a razor, he commenced to slash vigorously at the pale green silk upholstery of the couch and easy chairs. He was angry and vicious in his attacks upon the furniture, cutting and slashing everywhere in his triumph over the man who had refused to further assist him.

"The Eel" watched without uttering a remark. He had seen such explosions of anger before on the part of his companion when they were doing other "jobs." It is, indeed, well known to criminologists and to all police officials that the average burglar is never satisfied with mere theft, however great may be his *coup*, but that some force impels him to spend time in committing wanton damage to the furniture.

It was so with Ralph Ansell. He hated the Baron, therefore he slashed his furniture. In many other homes he had acted in a similar way, just as, indeed, Bonnemain always acted, carrying a keen knife for the purpose.

"Shall we risk going to his room?" whispered Adolphe, who approached him.

"Of course, my friend. A few of those papers will be worth thousands of francs to us," he replied in a low breath. "This is the job of our lives, *mon vieux*. I daresay there are papers there which the German Government would buy back at any price we chose to put on them."

"All right, then," was "The Eel's" reply. "If there's no great risk, then let us have a try."

"You've got your revolver—eh?"

"No. I never carry one now," was Adolphe's response.

"Never mind, I've got one; and I shall shoot—if necessary," Ralph replied. "I mean to have those papers at all costs. So don't lose your head."

"I never do."

"*Bien!* Then to work."

And the pair crept from the room without a sound, and along the dark, thickly-carpeted corridor.

X

Honour Among Thieves

They ascended the broad, dark staircase noiselessly and crept along to a door which *Fil-en-Quatre* opened cautiously, when they found themselves in the big salon, a spacious, luxuriantly-furnished room, where many of the notables of Paris, both social and political, were wont to assemble.

Society was in ignorance of the true *métier* of this wealthy Belgian, and as he entertained lavishly upon the money secretly supplied to him from Berlin, he was accepted at his own valuation, and was highly popular in the embassy set.

The little ray of light from Ralph's lamp travelled slowly around, revealing quantities of *bric-à-brac*; but so much booty had they already obtained that the pair only selected two gold spoons from a glass-topped specimen-table, with a little box, also of chased gold.

As Ralph looked around, he again became seized by that uncontrollable desire to commit damage for the mere sake of wanton destruction; therefore drawing his knife, he slashed quickly at a big ottoman covered with old rose silk damask, cutting it across and across. Afterwards he treated a down cushion in the same fierce fashion, causing the feathers to fly about the room.

"Come—enough!" whispered "The Eel" at his elbow. "Where is the Baron's room?"

"We've got to find it," was the reply. "And, by Heaven! if the spy moves, I'll put some lead into him!"

And together the pair stole forth on their tour of discovery.

The silent house was weird and full of distorted shadows. Through the long windows of stained glass which lit the great staircase the moon shone, its rays striking straight across the upper landing. Several of the doors were closed. They were bedrooms, evidently.

At one of them Ralph paused, raising his finger to command a halt. With the light touch of the expert he placed his fingers upon the door-handle, and, turning it, without raising the slightest click, he stole inside and stood in silence, listening attentively. All was dark, and there was no noise.

For a few moments he waited in patience. Then, hearing no sound of any sleeper, he switched on his little electric lamp, finding the apartment to be a small, well-furnished bedroom, but empty.

Both men examined it critically by the light of the torch, arriving at the conclusion that it contained nothing of worth.

Therefore, after Ralph had made a vicious slash at the satin-covered down quilt upon the bed, and also drawn his sharp knife across the carpet, severing it clearly, they went out to the next room, and to the next, with similar result.

Apparently the Baron did not sleep on that floor at all.

At last, however, they came to a locked door at the end of the corridor. A rapid examination showed that it had been locked from the inside, and the key was missing. Therefore, without further ado, Ralph knelt down at the lock, and with "The Eel" holding the little lamp, he commenced to attack the fastening with his skeleton keys. At such work he was an expert, for in three minutes the door stood open, and they found themselves standing in a small place, almost a box-room, for it only contained a plain little leather-covered table, set against the wall, and a chair; while in the opposite corner, upon a strong, wooden stand, stood a big, green-painted fireproof safe, about six feet in height.

Both men uttered ejaculations of surprise when their eyes fell upon it.

"The papers—the secrets of Germany—are in here!" Ralph exclaimed, in a whisper. "Come! There's no time to lose. Let's get at them. I hope this is the key. I suppose he preferred to keep it in hiding in the secret place in his writing-table than to carry it about with him."

Taking the bright little key from his pocket, he examined it critically by the light of the lamp. Then he examined the maker's name upon the brass plate on the safe.

"Yes," he said, "I think I'm right. And if so, we shall each be richer by a couple of hundred thousand francs."

"You don't seem to like the Baron, Ralph!" whispered his friend, with a smile.

"Like him! Why, I hate him! I've been here before—as his visitor."

"Is he really what you alleged—a German spy?"

"Yes. And I can prove it. Why, in doing what we are now we are acting as patriots, not as common burglars. We are acting for the honour of France."

"And for our pockets, my dear fellow," laughed his companion, as he bent beside him and watched him draw aside the brass cover of the lock and insert the key.

Gripping the big brass handle—for he knew the mechanism of that much-advertised make of safe—Ralph first turned it to the right. Then he turned the key, which worked evenly and easily, afterwards twisting the handle in an opposite direction.

Next moment, the bolts being shot back, the heavy, steel door came slowly open; but suddenly, at the same instant, a huge electric alarm bell in the main hall was set ringing.

At first so startled were they both that they did not move. But next second the truth dawned upon them.

"*Diable!* Let's fly!" cried Ansell. "It's all up! Across the garden and over the wall by the gate in the corner. Quick!"

Out of the room and down the stairs dashed the men like lightning. Along the corridor through the room by which they had entered, and out into the moonlight in the garden.

They heard loud shouts of alarm from the windows. Electric lights were being switched on everywhere, and loud cries were being raised of "Thieves! Assassins! Thieves!" while somebody fired three shots at them from a window as they crossed the grounds and sought concealment in the shadows.

As fast as their legs could carry them they made for the corner of the wall wherein was the Baron's secret exit, and, scaling the wall with quick agility, were soon on the other side—and clear away.

As they ran back in the direction of the Bois de Boulogne they could hear shouts and cries of the Baron and his servants. Twice were revolvers emptied to attract the police, and then the hubbub grew fainter, and at last, beneath the deep shadow of a wall, they halted to regain breath.

"Never mind, Adolphe!" laughed Ralph; "we've got a nice haul, and it was an easy job, after all. I never expected the spy to have an alarm attached to the door of his safe. He's a wary bird, after all!"

"Let's get back to your place at once," urged "The Eel." "It will be growing light soon, and we ought to be in before anyone gets about."

"You're right. Jean will be wondering where we are—poor, innocent little thing," he laughed, jeeringly. "I suppose she's been fretting—but fretting always does a woman good."

"Don't speak like that, old chap," said the other. "I don't like to hear it."

"Ah! You always take her part. You're too chicken-hearted where women are concerned. A woman will be your ruin one day, mark me," was Ralph's reply. "But come along."

And they hurried forward, in the direction of Ansell's house.

Half an hour later, just before the first flush of dawn, the two men entered the weedy courtyard, and Ansell let himself in with his key. Their movements were stealthy; but, nevertheless, Mother Brouet, in suspicion of the truth, for she had known *Fil-en-Quatre* for several years, put her head out of her door, asking:

"Halloa, my boys! Something on—eh?"

"Yes, mother," laughed Ralph lightly. "Something quite good. Keep your eyes open, and if anybody calls, we're not receiving visitors—you understand! And there's a couple of louis for you," he added with a grin.

The old woman grasped the coins with her claw-like hand, saying:

"*Tres bien, m'sieur*," and the head, adorned by curlers, disappeared.

The two men then mounted the stairs on tip-toe, and Ansell noiselessly unlocked the door of his apartment, believing Jean to be asleep.

But they found the lamp still burning as they had left it, the dirty plates still upon the table, and the atmosphere filled by the nauseous perfumes of petroleum.

Ralph's quick eye caught the letter lying upon the table.

"Halloa! What's this?" he cried, taking it up, glancing at the superscription, and tearing open the envelope.

He read through the brief, farewell message; then, crushing the paper in his hand fiercely, he stood for a few seconds without uttering a word.

"She's gone!" he exclaimed at last; "and a good job, too. I'm freer without her; but, by Heaven! I'll make her pay for deserting me like this! That I will!"

"Madame gone?" cried Carlier, starting in blank surprise.

"Yes."

"Well, and I don't wonder, after what you said to her last night. It was shameful."

"That's my own affair," the other said. "It don't concern you, so we need not discuss it."

"Where has she gone?"

"I don't know, and, moreover, I don't care. You, however, seem to take a particular interest in her."

"I hate to see a woman maltreated," replied Adolphe frankly.

"I tell you it is no concern of yours," replied the other, crushing Jean's letter into his jacket pocket and tossing away his cap, while Adolphe rebound his cut hand with the handkerchief which was already saturated with blood.

"Sit down and let's have a drink," said Ansell, lighting a candle, for the lamp was now very dim, and producing another bottle of red wine from the cupboard.

The pair seated themselves, and drank merrily to their own success, after which Ralph Ansell produced from his pockets the jewellery and the bundle of bank-notes, which he proceeded to examine.

Beneath the light of the single candle stuck in the tin candlestick the fine stones sparkled—diamonds, emeralds, and rubies—as "The American" produced them in a mass from his pocket and laid them upon the table.

"Quite a decent lot," he remarked. "Old Levy will give us twenty thousand francs for them, if we pretend we're not hard up. He went back to Amsterdam on Friday, but I'll wire him later on, and get him over."

"But we're not hard up," laughed "The Eel" with a grin of satisfaction.

"No—not quite," answered his companion, taking off the india-rubber band from the bundle of notes and carefully counting them, one by one. There were seventy-five blue and pink notes of the Bank of France for one thousand francs each—or three thousand pounds, as well as the loose cash.

Ralph Ansell swallowed another glass of wine.

"I'm sorry we had such horribly bad luck with that safe," he remarked. "But we were fortunate in getting away as we did. We were not a moment too soon, either."

"They saw us cross the garden," Adolphe said. "I don't like being fired at."

"By Jove! If I had met anyone he'd have gone down, I assure you," declared Ralph. "I had my revolver ready."

"A good job that we got out as we did. It is always a risky thing to try and get political papers. Remember the affair at the Austrian Ambassador's, when a stranger offered poor Bonnemain twenty thousand francs to get certain documents? I kept watch outside the Embassy that night, and we were nearly caught—all of us."

"Well—this is enough to keep the flag flying for a bit," said Ansell, as he proceeded to divide the bank-notes, placing fifty in his own pocket and giving Adolphe twenty-five.

The men had some sharp words, as thieves always have when it comes to a division of the spoils, but Ansell claimed a double share because he had been the instigator of the affair.

Adolphe Carlier protested vehemently, gesticulating wildly; but at last, finding argument of no avail, he shrugged his shoulders and accepted the inevitable. He had had previous experience of Ralph's overbearing American manners.

"Then you agree—eh?" asked Ansell, at last.

"I suppose I must," was the response, as "The Eel" thrust a thousand pounds into the inner pocket of his jacket.

"Must! Why, it is only fair!" declared Ansell. "Without my guidance you would never have brought off such a *coup*. Now this stuff," he added, indicating the jewellery. "I'll keep it till I get the money from old Levy—eh?"

"Very well," replied his companion. "But half shares of that, you know."

"Of course. That's agreed," responded the other, and both lifted the tumblers of wine in celebration of their success and safety.

"Phew! How warm I feel," exclaimed "The Eel."

"Take off your coat, old fellow, and wait here till the morning, Then we'll go out and wire to that old scoundrel, Levy," urged Ansell. "We can both do with an hour's rest after to-night's work."

"Right. But I'll bathe my hand first. It is very painful."

"Yes. Go into my room," said the other, indicating the door.

Therefore Adolphe threw off his coat, hung it upon a nail, and, unwrapping his injured hand, entered the adjoining room, closing the door after him.

"You'll find water in there," shouted his host, whose face, at the moment, relaxed into a hard, sinister smile.

He placed his hand in his jacket pocket, and it came into contact with Jean's letter.

The recollection of it maddened him. He remembered that the man in the room beyond had stood her champion, and had taken her part.

"Curse you!" he muttered, beneath his breath. "What business is it of yours—you soft-hearted fool?"

But scarce had the words fallen from his lips when the door opened suddenly, and the old woman from below, who acted as *concierge*, terrified and panting, entered, and with a loud whisper, cried:

"Ah, M'sieur Ansell. Quick! quick! The police are here! The commissary is asking for you. Quick! Get away, or you'll be caught like a rat in a trap. You know the way. Leave the rest to me!"

And without another word she disappeared, closing the door after her, while the wanted man stood staggered, pale, and dumb.

XI

THE VOW

For a second, pale with alarm, Ralph Ansell glanced around the room.

Suddenly an idea suggested itself. He was always resourceful.

Next moment he dashed across to the door and locked it, afterwards rushing to the door which led into the bedroom—the room in which his friend was bathing his wound. There was a bolt upon the door, and this he slipped, thus imprisoning the man who was, as yet, unconscious of danger.

Then, crossing to where Adolphe's jacket hung, he quickly drew out the twenty-five thousand francs in notes and placed them in his own pocket.

He held his breath and listened. As yet, all was quiet, save for a man's rough voice below. He was apparently in conversation with Mme. Brouet's husband.

That was sufficient for Ansell.

Quickly he pushed away the table from the centre of the room, and, kicking aside the Japanese grass-mats, there was revealed in the floor a trap-door with an iron ring in it.

Without more ado he lifted the heavy flap, disclosing the cavernous darkness of a kind of shaft which led to the cellar, whence there was a secret exit into a neighbouring street. Placing his foot upon the first rung of the rickety ladder, he quickly disappeared, closing the flap after him and bolting it from beneath.

Thus Adolphe, robbed and imprisoned by the man he had trusted so implicitly, was left to his fate.

Scarcely had the fugitive, carrying with him the whole of the booty, closed down the flap in the floor when Adolphe, whose hand was very painful and bleeding profusely, suddenly heard the voices below.

He started, crept to the window, and looked cautiously down into the courtyard.

Two men were there—men whom he instantly recognised as police agents in plain clothes.

"The Eel" listened for a second, then dashed to the door to warn Ralph.

He turned the handle, but, to his surprise and dismay, found the door bolted.

"Ralph! Ralph!" he cried. "Are you there? Quick! Let me in! The police!"

There was no response.

"Ralph!" he repeated. "Quick! The police are below!"

And he tugged frantically at the door. But it was securely fastened.

He was caught—like a rat in a trap!

Bending, he peered through the keyhole, surprised to discover that the table had been moved. He could see, too, that the matting had been cast aside, revealing the trap-door. That house had long been the abode of thieves. Bonnemain himself had lived in those same rooms for six years, and he had had the secret exit constructed. More than once it had been used, and the fugitive escaped by that secret way.

In a moment the grim truth flashed across Adolphe's mind. Ansell had for some reason bolted the door, and had forgotten to unlock it before escaping.

But why had he not warned him?

The voices outside were now raised, and he could hear the tramp of several other men over the moss-grown stones of the weedy courtyard.

Not a second was to be lost; therefore, taking up one of the rush-bottomed chairs and raising it above his head, he advanced to the door and brought it down with a crash upon the panel just over the lock.

A great crack showed, and by a second heavy blow the panel gave way sufficiently to allow him to insert his hand and draw the bolt from the opposite side.

He dashed across the living-room to where his coat hung, in order to seize his portion of the booty. Quickly he searched the pockets, but in vain!

The notes were gone!

Then, for the first time, he realised that he had been robbed, and from his dry lips there fell a fierce vow of vengeance against the man whose willing tool he had been—the man whose wife had left him because of his callous brutality.

Twice he searched his pockets, then he cast his coat from him in despair and, bending to the floor, tugged at the iron ring.

That, too, was secured. He could not lift it because the scoundrel had bolted it from beneath. Not only had he stolen his money, but he

WILLIAM LE QUEUX

had made him a prisoner, knowing that he must fall into the hands of the police.

With his long, black hair ruffled, his great, dark eyes starting from their sockets, and both fists clenched in desperation, he gazed wildly around for some means of escape. There were none. Heavy footsteps sounded upon the uncarpeted stairs, yet if he attempted to jump from the window he would fall into the arms of the police, who had by this time surrounded the house.

This was Ralph's revenge—because he had taken his poor little wife's part, because he had prevented him from striking her down!

A bitter thought arose in the young thief's heart. He bit his lip, and in an undertone declared:

"If ever I meet the cowardly blackguard I will kill him! That I swear. Not only has he robbed me, but he has also betrayed me to the police, knowing that I must be sent to prison, while he will remain safe!"

At that instant there came a heavy banging upon the door, while a loud, imperative voice cried:

"We are agents of police. Open—in the name of the law!"

The victim shrank back in terror. It was the end of his criminal career! He never dreamed that the police were so hot upon their track, and that they had been traced right over from Neuilly.

"Open—in the name of the law!" was again repeated, loud and commanding, followed by a sharp rapping.

For a few seconds Adolphe stood motionless, his fist still clenched, his terrified eyes fixed upon the door. He seemed rooted to the spot.

"Open this door—or we shall break it down!" shouted the police-officer on the stairs.

Then, finding resistance impossible, Ansell's victim was compelled to bow to the inevitable.

He crossed the room slowly, turned the key, and drew the bolt.

Next second three men in plain clothes and a couple of police-agents in uniform burst into the room, and Adolphe found himself seized roughly and secured.

"Just caught you, my young friend!" laughed the police-commissary, with satisfaction. He wore an overcoat and hard felt hat, and carried in his hand an ebony cane with silver knob.

Adolphe, in the hands of the two other men in plain clothes, made no reply, but at the moment Mme. Brouet entered at the door, with curiosity, to watch the proceedings.

The commissary, noticing the smashed panel of the bedroom door, ran inside, while the men in uniform quickly searched the place.

"Where is 'The American'?" asked the commissary, of Adolphe. "We know he is here, somewhere. You need not affect innocence, for your hand tells the truth. You and he did the job at the Baron de Rycker's, and you left a large blood-stain behind. What have you done with the stolen property—eh? Now, out with it! Give it up, and it will be better for you when in court."

"I haven't any," protested the young man. "Ralph has it all."

"Where is he?"

"I don't know. He locked me in yonder room and got away."

"Got away with the swag? Ah! Just like 'The American'! He did that same trick three years ago. I remember a complaint made by one of your fraternity whom I arrested at Versailles," replied the commissary. "How did he get away?"

Adolphe pointed to where the commissary was standing, and the official, looking down, saw, to his surprise, for the first time, the rusty ring in the floor.

He bent and tried to raise it, but found it firmly secured.

"He's gone!" he cried to the two agents in uniform, who were cyclists, wearing the flat-peaked caps with the arms of the City of Paris upon them. "Go out and scour all the streets in the neighbourhood. You may catch him yet!"

Without a second's delay, both men dashed out to do the bidding of their superior officer.

Adolphe Carlier was left with the two agents of the Sûreté—both dark, shrewd little men, broad-shouldered, and short of stature,—while the commissary, who wore the button of the Légion d'Honneur in his overcoat, made a tour of the apartment.

Another agent of police, in plain clothes, entered and saluted.

"Did you see anything of the fugitive, Leblanc?" asked the commissary eagerly.

"Nothing, m'sieur. I came along from the depôt, but met nobody."

"Search this place," he said. "There is some stolen stuff hidden in this rat-hole, I expect."

"I tell you Ralph Ansell has it all," declared the man held by the two officers, who were now allowing him to bandage up his hand, prior to putting handcuffs upon his wrists. "Arrest Ansell, and you will find everything upon him."

"Do you live here?" asked the commissary.

"No. Ansell lives here with his wife."

"His wife! Where is she?"

"I don't know. She was here at dinner-time, but now she's gone. She's left him."

"Why?"

"Because of his brutality." And Adolphe described the scene of the previous night.

"We must find her," said the commissary, decisively. "Perhaps she knows something. Ansell and you are the last two members of the Bonnemain gang. Am I not correct?"

"Quite, m'sieur."

"I thought I was," and the commissary smiled. "Well," he added, "your friend robbed you and threw you right into our hands. No wonder you are ready to give him away."

The commissary well knew the ways of criminals, and was also aware with what murderous hatred a man was regarded who robbed his accomplice.

"Do not discuss him, m'sieur," replied the man under arrest. "He has placed me in your hands, and I am helpless. I suppose I shall only get what I deserve," he added, in a low, pensive tone.

"You are reasonable, Carlier, and I'm glad to see it," responded the commissary in a softer tone. "Your friend is an arrant blackguard to have treated his wife as he has, and to have betrayed you because you took her part. But you surely knew how unscrupulous he was, and also that he was a most dangerous character. We know of one or two of his exploits, and I may tell you that if he is caught, there are two charges of murder against him."

"I know," replied the thief, briefly. "Though you have arrested me, I can truly say that I have never raised a knife, or fired a revolver, or attempted to take the life of any man."

"You will not be charged with any crime more serious than burglary, Carlier," replied the official. "But besides the Baron's affair to-night, there is also the robbery at the widow's apartment in the Rue Léonce Reynaud, the theft from the Château des Grandes Vignes, out at Moret in the Forest of Fontainebleau, and the safe-breaking at Thessier's in the Boulevard des Italiens. You were in all of them, remember."

"M'sieur knows," replied Adolphe with a grim smile.

"It is my duty to know, eh?" was the rather sympathetic reply, for the commissary had quickly seen that this member of the broken Bonnemain gang, which had for years given such trouble to the Sûreté, was, though a criminal and outwardly a rough scoundrel of the Apache type, yet nevertheless a man possessed of better feelings than the ordinary thief.

The treatment that Carlier had received at his friend's hands had crushed him. He did not crave for mercy, as so many criminals did when suddenly cornered and placed under arrest. He merely regarded it as a stroke of ill-luck, and with the true sportsman-like air "faced the music."

As a matter of fact, he was wondering at that moment what had become of little Mme. Ansell, and whether the efforts of the police to discover her would be successful. No doubt they would, for one cannot travel far in Paris if one is searched for by the Sûreté, unless one is a professional thief, and therefore knows the holes in the underworld of Parisian life in which to hide successfully.

The commissary, pointing with his stick at the movable cupboard, ordered one of the agents to search it, and then, moving from one object to another, he had everything turned upside down in search of any property which might be concealed. The cupboard and sideboard were shifted away from the wall, the chairs were examined, the pictures taken down and pulled from their frames; indeed, no stone was left unturned.

When the French police make a search, they do so with a creditable thoroughness.

Adolphe, the gyves upon his wrists, craved a cigarette, and a police-officer took one from the packet lying upon the sideboard. Then, with both hands, the prisoner lit it, and sat upon a chair watching them turn the place upside down.

In the adjoining room they investigated everything. They even cut open the mattress and searched for stolen jewellery or bank-notes.

"It's no use, m'sieur; there is nothing here," Carlier assured the commissary. "We have not done a job for a long time."

"Are you sure that 'The American' has it all?" asked the official earnestly.

"I've already told m'sieur," was "The Eel's" reply. "And, further, may I crave a favour?"

"What is that?"

"To speak alone with you just for a moment. I want to tell you something—for your ear alone."

The official was instantly suspicious. But, as the prisoner was securely handcuffed, there was, he saw, no danger.

So he permitted him to pass inside the disordered bedroom, and then he closed the broken door.

XII

The Fate of "The American"

Monsieur," said Carlier, in a low, confidential voice, when they were alone, "though I may be a thief, and under arrest, I am still a son of France, am I not?"

"I suppose so," replied the commissary, rather puzzled.

"Well," said the man before him, "if you keep observation upon the Baron de Rycker, you will find that what he has lost he well deserved to lose."

"What do you mean?"

"I mean that the Baron is a spy—a secret agent of Germany."

The commissary looked at him sharply, and asked:

"How do you know that?"

"Ansell told me."

"Are you quite certain?"

"Quite. Ansell has done some jobs for him, and has been well paid for them. He has acted as a spy for our enemies."

"A spy as well as a thief—eh?"

"Exactly, m'sieur. Ansell has been in the Baron's pay for nearly two years."

"But this allegation is quite unsubstantiated. The Baron de Rycker is well known and highly popular in Paris. He moves in the best society, and the Ministers frequently dine at his table."

"I know that, m'sieur. But search that safe in the little room upstairs—the safe we opened. Go there in pretence of examining our finger-prints, and you will find in the safe quantities of compromising papers. It was that collection of secret correspondence which we were after when the alarm-bell rang. We intended to secure it and sell it back to Germany."

"If what you say is really true, Carlier, our friends in Berlin would probably give you quite a handsome price for it," replied the official thoughtfully.

He had watched the thief's face, and knew that he was telling the truth.

"Will you have inquiries made?" urged the thief.

"Most certainly," was the reply. "And if I find you have told the truth, I will endeavour to obtain some slight favour for you—a shorter sentence, perhaps."

"I have told you the truth, m'sieur. It is surely the duty of every Frenchman, even though he be a thief like myself, to unmask a spy."

"Most certainly," declared the official. "And I am very glad indeed that you have told me. I shall make a report to the Prefect of Police this morning, and tell him the name of my informant. The matter will be dealt with at once by the political department of the Sûreté."

"The Baron will not be told who informed against him?" asked Adolphe anxiously.

"Certainly not. But if Ralph Ansell is arrested, he will be charged with assisting foreign spies—a charge quite as serious as breaking into the Baron's house."

"He hated the Baron because the latter had discharged him from his secret service."

"What were his duties?"

"Ah! that I do not quite know, except that he performed delicate missions, and sometimes went abroad, to Holland, England, Norway, and other places."

"Ansell evidently knew the arrangements of the house—eh?"

"He had been to see the Baron in secret many times."

"And been well paid for his work, I suppose?"

"Oh, yes; heavily paid."

"Well," remarked the police official, "you may rest assured that the Baron will, in future, be well watched. We have no love for foreign spies in Paris, as you know."

And then the commissary went on to question Carlier closely regarding his antecedents and his connection with the notorious Bonnemain gang, which had now been so fortunately broken up.

To all his questions Adolphe replied quite frankly, concealing nothing, well knowing that his sentence would not be made heavier if he spoke openly.

"I've heard stories of you for a long time, Carlier," the commissary said at last. "And I suppose we should not have met now, except for the blackguardly action of this man who posed as your friend."

"No. I should have escaped, I expect, just as I have done so often that my friends call me 'The Eel,' on account, I suppose, of my slipperiness!" And he grimaced.

The official laughed, and, with a word of thanks for the information concerning the Baron, both captor and prisoner passed back into the living-room, where the police-agents were concluding their searching investigations.

Nothing had been found of an incriminating nature, and the commissary now saw that the man arrested had spoken the truth.

While Ansell's house was being turned upside down and Adolphe and the commissary were exchanging confidences, "The American" was having a truly hot and exciting time, as indeed he richly deserved.

Having entered the shaft, after securing the trap-door with its stout, iron bolt, he descended the rickety ladder to the cellar; thence, passing by a short tunnel, which Bonnemain had constructed with his own hands, he ascended a few rough wooden steps, and found himself in a lean-to outhouse close to a door in a high wall which led into a side street.

Creeping to the door he drew the bolt, and in a moment was free.

Turning to the left, he took to his heels, and ran as fast as his legs would carry him, intending, if possible, to get away to the country.

He was elated at his narrow escape, and how cleverly he had tricked his friend, with whom he knew the police would be busy and so allow him time to get clean away.

He was lithe and active, and a good runner. Therefore in his rubber-soled shoes he ran swiftly in the grey light of early morning, turning corner after corner, doubling and re-doubling until he came to a main thoroughfare. Then, walking slowly, he crossed it, and dived into a maze of small turnings, all of which were familiar to him.

His first idea had been to seek refuge in the house of a friend—a thief, like himself, named Toussaint—but such a course would, he reflected, be highly dangerous. The police knew Toussaint to be a friend of his, and would, perhaps, go there in search of him.

No. The best course was to get away into the country, and then to Belgium or Spain. With that snug little sum in his pocket, he could live quietly for at least a year.

At last, out of breath, he ceased running, and, moreover, he noticed some men, going to their work early, look askance at his hurry.

So he walked quietly, and lit a cigarette so as to assume an air of unconcern.

"'The Eel' has been trapped at last," he laughed to himself. Then, as he put his hand into the outside pocket of his jacket, it came into contact with Jean's letter of farewell.

He drew it out, glanced at it, and put it into his inner pocket with an imprecation followed by a triumphant laugh.

Then he whistled in a low tone to himself a popular and catchy refrain.

He was walking along briskly, smiling within himself at his alert cleverness at escaping, when, on suddenly turning the corner of a narrow street close to the Seine, he found himself face to face with two agents of police on cycles.

They were about a hundred yards away and coming in his direction. They instantly recognised him. They were the two men sent out by the commissary.

In a moment, by the attitude of the two officers, Ralph Ansell realised his danger. But too late. They threw down their cycles and fell upon him.

For a few seconds there was a fierce struggle, but in desperation Ansell drew his revolver and fired point-blank at one of his captors, who staggered and fell back with a bullet-wound in the face.

Then in a moment the thief had wrenched himself free and was away.

The sound of the shot alarmed two other police-cyclists who were in the vicinity, and, attracted by the shouts of the injured man's companion, they were soon on the scene, and lost no time in pursuing the fugitive.

The chase was a stern one. Through narrow, crooked streets "The American" ran with all speed possible, his endeavour being to reach a narrow lane protected from wheeled traffic by posts at either end, where he knew the cyclists would be compelled to dismount.

The quarter where he was, chanced to be a not altogether respectable one, therefore the wild shouts of the pursuing cyclists brought no assistance from the onlookers. Indeed, the people shouted to the fugitive, crying:

"Run, young fellow! Run on and they won't get you! Run!"

And men and women shouted after him encouragingly.

With their cries in his ears, Ansell mended his pace, but his pursuers were fast gaining upon him, and had almost overtaken him when he reached the narrow passage between two high, dark-looking houses, close to the river.

He was now near to the river-bank, and within sight of the Pont des Peupliers, which crosses the Seine to Issy. The two police-agents threw aside their cycles and sped after him, but he was too quick for them, and when they had passed through the passage, they saw him dashing along by the edge of the river.

In his mad haste he stumbled and fell, and his pursuers were instantly upon him. But ere they could reach him he had jumped again to his feet and, levelling his revolver, fired point-blank at them.

The bullet passed them harmlessly, but a group of men on their way to work, attracted by the shot and seeing the thief fleeing from justice, again shouted to him encouragingly, for the police of Paris are not in good odour with the public, as are the police of London.

"Keep on, brave boy!" they shouted. "Go it! Don't give up!" And so on.

The police-cyclists proved, however, to be good runners. They took no heed of the men's jeers. One of their colleagues had been shot; therefore they intended to arrest his assailant, alive or dead.

Indeed, the elder of the two men had drawn his heavy revolver and fired at Ansell in return.

"Coward!" cried the men, reproachfully. "You can't catch the man, so you'd shoot him down. Is that the justice we have in France?"

On went the hunted thief, and after him the two men, heedless of such criticism, for they were used to it.

At last, as they neared the bridge, Ralph Ansell felt himself nearly done. He was out of breath, excited; his face scarlet, his eyes starting out of his head.

He was running along the river-bank, and within an ace of arrest, for the two men had now out-run him.

They were within a dozen feet of his heels, one of them with a heavy, black revolver in his hand.

Should he give up, or should he make still one more dash—liberty or death?

He chose the latter, and ere his pursuers were aware of his intention, he halted on the stone edge of the embankment.

For a second he paused, and laughing back triumphantly at the agents, who had cornered him, he raised his hands above his head and dived into the swiftly flowing stream.

The men who had chased him drew up instantly, and the elder, raising his weapon, fired at the thief's head as it appeared above the water. Three times he fired, and had the satisfaction of seeing the head disappear beneath the surface close to the dark shadow of the bridge.

That he had wounded him was plainly evident. Therefore, in satisfaction, the two men stood and watched to see the fugitive rise again.

But they watched in vain.

If he did rise, it was beneath the great bridge, where the dark shadow obscured him, for it was not yet daylight.

Ralph Ansell, alias "The American," and alias half-a-dozen other names, known in criminal circles in Paris, London, and New York, sank in the swift, muddy Seine flood—and disappeared.

XIII

SISTERS IN SILENCE

Just before eleven o'clock on the following morning two sisters of the Order of Saint Agnes, one of the religious Orders which devote themselves to nursing the poor, were passing through the Tuileries Gardens, sombre figures in their ample plain, black habits, black head-dresses, and deep, white collars, their hands beneath their gowns and gaze downturned, when one of them chanced to note the frail, pathetic little figure of a woman resting upon one of the seats.

It was Jean Ansell. Worn and weary after hours of aimless wandering, she had entered those gardens so beloved of Parisian *bonnes* and children, and sunk down upon that seat just within the high railings skirting the busy Rue de Rivoli, and had then burst into bitter tears. Her young heart was broken.

Within sound of the hum of the never-ceasing motor traffic, up and down that fine, straight street of colonnades to the great Place de la Concorde, where the fountains were playing, the stream of everyday life of the Gay City had passed her by. None cared—none, indeed, heed a woman's tears.

Men glanced at her and shrugged their shoulders, and the women who went by only grinned. Her troubles were no concern of theirs. Hatless, with only an old black shawl about her, and with her apron still on, she found herself hungry, homeless, and abandoned. Moreover, she was the wedded wife of a dangerous criminal!

Those who passed her by little dreamed of the strange tragedy that was hers, of the incidents of the past night, of the burglary, the betrayal, the arrest, the flight, and the crowning tragedy. Indeed, she herself sat in ignorance of what had happened to the pair after they had left the house.

She was only wondering whether Ralph had found her note, and whether on reading it, he had experienced any pang of regret.

She was only an encumbrance. He had bluntly told her so.

And as she again burst into tears, for the twentieth time in the half-hour she had rested upon that seat, the two grave-faced sisters noticed her. Then, after discussing her at a distance, they ventured to approach.

She was sitting in blank despair, her elbow upon the arm of the seat, her head bent, her hand upon her brow, her whole frame convulsed by sobs.

"Sister, you are in trouble," exclaimed the elder of the two thin-faced, ascetic-looking women, addressing her as she placed a hand tenderly upon her shoulder. "Can we be of any assistance?"

Poor Jean looked up startled, dazed for the moment. She was amazed at sight of them. Ah, only those who have been adrift in Paris— the bright, laughter-loving, gay city of world-wide fame—know how hard, cruel, and unsympathetic Paris is, how the dazzling shops, the well-dressed crowds, the brilliantly-lit boulevards, the merry *cafés*, and the clattering restaurants all combine to mock the hungry and weary, the despairing, the penniless.

The girl looked up into the kind, rather sad features framed by the white linen head-dress, and tried to speak. She endeavoured to reply, but so weak was she after a whole day and night without food, that she suddenly fainted.

It was some time before she recovered consciousness, but as soon as she was sufficiently calm she gave them a brief account of what had happened. She said nothing about her husband's latest exploit, but merely told them how she had left him because of his neglect and brutality, combined with the fact that she had made the astounding discovery that he was a thief.

They sat beside her, listening attentively to her story, and expressing the deepest sympathy.

Then, after a quarter of an hour's conversation, the two sisters agreed that they could not leave her there alone, and suggested that she should accompany them to the convent, situated a few kilometres out of Paris, close to Enghien.

So, after taking her to a small restaurant near and giving her some food, they took a taxi to the Gare du Nord, and half an hour later entered the big convent of the Order, a grey, inartistic, but spacious place, with large shady gardens at the rear, sloping down to the Lake of Enghien.

In the heavy door was a small grille, and when one of the sisters rang the clanging bell a woman's face peered forth at them with curiosity before admitting them.

Jean, in her weak, nervous state, had visions of long, stone corridors, of ghostly figures in black habits and white caps moving noiselessly, and of a peace and silence entirely strange to her. Inside, no one spoke. Save those conducting her to the rooms of the Mother Superior, all were mute.

On every wall was a crucifix, and at each corner in a small niche stood a statue of the Holy Virgin.

They passed by the fine chapel, and Jean saw the long, stained-glass windows, the rows of empty chairs, and the Roman Catholic altar, the burning candles reflecting upon the burnished gilt, and the arum lilies in the big brass vases on either side.

At last, shown into a large bare room, the walls of which were panelled half-way up—a room bare, austere, and comfortless, with an utter lack of any attempt at decoration—Jean sank into a big leather-covered arm-chair, and one of the sisters took the old black shawl from her shoulders.

A few minutes later there entered an elderly, stately woman, with hard mouth and aquiline nose, yet in whose eyes was a pleasant, sympathetic expression—a woman very calm, very possessed, even austere. She was the Mother Superior.

With her was another sister, also a probationer in the white dress, big apron, and cap with strings, proclaiming her to be a nurse.

The two sisters who had found the poor girl introduced her to the Mother Superior, who at first looked askance at her and whose manner was by no means cordial.

She heard all in silence, gazing coldly at the girl seated in the chair.

Then she questioned her in a hard, unmusical voice.

"You have been brought up in London—eh?"

"Yes, madame. I was a modiste, and my father was a restaurant keeper."

"You speak English?"

"Quite well, madame. I have lived there ten years."

"We have a branch of the sisterhood in England—near Richmond. Perhaps you know it?"

"Yes, madame. I remember my father pointing the convent out to me."

"Ah, you know it!" exclaimed the elder woman. "I was there last year."

Then she reverted to Jean's husband, asking where they were married, and many details concerning their life since that event.

To all the questions Jean replied frankly and openly. All she concealed was the fact that Ralph and Adolphe had committed a burglary on the night when she had taken her departure.

"I could not stand it any longer, madame," she assured the Mother

Superior, with hot tears in her big eyes. "He tried to strike me, but his friend prevented him."

"His friend sympathised with you—eh?" remarked the woman, who had had much experience of the wrongs of other women.

"Yes, madame."

"In love with you? Answer me that truthfully!" she asked sternly.

"I—I—I really don't know," was the reply, and a hot flush came to her pale cheeks.

The questioner's lips grew harder.

"But it is plain," she said. "That man was in love with you! Did he ever suggest that you should leave your husband?"

"No—never—never!" she declared very emphatically. "He never made such a suggestion."

"He did not know your intention of leaving your home?"

"No. He knew nothing."

The Mother Superior was silent for a few moments, surveying the pale, despairing little figure in the huge carved chair; then, with a woman's sympathy, she advanced towards her and, placing her hand upon her shoulder, said:

"My child, I believe your story. I feel that it is true. The man who was a criminal deceived you, and you were right to leave him to his own devices, if he refused to listen to your appeal to him to walk in the path of honesty. To such as you our Order extends its protection. Remain here with us, child, and your home in future shall be a home of peace, and your life shall be spent in doing good to others, according to the Divine command."

At her words the three sisters bent to her enthusiastically, calling her by her Christian name; while Jean, on her part, raised the thin, bony hand of the Mother Superior and kissed it in deep gratitude.

From that moment she became a probationer, and joined the peaceful, happy circle who kept their religious observations so rigidly, and who, during the hours of recreation, chattered and made merry together as women will.

In her white dress, linen apron, and flat cap with strings, her first duties were in the linen-room, where she employed her time in sewing, with three other probationers as companions, while each day she attended a class for instruction in first aid in nursing.

Thus the weeks went on until, in the month of November, the Mother Superior came to her one afternoon with the news—not altogether welcome—that as she spoke English so well, it had been arranged that she should be transferred to the branch in London, and that she was to leave in two days' time.

So attached had she become to them all that she burst into tears and appealed to be allowed to remain. The matter, however, had been decided by the Council of the Order, therefore to stay was impossible. The only hope that the Mother Superior held out was that she might come back to Paris at frequent intervals as a visitor.

Long and many were the leave-takings, but at last came the hour of her departure.

Then, with a final farewell to the Mother Superior, she entered the taxi with her small belongings and drove to the Gare du Nord, where, in the black habit of the Order, she took train for London.

The journey by way of Calais and Dover had no novelty for her. She had done it several times before. But on the arrival platform at Charing Cross she saw two sisters of her Order awaiting her, and was quickly welcomed by them.

Then, hailing a taxi, the three drove at once away through Kensington, across Hammersmith Bridge, along Castlenau, across Barnes Common, and at last into Roehampton Lane, that long, narrow thoroughfare which, even to-day, retains a semi-rural aspect, its big, old-fashioned houses surrounded by spacious grounds, and its several institutions which have been built on sites of mansions demolished during the past five years or so.

The Convent of Saint Agnes was a big building, constructed specially by the Order some twenty years ago. Shut off from the dusty, narrow roads by a high, grey wall with a small, arched door as the only entrance, it stood about half-way between the border of Barnes Common and Richmond Park, a place with many little arched windows and a niche with a statue of the Virgin over the door.

Here the Mother Superior—a woman slightly older than the directress in Paris, but with a face rather more pleasant—welcomed her warmly, and before the next day had passed Jean had settled down to her duties—the same as those in Paris, the mending of linen, at which she had become an adept.

In the dull November days, as she sat at the window of the linen-room overlooking the frost-bitten garden with its leafless trees and dead flowers, she fell to wondering how Ralph fared. She wondered how all her friends were at the Maison Collette, and who was now proprietor of her dead father's little restaurant in Oxford Street.

Through the open windows of her little cubicle, in the silence of night, she could see the red glare over London, and could hear the distant roar of the great Metropolis. Oft-times she lay thinking for hours, thinking and wondering what had become of the man she so unwisely loved—the man who had destroyed all her fondest hopes and illusions.

December went on, a new year dawned—a year of new hopes and new resolutions.

She had settled down in her new home, and, among the English sisters, found herself just as happy as she had been at Enghien. No one in the whole sisterhood was more attentive to her instruction, both religious and in nursing, for she was looking forward with hope that by March she would pass from the grade of probationer to that of nurse, and that she would soon go forth upon her errands of mercy among the poor and afflicted.

And so, after the storm and stress of life in the underworld of Paris, Jean Ansell lived in an atmosphere of devotion, of perfect happiness, and blissful peace.

XIV

Jean Learns the Truth

Months—months of a quiet, peaceful, uneventful life went by, and Jean had become even more popular among the English sisters than she had been in Paris.

Though her life had so entirely changed, and she had naught to worry her, not a thought nor a care beyond her religious duties and her nursing, in which she was now growing proficient, she would sometimes sit and think over her brief married life, and become filled by wonder.

Where was her husband? Where, too, was the low-born thief who had taken her part and prevented the blow upon that never-to-be-forgotten night?

Sometimes when she reflected upon it all she sat horrified. And when she recollected how shamefully she had been deceived by the man she so implicitly trusted and so dearly loved, tears would well in her great, big eyes. Sister Gertrude, one of the nurses, a tall, fair woman, who was her most intimate friend, often noticed the redness of her eyes, and guessed the truth.

Seldom, if ever, Jean went out farther than across Barnes Common or into Richmond Park for exercise, and always accompanied by Sister Gertrude, the latter wearing the black habit of the Sisterhood, while Jean herself was in a distinctive garb as a nurse of the Order of Saint Agnes.

Never once in all those months had she been in London. All she saw of it was the red glare upon the night sky. But she was happy enough. London, and especially the neighbourhood of Regent Street, would remind her too vividly of Ralph and of her dear father.

One spring afternoon, while seated at the open window finishing some needlework destined for a poor family living in a back street off the Hammersmith Broadway, she was chatting merrily with Sister Gertrude. Over their needlework the rules allowed them to chatter, and in that barely-furnished little room she and Sister Gertrude enjoyed many a pleasant gossip.

Outside, the garden was gay with daffodils and hyacinths, and the trees were just bursting into bud, the fresh green rendered the brighter by the warm sunshine.

Jean concluded her work at last, placed her needle in the cushion, and removed her thimble.

"At last!" she sighed. "I've been over this a whole week," she added.

"Yes; you've been most patient," declared her friend. "Soon you will abandon needlework and be sent out nursing. I heard the Mother Superior talking about it with Sister Lilian after vespers last night. Now that Sister Hannah has gone back to Paris we are one nurse short, and you are to take her place."

"Am I?" cried Jean, with delight, for she had studied long and diligently in the hope that soon outside work would be given her. She was devoted to nursing, and had made herself proficient in most of the subjects.

"Yes. I believe you will hear something in the course of a few days. But," added Sister Gertrude, "I know another secret. Your friend, the Mother Superior in Paris, is coming here, and ours has been transferred to Antwerp. The change will be announced, I expect, to-morrow."

At this news Jean expressed the greatest satisfaction, for the grave, yet rather hard-faced, directress of the convent at Enghien had been so good and generous that she had become devotedly attached to her. Indeed, to her she owed her life, for in her despondent state on that morning when found in the Tuileries Gardens she had seriously contemplated throwing herself into the Seine.

Jean was therefore loud in praise of the directress from Enghien, and highly delighted at the thought of her coming to take over the direction of the English branch of the Order.

"Here is some paper and string to wrap up your work," Sister Gertrude said at last, handing her an old copy of the *Daily Telegraph*. "I am taking it with me to Hammersmith this evening."

And then she left the room, promising to return in a few minutes.

Alone, Jean, standing at the window, gazed idly at the newspaper, the date of which was a Monday in the previous October.

It was strictly against the rules of the Order to read any newspaper, but as she turned it over, a column headed "Paris Day by Day" caught her eye. The temptation proved too much, and she scanned it down as she had been in the habit of scanning the paper each evening in the days when she had lived at home.

Suddenly a paragraph caught her eye. Her mouth stood open, her eyes started from their sockets as she read. Then she held her breath, placing her left hand to her breast as though to stay the beating of her heart.

Her countenance was blanched to the lips. The words she read were as follows:

"The daring exploits of the notorious criminal, Ansell, alias 'The American,' and Carlier, alias 'The Eel,' are at an end. Yesterday, in Paris, Carlier was sentenced to seven years' hard labour, and Ansell, it will be remembered, was shot by the police while swimming the Seine, but his body was never recovered."

"Dead!" she gasped, white as death. "Shot down by the police—*my husband!*"

She staggered, clutching at the small deal work-table for support, or she would have fallen.

"And Adolphe has been sent to prison for seven years!" she went on, speaking to herself in a low mechanical tone. "Was it for the crime committed on that night, I wonder? Were my fears well-grounded, and did my prediction of discovery come true? Ah, if Ralph had but listened to my appeal!" she cried in agony. "But he is dead—dead! Shot by the police—shot down like an animal. Ah, what an ignominious end!"

The newspaper fell from her fingers. The blow had stunned her.

She stood swaying slightly, her white face turned towards the open window, her eyes staring straight before her—silent, motionless, aghast.

Sister Gertrude entered, but so preoccupied was she that she was utterly unconscious of her presence.

"You are unwell, Jean," she said, in her soft, refined voice, for before entering the convent five years ago she had moved in society, being the daughter of a well-known Paris banker. "Tell me, dear, what ails you?"

Jean started, and stared at her in amazement.

"I—I—oh, there is nothing," she faltered. "I don't feel very well—that's all."

The newspaper lay on the floor, where it had fallen from her white, nerveless fingers.

In Jean's face was a hard, haggard look, and Sister Gertrude, a woman of the world, noted it, and wondered what could have affected her in those few moments of her absence.

"Tell me, dear, how you feel? Can I get you anything?" she asked her friend, to whom she was so much attached.

"Nothing, thanks," was her reply, with a great effort. "I shall be quite well soon, I hope."

Sister Gertrude advanced towards her, and, placing her hand upon the girl's shoulder tenderly, said:

"You will soon be all right again, dear, I hope. But why keep your secret? Why not confide in me?"

"Secret!" she echoed. "It is no secret!"

"Then why not tell me the truth right out? What has upset you?"

Jean clenched her teeth. How could she confess that she was the wife of a notorious thief—a man who had been shot like a dog by the police?

No. Her secret was hers, and it should remain so. Her past from that moment was buried. None, save the Mother Superior at Enghien and the two sisters who had found her in the Tuileries Gardens, knew the truth. And none should now know.

"Really, you are a little too solicitous of my welfare," she laughed, well feigning amusement at the situation. "I am quite well now. Quite well, I assure you."

And picking up the old copy of the newspaper, she resumed the wrapping up of the parcel of underclothing which she had made with her own hands for charitable purposes.

And the big bell having clanged out for tea in the refectory, Jean and Sister Gertrude passed arm-in-arm through the long stone corridor to the big, vaulted hall, where all the inmates of the convent had assembled and the Mother Superior was presiding over the four shining tea-urns at the top table.

But Jean sat silent and thoughtfully sipping her tea, heedless of all about her.

Her mind was full of that terse announcement which she had read, the obituary notice of the notorious thief known in Paris as "The American"—the man whom she loved and who was her husband.

She was thinking, too, of *Fil-en-Quatre*, the shock-headed, rather uncouth Parisian loafer—the man who had been sentenced to seven years' hard labour. That meant Cayenne, without a doubt—drudgery at Devil's Island, that ill-governed penal settlement established by the Republic of France.

She remembered him. Ah, how often he had sympathised with her! How frequently he had uttered cheering words to her in secret, although he had never once betrayed his friend's real profession, nor had he ever once spoken of the great and fervent affection which he had borne her.

Though he was a thief, a scoundrel of the underworld of Paris, ingenious, unscrupulous, and even dangerous if cornered, he was nevertheless loyal and honest towards his friend, and behaved as a gentleman towards his friend's wife.

Yes, Adolphe Carlier, though a thief, was still a gentleman in the true sense of the word.

The weeks went by, and poor Jean, a widow in secret—for she told no one of what had occurred—was sent forth daily in the poorer districts of London on her mission to the sick, to whom she carried food and delicacies prepared by the kind hands of the sisters.

The slums she visited in Clerkenwell and other places often reminded her of those last few days of her married life, those days before she parted for ever from "Le Costaud." Where men feared to venture, and where no police-constable cared to go alone, she went without fear, down into the deepest depths of the unknown underworld of London, and through months she worked hard each day amid the most sordid and poverty-stricken surroundings, returning each night to the convent fagged and hungry. But now that she knew the bitter truth, her whole life was devoted to her work of mercy and to her religious duties. Her sweetness of disposition, her calm patience, her soft voice, and her cheerful manner all endeared her to those whom she tended with such unremitting care.

Thus she passed the long summer days in the stifling slums of London.

So devoted was she, and so hard did she work, that at last a serious illness was threatened, in consequence of which she was sent by the Mother Superior to the West of England branch of the Order, who had a small convent at Babbacombe, near Torquay, and in the latter town, in better air, she continued her labours.

Not far from the convent, on the road leading to Newton Abbot, was the ivy-covered lodge and great, handsome gates of ornamental iron leading to Bracondale Park, the seat of the Right Honourable the Earl of Bracondale, K.G.

The park, a spacious domain with great oaks and elms, was situated high up, overlooking the English Channel, and away in the distance the long, rather low-built mansion with a square, castellated turret at the western end. The fine domain of the Bracondales, one of the most ancient families in England, extended over many thousands of fertile acres in Devon, besides which the Earl possessed a deer forest near Grantown, in the Highlands; a pretty winter villa at Beaulieu, close to Nice; the old-fashioned town house in Belgrave Square, and a pretty seaside villa in the new and fashionable little resort, Saint-Addresse, near Havre.

But, as His Majesty's Principal Secretary of State for Foreign Affairs, the Earl of Bracondale had but little time in which to enjoy his beautiful residences. True, he spent a few weeks on the Riviera in winter, shot once or twice over the Bracondale coverts in the season, and spent an annual fortnight up at the shooting lodge in Scotland; but he was usually to be found either at Downing Street or down at Bracondale immersed and absorbed by the affairs of State.

His one hobby was motoring, and he frequently drove his own car—a big six-cylinder open one. Years ago, on the introduction of the motor-car, he had been a young man, and had quickly become an enthusiast. He had motored ever since the early days, and was still an expert driver. Once he had held a world's distance record, and nowadays, even with the heavy responsibilities upon him, he was never so happy as in overcoat and cap at the steering-wheel. And in this recreation he found a very beneficial change after so many hours of studying complicated reports and worrying despatches from the Embassies abroad.

One summer's night he had been addressing a big political meeting at Plymouth, and at ten o'clock he turned out of the garage of the Royal Hotel, and alone drove through the brilliant, starlit night back to Babbacombe. Usually when he went out at night he took Budron, the head chauffeur, with him. But on this occasion he had left the man in London, superintending some repairs to one of the other cars. Hence he put on a cigar, and, alone, drove leisurely along the rather narrow, winding high road which leads from Plymouth through Plympton and Ivybridge.

The distance was twenty-five miles or so, and he travelled swiftly during the last portion of it.

It was nearly half-past eleven when he passed through Torquay, then silent and deserted, and ascending the hill, was quickly on the Babbacombe road.

Suddenly, however, when within half a mile of his own lodge gates, at a sharp bend in the narrow road along the cliffs, he found himself facing a heavy wagon, the driver of which was asleep.

There was the crash of a heavy impact, a shattering of glass, a rearing of horses, and next second his lordship, shot out of his seat, was lying on the other side of a low hedge, doubled up and quite still, while the car itself was overturned and completely wrecked.

XV

His Lordship's Visitor

The two doctors, summoned by telephone from Torquay, stood beside Lord Bracondale's bed, and after careful examination and long consultation, grew very grave.

His lordship had been carried unconscious to the park and upstairs into his own tastefully-furnished room, where he still remained motionless and senseless, though two hours had now passed.

In addition to severe contusions, his shoulder was badly dislocated, and it was also feared that he had suffered severe internal injury through being thrown against the steering-pillar of the car. The examination had occupied a long time, and the greatest consternation had been caused in the big household, the servants going about pale and scared.

Dr. Wright-Gilson, the elder of the two medical practitioners, a rather bent, grey-bearded man, addressing his colleague, said, after a long discussion:

"I really think that Morrison should see him. If I telephoned to him at Cavendish Square he could be down here by ten o'clock to-morrow. We could then have a consultation, and decide whether to operate or not."

To this the younger man agreed; therefore Wright-Gilson went into the library with Jenner, the stout, white-headed old butler, and, using the private telephone to Downing Street, which stood upon the big, littered writing-table, he was quickly put on to the house of Sir Evered Morrison, the great surgeon.

The specialist, who was asleep, answered the telephone at his bedside, and, hearing of the accident, promised he would catch the next train from Paddington. Then he rose, dressed hurriedly, and left by the newspaper-train.

At eleven o'clock the next morning—by which hour the world knew of his lordship's accident—the great specialist had made his examination and was seated in the library with the two Torquay doctors.

"No," said Sir Evered, a tall, thin, clean-shaven man, who was a personal friend of Lord Bracondale's. "In my opinion an operation is not advisable. The case is a serious one, and full of grave danger. But

I do not think we need despair. I'll remain here, and by this evening I shall hope to see consciousness restored." Then he added: "By the way, are there any good nurses in Torquay?"

"The Convent of Saint Agnes is quite close. They are a Nursing Order, as you know," replied Dr. Wright-Gilson.

"Yes, and usually most excellent. We had better send for the Mother Superior and get her to give us two trustworthy nurses. Having myself had experience of them, I have always found them most painstaking, and in every way excellent."

"That is also my own experience, Sir Evered. Several of my patients have employed them with great success."

"Very well; we will have them." And Jenner was at once called and sent with a note from the great surgeon to the Mother Superior.

Twenty minutes later the grave-faced directress, who wore her black habit and wide, white collar, and spoke with a very pronounced French accent, arrived, accompanied by Jean and Sister Gertrude, whom she introduced to the three medical men standing in the library.

And very soon afterwards Jean found herself installed in the big, handsome bedroom beside the unconscious Cabinet Minister.

The white, inanimate face lay upon the pillow with the pallor of death upon it, the sheet edged with broad lace having been turned down and carefully arranged by the head housemaid.

Many and precise were the instructions which Sister Gertrude and Jean received from the great surgeon, who first explained to them the injuries from which his distinguished patient was suffering, and the nature of the treatment he intended to adopt.

The Honourable John Charlton, his lordship's private secretary, arrived post-haste from London at midday, and took over many of the confidential papers and other documents which were lying about upon the library table.

He was anxious for the Earl to recover consciousness in order to obtain instructions concerning the attitude to be adopted towards Austria, regarding whom a ticklish point of policy had on the previous evening arisen. The political horizon of Europe changes from hour to hour.

Our Ambassador in Vienna had wired in cipher urgently requesting a response, and this only the Foreign Minister himself could give.

But the doctors would not allow him to be disturbed.

A warm, anxious day went by, and Jean found herself amid surroundings so luxurious and artistic that she gazed about her open-mouthed in wonder.

As a nurse she soon showed her proficiency and her business-like methods—a manner which at once impressed Sir Evered.

But, alas! The Earl of Bracondale still remained unconscious. His pulse was feeble, his heart was just beating; the spark of life was still aglow.

From all quarters of the world, from every one of the Chancelleries of Europe, telegrams of regret arrived. Kings, statesmen, politicians of all grades, and all parties, lawyers, diplomats; in fact, all classes, sent messages, and all day long boys kept continually cycling up the long drive through the park bearing sheaves of orange-coloured envelopes, which were opened one after the other by the Honourable John Charlton.

Not before the following afternoon did consciousness return to the injured man, and then Jean's real work commenced.

His eyes, when they first opened, met her calm, anxious gaze.

He looked at her in astonishment, and then glanced at the other faces of the doctors around.

Sir Evered spoke as he bent over him.

"You know me—eh? Come, you're a lot better now, my dear fellow. Just drink this," and he took a glass from Jean's hand.

The prostrate man swallowed the liquid with an effort. Then, staring about him with an air of astonishment, he said:

"Why—it's you, Evered. You!"

"Yes; I'm here looking after you, and with good nursing you'll soon be quite right again."

His lordship drew a long breath, and for a few moments remained silent. Then he asked, in a low, weak whisper:

"What's happened?"

"Oh, nothing very much. Don't bother about it," was the great specialist's reply. "You were thrown out of your car, that's all. No bones broken."

"Ah! yes," he replied, slowly raising a hand to his brow. "Ah! yes—now I remember. That wagon—right across the road—and no light upon it! Yes—I—I remember!"

"Don't bother. That's enough now. Just go to sleep again, my dear fellow," said Sir Evered, soothingly, placing his hand upon his patient's brow. "Don't try and think. Just rest for the present."

And thus advised, his lordship closed his eyes wearily, and was soon asleep.

"Excellent," declared Sir Evered, much gratified when outside the room with the others, leaving Jean alone with the sleeper. "He'll recover—no doubt he will."

And five minutes later he was in the library, speaking over the telephone to the Prime Minister at Downing Street, while that same evening the papers gave the welcome news to the world that there was every hope of the Foreign Minister's restoration to health.

The three medical men had strapped up the injured shoulder and applied various remedies, therefore the patient that night was in no pain, though Sister Gertrude took Jean's place at ten o'clock and sat by his bedside all night, receiving hourly visits from the doctors.

Bracondale Park was a house of breathless anxiety through the days which followed. Sir Evered, though his presence was required hourly in London—as is the presence of such a great surgeon—remained at the bedside of his friend. They had been at Cambridge together, and ever since their undergraduate days had been intimate chums.

His lordship's illness proved of longer duration than was at first anticipated. Sir Evered remained at Bracondale a whole week, and then, finding that his patient was progressing favourably, returned to London, leaving the case in the hands of Dr. Wright-Gilson and Dr. Noel Tanner, while Sister Gertrude and Jean did the nursing.

Life at Bracondale Jean found extremely pleasant. The great house, with its luxuriously-furnished rooms, its fine picture-gallery, where, often, in her hours of recreation, she wandered; the big winter-garden with palms and exotic flowers, the conservatories, the huge ballroom—wherein long ago the minuet had been danced by high-born dames in wigs and patches—the fine suites of rooms with gilded cornices—all were, to her, full of interest.

The great house was built by the second Earl of Bracondale, who was the famous Chancellor of the Exchequer in the reign of Charles I., and ever since the Bracondales had borne their part in the government of England.

The room allotted to Jean was a visitor's room—a large, old-fashioned sitting-room, with a bed in one corner screened off; a room the long, leaded windows of which afforded beautiful views across the extensive, well-wooded park to the blue sea beyond. It was a place with a quiet, old-world atmosphere—a room that had never been changed for a century past. The old chintzes were of the days of our grandmothers, while the Chippendale chairs and tables would have fetched hundreds of pounds if put up at Christie's.

The elderly housekeeper, in her black silk cap, did all she could to make her comfortable, and treated her with the greatest consideration and respect—more so, perhaps, than she did Sister Gertrude, who, of course, wore the habit of the Order, while Jean still wore her French nurse's uniform.

Old Jenner, on the other hand, looked upon "them dressed-up Sisters o' Mercy," as he termed them in the servants' hall, as interlopers, and was often sarcastic at their expense. As an old servant of the family, he felt jealous that they should wait upon his master while his presence was not permitted in the sick-room.

All his life he had been used to wait upon "his young lordship," and he was annoyed that he was not allowed to do so at that critical hour.

As soon as the injured man was sufficiently well to talk and to recognise that he was being tended by sisters from the neighbouring convent, he treated both with the greatest consideration. A car was placed at their disposal every afternoon so that they might take an airing, while the whole house was thrown open to them to wander where they liked.

The library, however, was Jean's favourite room. It was a big, sombre, restful place, with high windows of stained glass, a great carved overmantel, and electric lights set in the ancient oaken ceiling. Lined from ceiling to floor with books, and with several tables set about the rich Turkey carpet, it was a cosy, restful place, where one could lounge in a big arm-chair and dream.

Jean's duties in the sick-room were never irksome. The pair took it in turns to sit with the patient every other night, and it was only then that the hours in the green-shaded night-light seemed never ending. By day she found Bracondale always interesting and frequently amusing.

After he had been in bed a fortnight the doctors allowed him to see visitors, and several distinguished men called and were admitted by Jean. These included the Prime Minister, politicians, and magnates of commerce. And there were some mysterious visitors also, including a Mr. Darnborough, who called one afternoon, being shown up by Jenner.

Jean, in surprise, found the butler and the visitor outside the door, whereupon Jenner explained:

"This is Mr. Darnborough, nurse, a very great friend of his lordship. He must see him alone, as they have confidential business to transact."

"Thank you, Jenner," replied Jean, rather stiffly. "If his lordship wishes to see Mr. Darnborough alone he will probably tell me so."

And, surveying the visitor with some suspicion, she ushered him to the sick man's side.

"Ah! my dear Darnborough!" cried his lordship, gaily, as soon as he recognised him. "I'm very glad to see you. I heard that you were in Cairo a week ago. Well, how are things in Egypt?"

"Just as full of trouble as ever," was the reply; "but—" and he glanced inquiringly at Jean.

"Oh, yes, I forgot," exclaimed the Earl. "Nurse Jean, might I ask the favour that you leave Mr. Darnborough to talk with me alone for half an hour? I shall be all right—and my medicine is not due until five o'clock."

Jean smiled at the pair.

"Certainly; I will come back when it is time for your lordship to have the next dose," she answered.

And with that she passed noiselessly out of the room, the Earl's dark eyes following her.

The door having closed, the pair were left alone. Then the Earl lay listening attentively to the all-important secret report which Darnborough had travelled down there to make.

XVI

JEAN HAS A SURPRISE

Jean, thus dismissed, descended to the library, where, across the dark crimson carpet, the last rays of the gorgeous sunset slanted in through the high windows in which were set the armorial bearings of the dead-and-gone Bracondales in stained-glass escutcheons.

She crossed the great sombre apartment and stood gazing through the diamond panes away over the level green of the broad park to where the sea lay bathed in the golden light of the dying day.

Her eyes were fixed vacantly into space. She was thinking—thinking again of that fateful paragraph in the paper—the unexpected news which had rendered her a widow. And poor Adolphe? Alas! though he had been her only friend and full of sympathy for her, yet he was now wearing out his days in penal servitude at the dreaded Devil's Island.

She thought of him often with feelings of pity. Though a criminal of a criminal stock, ill-bred, and with scarcely any education, yet he had behaved to her as few men had behaved. He had always held her in high esteem and respect. Even as she stood there she could hear his high-pitched voice addressing her as "Madame."

Upstairs, by the bedside of the sick Cabinet Minister, the thin, grey-faced man, "the eyes and ears of the Cabinet," was making a secret report to his lordship.

Though the Earl of Bracondale, K.G., was His Majesty's Principal Secretary of State for Foreign Affairs, yet Darnborough, the ever-astute, sleepless man of secrets, was the keeper of Great Britain's prestige abroad. Though his name never appeared on the roll of Government servants, and did not draw any salary as an official, yet he was the only man in England who could demand audience of the Sovereign at any hour by day or by night, or who had the free *entrée* to the Royal residences and could attend any function uninvited.

As a statesman, as a secret agent, as an ingenious plotter in the interests of his country, he was a genius. He was a discovery of the late Lord Salisbury in the last days of the Victorian Era. At that time he had been a Foreign Office clerk, a keen-eyed young man with a lock of black hair hanging loosely across his brow. Lord Salisbury recognised in him a man of genius as a diplomat, and with his usual bluntness called him one day to Hatfield and gave him a very delicate mission abroad.

Darnborough went. He had audience with the Shah of Persia, juggled with that bediamonded potentate, and came back with his draft of a secret treaty directed against Russia's influence safely in his pocket. He had achieved what British Ministers to Teheran for the previous fifteen years had failed to effect. And from that moment Darnborough had been allowed a free hand in international politics.

Lord Rosebery, Lord Lansdowne, and Sir Edward Grey had adopted the same attitude towards him as the great Lord Salisbury. He was the one man who knew the secret policy of Britain's enemies, the man who had so often attended meetings of the Cabinet and warned it of the pitfalls open for the destruction of British prestige.

At that moment the renowned chief of the Secret Service was explaining the latest conspiracy afoot against England, a serious conspiracy hatched in both Berlin and Vienna to embroil our nation in complications in the Far East. Darnborough's agents in both capitals had that morning arrived at Downing Street post-haste and reported upon what was in progress, with the result that their chief had come to place before the Foreign Minister the latest iniquity of diplomatic juggling.

His lordship lay in bed and listened to the man of secrets without uttering a word.

At length he turned his head restlessly on the pillow and, with a weary sigh, remarked:

"Ah! Darnborough, I fear that each day brings us nearer the peril, nearer the day of Germany's attack. The exposure of those confidential reports upon our naval manoeuvres was serious enough to our diplomacy. The policy of the Government is, alas! one of false assurance in our defences. The country has been lulled to sleep far too long. False assurances of our national security have been given over and over again, and upon them the Cabinet have pursued a policy of bluff. But, alas! the days of Palmerston and Salisbury are past. Europe can gauge the extent and strength of our national defence, and, with the navigation of the air, we live no longer upon 'the tight little island' of our revered ancestors."

"Yes," replied the man seated in the chair by the bedside, as he stretched his legs forward and folded his arms. "In all the capitals it is to-day the fashion to laugh at England's greatness, and to speak of us as a declining Power. I hear it everywhere. The Great Powers are in daily expectation of seeing the tail of the British lion badly twisted, and

I quite agree that the most unfortunate leakage of a national secret was that report upon the last naval manoeuvres. The bubble of our defensive and offensive power has burst."

"And poor Richard Harborne lost his life," remarked the Earl.

"Yes," replied the other, thoughtfully.

"He was a fine fellow, Darnborough—a very fine young fellow. He came to see me once or twice upon confidential matters. You sent him to Mexico, you'll remember, and he came to report to me personally. I was much struck by his keen foresight and cleverness. Have you gained any further information concerning his mysterious end?"

"I have made a good many inquiries, both at home and abroad, but Harborne seems to have been something of a mystery himself. He was strangely reserved, and something of a recluse in private life—lived in chambers in the Temple when not travelling abroad, and kept himself very much to himself."

"For any reason?"

"None, as far as I can tell. He was a merry, easy-going young fellow, a member of the St. James's, and highly popular among the younger set at the club, but he held aloof from them all he could. As I told you some time ago, there was a lady in the case."

His lordship sighed.

"Ah! Darnborough, the best of men go under for the sake of a woman!"

"In this case I am not sure that Harborne was really a victim," replied his visitor. "Only the other day, when in Borkum, I ascertained that Harborne had been in Germany and met by appointment a young foreign woman named Fräulein Montague. She was French, I was told, and very pretty. It was she who carried on the negotiations for the purchase of the secret of the new Krupp aerial gun."

"You ought to find her. She might tell you something."

"That's just what I am striving my utmost to do. I have learnt that she was the daughter of a French restaurant-keeper, living somewhere in London, and that after Harborne's death she married a Frenchman, whose name I am unable, as yet, to ascertain."

"You will soon know it, Darnborough," remarked the Earl with a faint smile. "You always know everything."

"Is it not my profession?" the other asked. "Yes, I shall try to discover this lady, for I have a theory that she knows something which we ought to know. In addition, she knows who killed Richard Harborne."

"I sincerely hope that you will be successful," declared the Foreign Minister. "By Harborne's death Britain has lost a fearless patriot, a man who served his country as truly and as well as any bedecorated general, and who had faced death a dozen times unflinchingly in the performance of his duties to his country and his sovereign."

"Yes," declared Darnborough, "if any man deserved a C.M.G. or a knighthood, Dick Harborne most certainly did. I am the only person who is in the position of knowing how devotedly he served his country."

"I know, I know!" exclaimed the Earl. "And if he had lived it was my intention of including his name in the next Birthday Honours list."

"Poor fellow," remarked his chief. "I wonder who that woman Montague was, and whether she really had any hand in the crime? That he was fond of her I have learned on good authority, yet Dick was, after all, not much of a ladies' man. Therefore I am somewhat surprised at the nature of the information I have gathered. Nevertheless, I mean to find the woman—and to know the truth."

"Have you any clue whatever to her identity?" inquired the Earl, looking at him strangely.

"None, save what I have told you," was the slow, deliberate reply. "But I think I shall eventually find her."

"You will, Darnborough. I know well what you mean when you reply in those terms. I have experienced your vague responses before," laughed his lordship.

But the great secret agent only grinned, and his grey face broadened into a smile, while the Earl lay wondering whether, after all, his visitor knew more concerning the mysterious female friend of Harborne than he had admitted.

Darnborough went on with his secret report, placing before the Secretary of State the exact nature of the war-cloud which once again threatened to arise over Europe, and of which our Embassies in Berlin and Vienna, with all the pomp of their officialdom, were as yet in ignorance.

And while the chief of the Secret Service was closeted with the Foreign Minister, and the latter was scribbling some pencil notes of his visitor's report, Jean waited downstairs in the library for the Earl's permission to return to his room.

As the soft after-glow of early autumn spread over the western sea before her, she turned at last from the long window and crossed the big room, wherein deep shadows were now falling.

The Earl's mysterious visitor had been shown in there by Jenner before being conducted to his lordship's room, and upon the Earl's pedestal writing-table, set in an alcove overlooking the terrace, stood a small, well-worn despatch-box of green enamelled steel, covered with dark green canvas.

It had been brought by Darnborough, and stood unlocked and open, just as he had taken from it the written reports of the agents of the Secret Service who had arrived at Charing Cross early that morning from the Continent.

Curiosity prompted Jean to pause and peer into it. She wondered what business that rather sour-faced man had with the Earl, and what that portable little steel box could contain.

A photograph—the photograph of a young and handsome woman—which was lying face upwards, first attracted her attention. Curious, she thought, that the man towards whom old Jenner had been so deferential should carry about the picture of a pretty woman.

She took it in her fingers and held it in the light in order to examine it more closely. Then, in replacing it, she glanced at the file of papers uppermost, a thick bundle of various documents, stamped with the arms of England and the words, "Foreign Office," and upon the outside of which was written in a bold, clerkish hand, "*Re* Richard Harborne, deceased."

Richard Harborne! Sight of that name caused her to hold her breath.

She took out the file of papers with trembling hand and bent to examine them in the light.

She saw there were newspaper cuttings, and long reports both in writing and typed—reports signed by persons of whom she had no knowledge.

In one paper at which she glanced Dick was referred to as "The Honourable Richard Davies Harborne, late of His Britannic Majesty's Secret Service."

She read eagerly, hoping to discover something to throw light upon the poor fellow's sad end, but the writing was small, cramped, and difficult for her to decipher.

Yet, so deeply interested did she become that she did not hear the door open.

Suddenly she heard a footstep behind her, and, starting quickly, turned to find his lordship's mysterious visitor standing facing her with a look of severe inquiry upon his grey, furrowed countenance.

"Oh! I—I—I'm so very sorry!" was all she could say, as she quickly replaced the file of papers in the despatch-box. "I—I—"

But further words failed her, and she stood abashed, confused, and ashamed.

XVII

The Darkening Horizon

W ell, nurse, I hardly expected that," he said, reprovingly, his serious eyes fixed upon hers.

Jean turned scarlet, and then admitted, as she stood with her back to the writing table:

"I saw the photograph in your despatch-box, and it attracted me. Then I saw those papers."

"And they seem to have greatly interested you, nurse—eh?" Darnborough remarked.

"A woman is always interested in what does not concern her," she replied with a forced smile.

"Well, forgive me for saying so, but I consider it gross impertinence on your part to have pried into my papers, young lady," exclaimed the chief of the Secret Service, with some asperity.

"I trust you will forgive me, Mr. Darnborough, but, truth to tell, I could not resist the temptation."

"Just as many other people could not resist—if they knew what secrets this despatch-box of mine sometimes contains," he laughed. "Well, nurse, I forgive you," he added cheerfully, his manner changing. "Go back to Lord Bracondale, and make haste and get him well again. England is sorely in need of him to-day—I can assure you."

"Does he wish for me?"

"Yes, he gave me a message asking you to return to him at once."

"I'll go, then," she replied. "I'm so glad you've forgiven me. My action was, I know, horribly mean and quite unpardonable. Good evening."

"Good evening, nurse," Darnborough responded, as he busied himself repacking his papers. She left the room.

The great man of secrets was, as yet, in ignorance that the pretty, graceful, half-French nurse and Fräulein Montague, Dick Harborne's friend, were one and the same person.

At that moment he had been talking with the very woman whom his agents had been hunting the whole of Europe to find. Yet he bowed her out of the room in entire ignorance of that fact.

And as she ascended the great, broad, thickly-carpeted staircase to the sick man's room she was filled with regret that Darnborough had not entered five minutes later, when, by that time, she would have learnt the secret of what was contained in those papers concerning Dick Harborne's death.

Her head swam as she recalled that tragic afternoon and also the afternoon succeeding it, when she had witnessed the terrible accident to Noel Barclay, the naval aviator. She recollected how Ralph had been at her side in the cab when they had both witnessed the collapse of the aeroplane, and how utterly callous and unmoved he had been.

For the thousandth time she asked herself whether Ralph Ansell, her dead husband, had ever discovered her friendship with Richard Harborne. It was a purely platonic friendship. Their stations in life had been totally different, yet he had always treated her gallantly, and she had, in return, consented to assist him in several matters—"matters of business" he had termed them. And in connection with one of them she had gone to Germany as Fräulein Montague and met him on that memorable day when she acted as a go-between.

Had Ralph found this out? If so, had Dick died by her husband's hand?

She was at the door of his lordship's room, a pretty figure in her blue cotton gown and white nursing-apron and cap. For a moment she paused to crush down all recollections of the past. Then she turned the handle and entered on tip-toe, fearing lest her patient might be asleep.

But he was very wideawake—planning a line of policy to defeat the suggested Austro-German alliance against Great Britain. Prompt measures were necessary. At eight o'clock in the morning two King's Messengers would be at Bracondale ready to take the cipher despatches—autograph instructions to the British Ambassadors to the Courts of both Empires.

Though the Earl of Bracondale was confined to his bed, the foreign policy of the nation had still to be conducted, and he had resumed control of affairs as soon as ever his hand could use a pen.

A whole stream of officials from Downing Street, and others, called at Bracondale daily and passed through his room. And to each and sundry he gave precise and implicit instructions, the marvellously ingenious policy evolved by his remarkable brain.

"It is time for your medicine," Jean said, in a soft voice, as she entered.

"It was due half an hour ago, but I hesitated to disturb you with your visitor."

"Quite right, nurse. Never disturb me when Mr. Darnborough calls. My business with him is always of the very highest importance, and always strictly confidential."

Jean crossed to the small round table whereon stood the bottle and medicine-glass, and after measuring the mixture carefully, handed it to him, asking:

"Is your shoulder quite easy now?"

"Quite, nurse," was his reply, as, raising himself on his other elbow, he tossed off the medicine, pulling a wry face afterwards. Then, with a calm, set expression upon his countenance, he looked at her, and remarked:

"I should think nursing must be a terribly dull, monotonous life, isn't it? Surely the continual atmosphere of the sick-room is very depressing?"

"I do not find it so," she replied brightly, with her pretty French accent. "I am devoted to my calling."

"I quite recognise that," said his lordship, looking into her sweet, serious eyes. "Yet it requires a good deal of self-denial, I should imagine."

"Perhaps," and she smiled. "But self-denial is one of the first lessons learnt in our Sisterhood."

"You joined the Sisterhood in France, did you not?" he asked.

"Yes; at the chief convent at Enghien, near Paris. But, of course, I have not yet taken my vows as a nun."

"You intend to do so, I suppose?"

She was silent a few seconds; then, with her eyes averted, she answered frankly:

"It is more than possible."

"Would it not be a great sacrifice? Remember, you are young. Why should you cut yourself off so entirely from the world?"

Again she was silent. Then, seeing that he awaited her reply, she answered:

"If I take the vows I shall do so because I have certain reasons for so doing."

"Strong reasons?" he asked, still looking into her face.

She raised her fine eyes to his again, and nodded in the affirmative.

Then she turned and walked towards the table to put down the empty glass.

Lord Bracondale for the first time realised that the nurse by whom during the past few days he, confirmed bachelor that he was, had become so strangely attracted, possessed a chapter of her life which she hoped was closed for ever.

The curious situation attracted him. What, he wondered, could be the nature of the secret of such a good, pure-minded, honest woman?

His eyes followed her as she moved about the room in silence. He was wondering.

The autumn days passed slowly. His was a long illness.

Out in the great park the golden leaves, in falling, were swept along the wide avenue by the strong winds from the sea, and the face of the country had now become brown and desolate.

Jean, when she took her walk alone each afternoon, when off duty, wandered over the bare fields or beside the grey, chill sea until, so dispiriting did she find the scene, that she preferred to spend her hours of rest in the big, well-warmed house or at the convent itself.

His lordship's recovery was very slow.

Sir Evered Morrison had been down three times from London and seen the patient, and on the last occasion had been accompanied by another renowned surgeon.

Though it was kept a profound secret, the truth was that the Earl was not progressing as well as had been expected. Perhaps the strain of State affairs was too heavy upon him, for though far from recovered, he worked several hours with Mr. Charlton, his secretary, who sat at a table at his bedside, writing despatches as his lordship dictated them.

Thus three months went by. November came and went, and still the Earl had not left his room, although he was allowed to sit by the fire in his dressing-gown for two hours each day.

The room had been transformed into a small library, and here his lordship received callers who came from London upon official business. Indeed, he on more than one occasion received an ambassador of one of the Great Powers.

To Jean it was all a very novel and strange experience. At her patient's bedside she met some of the greatest of the land, men whose names were as household words. Even a royal prince called one day in his motor-car and sat beside the fire with the invalid. And if the truth be told, scarcely a person who visited the Earl did not remark upon his nurse's grace, sweetness, and good looks.

Inwardly, the Earl of Bracondale was much mystified. Unconsciously, though occupied with State affairs, he found himself thinking of her, and when she was absent for rest he looked forward eagerly to her return. To Sister Gertrude he spoke but little, while to Jean he was always frank, open, and exceedingly chatty.

Yet constantly did the suspicion arise in his mind that she was in possession of some dread secret, that there was a chapter in her past which she was undesirous of revealing.

In the middle of December he grew convalescent, and Sir Evered one day announced that he would, with care, completely recover.

The daily bulletins in the newspapers ceased to appear, and the world then knew that the renowned Foreign Secretary was on his way back to health.

This he attributed to Jean's careful nursing. To every one he was loud in her praises. Indeed, he often spoke of her in eulogistic terms while she was present, and on such occasions she would blush deeply and declare that she had only performed her duty.

In those weeks they had been constantly in each other's society. The long days in which she sat at his bedside reading or doing needlework, and the nights when each quarter of an hour she stole in stealthily to see that all was well, she had grown very partial to his society. He was so bright and intellectual, and possessed such a keen sense of humour when his mind was not overshadowed by the weight of political events. Often he would chat with her for hours, and sometimes, indeed, he would put a subtle question upon the matter in which he now took so keen an interest—her past.

But to all his cleverly-conceived inquiries she remained dumb. Her wit was as quick as his, and he saw that whatever was the truth, her intelligence was of a very high order. She would speak freely upon every other subject, but as to what she had done or where she had been before entering the Sisterhood she refused to satisfy him.

The past! To her it was all a horrible nightmare. Often, when alone, the face of Ralph Ansell, the man who had been shot like a dog by the police, arose before her. She tried to blot it out, but all was, alas! of no avail.

Sometimes she compared her patient with her dead husband. And then she would sigh to herself—sigh because she held the Earl in such admiration and esteem.

Just after Christmas another diplomatic bombshell burst in Europe. Darnborough came to and fro to Bracondale half a dozen times in the course of four or five days. Once he arrived by special train from Paddington in the middle of the night. Many serious conferences did he have with his chief, secret consultations at which Jean, filled with curiosity, of course was not present, though she did not fail to note that Darnborough usually regarded her with some suspicion, notwithstanding his exquisite politeness.

More than once in those last days of the year Jean suggested that her presence at Bracondale was no longer required. But her patient seemed very loath to part with her.

"Another week, nurse," he would say. "Perhaps I will be able to do without you then. We shall see."

And so indispensable did his lordship find her that not until the last day of January did she pack her small belongings ready to be carried back to the convent.

It was a warm, bright evening, one of those soft, sunny winter days which one so often experiences in sheltered Torquay, when Jean, having sent her things down by Davis, the under chauffeur, put on her neat little velvet hat and her black, tailor-made coat, and carrying her business-like nursing-bag, went into the huge drawing-room, where she had learnt from Jenner the Earl was reading.

The big, luxurious, heavily-gilded apartment was empty, but the long, French windows were open upon the stone terrace, and upon one of the white iron garden chairs the Earl, a smart, neatly-dressed figure in black morning coat, widely braided in the French manner—a fashion he usually affected—sat reading.

Jean walked to the window, bag in hand, and paused for a few seconds, looking at him in silence.

Then, as their eyes met and he rose quickly to his feet, she advanced with outstretched hand to wish him farewell.

XVIII

LORD BRACONDALE'S CONFESSION

W hat!" he cried, with a look of dismay upon his pale face. "Are you really leaving, nurse?"

"Yes, Lord Bracondale. I have already sent my things back to the convent. I have come to wish you good-bye."

"To wish me good-bye!" he echoed blankly, looking her straight in the face. "How can I ever thank you—how can I ever repay you for all your kindness, care, and patience with me? Sir Evered says that I owe my life to your good nursing."

She smiled.

"I think Sir Evered is merely paying me an undeserved compliment," was her modest reply.

He had taken her small, white hand in his, and for a moment he stood mute before her, overcome with gratitude.

"Sir Evered has spoken the truth, Nurse Jean," he said. "I know it, and you yourself know it. In all these weeks we have been together we have begun to know each other, we have been companions, and—and you have many a time cheered me when I felt in blank despair."

"I am very pleased if I have been able to bring you happiness," she replied. "It is sometimes difficult to infuse gaiety into a sick-room."

"But you have brought me new life, new hope, new light into my dull, careworn life," he declared quickly. "Since I found you at my bedside I have become a different man."

"How?" she asked, very seriously.

"You have inspired in me new hopes, new aspirations—and a fresh ambition."

"Of what?"

He raised her ungloved hand and kissed it fervently.

She tried to snatch it away, but he held it fast, and, looking into her dark, startled eyes, replied:

"Of making you my wife, Jean."

"Your wife!" she gasped, her face pale in an instant, as she drew back, astounded at the suggestion.

"Yes. Listen to me!" he cried, quickly, still holding her hand, and drawing her to him as he stepped into the huge room upholstered with pale blue silk. "This is no sudden fancy on my part, Jean. I have watched you—watched you for days and weeks—for gradually I came to know how deeply attached I had become to you—that I love you!"

"No, no!" she exclaimed. "Let me go, please, Lord Bracondale! This is madness. I refuse to hear you. Reflect—and you will see that I can never become your wife!"

And upon her sweet face there spread a hard, pained expression.

"But I repeat, Jean—I swear it—I love you!" he said. "I again repeat my question—Will you honour me by becoming my wife? Can you ever love me sufficiently to sacrifice yourself? And will you try and love me—will you—"

"I cannot bear it!" she cried, struggling to free herself from his strong embrace, while he held her hand and again passionately raised it to his lips. "Please recall those words. They are injudicious, to say the least."

"I have spoken the plain truth. I love you!"

Her eyes were downcast. She stood against a large, silk-covered settee, her hand touching the silken covering, her chest heaving and falling in deep emotion, so unprepared had she been for the Earl's declaration of affection.

Through her mind, however, one thought ran—the difference in their social status; he—a Cabinet Minister; and she—the widow of a thief!

Recollection of that hideous chapter of her life flashed upon her, and she shuddered.

Bracondale noticed that she shivered, but, ignorant of the reason, only drew her closer to him.

"Tell me, Jean," he whispered. "May I hope? Now that you are leaving, I cannot bear that you should go out of my life for ever. I am no young lover, full of flowery speeches, but I love you as fervently, as ardently, as any man has ever loved a woman; and if you will be mine I will endeavour to make you contented and happy to all the extent I am able."

"But, Lord Bracondale," she protested, raising her fine eyes to his, "I am unworthy—I—"

"You are worthy, Jean," he declared, earnestly. "You are the only woman in all my life that I have loved. For all these years I have been a bachelor, self-absorbed in the affairs of the nation, in politics and diplomacy, until, by my accident, I have suddenly realised that there is still something more in the world to live for higher than the position I hold as a member of the Cabinet—the love of a good woman, and you are that woman. Tell me," he urged, speaking in a low whisper as he bent to her, "tell me—may I hope?"

Slowly she disengaged the hand he held, and drew it across her white brow beneath her velvet hat.

"I—I—ah! no, Lord Bracondale," she cried. "This is all very unwise. You would soon regret."

"Regret!" he echoed. "No, I shall never regret, because, Jean, I love you!"

"Have you ever thought that, while you are a peer and a Cabinet Minister, I am only a nurse?"

"Social status should not be considered when a man loves a woman as truly and devotedly as I love you. Remember, to you I owe my recovery," he said frankly. "In the weeks you have spent at my side I have realised that life will now be a blank when you have left my roof. But must it be so? Will you not take pity upon me and try to reciprocate, in even a small degree, the great love I bear you? Do, Jean, I beg of you."

She was silent for a long time, her eyes fixed across the terrace upon the pretty Italian garden, to the belt of high, dark firs beyond.

"You ask me this, Lord Bracondale, and yet you do not even know my surname!" she remarked at last.

"Whatever your surname may be, it makes no difference to me," was his reply. "Whatever skeleton may be hidden in your cupboard is no affair of mine. I ask nothing regarding your past life. To me, you are honest and pure. I know that, or you would not lead the life you now lead. I only know, Jean, that I love you," and, again taking her soft hand tenderly, he once more raised it to his lips and imprinted upon it tender kisses.

His words showed her that his affection was genuine. His promise not to seek to unveil her past gave her courage, for she had all along been suspicious that he was endeavouring to learn her secret. What would he say, how would he treat her, if he ever knew the ghastly truth?

"Now, I wish to assure you," he went on, "that I have no desire whatever that you should tell me the slightest thing which you may wish to regard as your own secret. All of us, more or less, possess some family confidence which we have no desire to be paraded before our friends. A wife should, of course, have no secrets from her husband after marriage. But her secrets before she becomes a wife are her own, and her husband has no right to inquire into them. I speak to you, Jean, as a man of the world, as a man who has sympathy for women, and who is cognisant of a woman's feelings."

"Do you really mean what you say, Lord Bracondale?" she asked, raising her serious eyes inquiringly to his.

"I certainly do. I have never been more earnest, or sincere, in all my life than I am at this moment."

"You certainly show a generous nature," she replied. His assurance had swept away her fears. She dreaded lest he should know the truth of the tragedy of her marriage. She held Darnborough in fear, because he seemed always to suspect her. Besides, what could that file of papers have contained—what facts concerning her friend's tragic end?

"I hate to think of your wearing your life out in a sick-room, Jean," he said. "It is distressing to me that you, whom I love so dearly, should be doomed to a convent life, however sincere, devout, and holy."

"It is my sphere," she replied.

"Your proper sphere is at my side—as my wife," he declared. "Ah, Jean, will you only give me hope, will you only endeavour to show me a single spark of affection, will you try and reciprocate, to the smallest extent, my love for you? Mine is no boyish infatuation, but the love of a man whose mind is matured, even soured by the world's follies and vanities. I tell you that I love you. Will you be mine?"

She still hesitated. His question nonplussed her.

How could she, the widow of a notorious thief dare to become Countess of Bracondale!

He noticed her hesitation, and put it down to her natural reticence and shyness. He loved her with all his heart and soul. Never, in all his career, had he ever met, in society or out of it, a woman to whom he had been so deeply devoted. He had watched her closely with the keen criticism of a practised mind, and he had found her to be his ideal.

She was still standing against the pale blue settee, leaning against it for support. Her face was pale as death, with two pink spots in the centre of the cheeks betraying her excitement and emotion. She dare not open her mouth lest she should betray the reason of her hesitation. It was upon the tip of her tongue to confess all.

Yet had he not already told her that he had no desire to probe the secret of her past—that he only desired her for herself, that her past

WILLIAM LE QUEUX

was her own affair, and that his only concern was her future, because he loved her so? She recognised how good, how kind, how generous, and how every trait of his character was that of the high-born English gentleman. In secret she had long admired him, yet she had been careful not to betray an undue interest beyond that of his accident. In such circumstances a woman's diplomacy is always marvellous. In the concealment of her true feelings, woman can always give many points to a man.

Bracondale was awaiting her answer. His eyes were fixed upon hers, though her gaze was averted. He held her in his arms, and again repeated his question in a low, intense voice, the voice of a man filled with the passion of true affection.

"Will you be mine, dearest?" he asked, a second time. "Will you trust in me and throw in your lot in life with mine?"

She shook her head.

"No, Lord Bracondale; such a marriage would, for you, be most injudicious. You must marry one of your own people."

"Never!" he cried in desperation. "If I marry, it will be only your own dear self."

"But think—think what the world will say."

"Let the world say what it likes," he laughed. "Remember my policy and my doings are criticised by the Opposition newspapers every day. But I have learned to disregard hard words. I am my own master in my private life as well as in my public life, and if you will only consent to be my wife I shall tackle the difficult European problems with renewed vigour, well knowing that I have at least one sympathiser and helpmate—my wife."

He paused, and looked into her dark eyes for quite a long time.

Then, bending till his lips almost touched hers, and placing his arm tenderly about her waist, he asked breathlessly:

"Jean, tell me, darling, that you do not hate me—that you will try to love me—that you will consent to become my wife. Do, I beg of you."

For a few seconds she remained silent in his embrace, then slowly her lips moved.

But so stirred by emotion was she that no sound escaped them.

"You will be mine, darling, will you not?" he urged. "Jean, I love you—I'll love you for ever—always! Do, I beseech of you, give me hope. Say that you love me just a little—only just a little."

Tears welled in her great, dark eyes, and again her chest heaved and fell.

Then, of a sudden, her head fell upon his shoulder and she buried her face, sobbing in mute consent, while he, on his part, pressed her closely to him and smothered her cheek with burning kisses.

XIX

The Garden of Love

S ix years later.

The years had gone by—happy, blissful years, during which the Countess of Bracondale had become a popular society and political hostess.

At Bracondale, and in Scotland, the Earl and his wife had on three occasions entertained the Sovereign at shooting-parties, and no social function was complete without the handsome, half-French Lady Bracondale.

After her marriage, though she had no ambition to enter that wild world of unrest which we call modern society, she realised that, in order to assist her husband in his political and diplomatic work, she was compelled to take her place in London life. So she had entered upon it cheerfully; the town house had been redecorated, and many brilliant functions—dinners, balls, diplomatic receptions, and the like—had been given, while at the Foreign Office receptions her ladyship always acted as hostess to the *corps diplomatique*.

The society newspapers gave her portrait constantly, and declared her to be among the most beautiful women in England.

Wealth, position, popularity, all were hers, and, in addition, she had the great love of her devoted husband, and the comfort of her sweet little daughter, Lady Enid Heathcote—a child with pretty, golden hair—whom she adored. The happiest of wives and mothers, she also bore her part as one of the great ladies of the land, and her husband was ever proud of her, ever filled with admiration.

It was eight o'clock on a warm, August morning at Bracondale, where Jean and her little daughter, with Miss Oliver, the governess, were spending the summer.

Jean came down to breakfast in a pretty gown of Japanese silk embroidered with large, crimson roses, and passed through the dining-room out upon the terrace overlooking the park, where, on warm mornings, it was their habit to take their coffee in Continental style.

As she went along to where the table was set, little Enid, with her hair tied at the side with blue ribbon, and wearing a pretty, cotton frock, came dancing along the terrace, where she was walking with her governess, crying in her childish voice:

"Good morning, mother, dear. I wish you many happy returns of your birthday."

"Thank you, darling," replied Jean, catching the child up in her arms and kissing her, while Miss Oliver, a tall, discreet, and rather prim person, at that moment came up with a great bunch of fresh roses which she had just cut for the table.

Bracondale had been absent on official duties at Downing Street for a week, but had returned by special train from Paddington, arriving at Torquay at half-past three in the morning. He had indeed placed aside some most pressing affairs of State in order to spend his wife's birthday in her company.

And hardly had she kissed her child before he stepped forth from the dining-room, exclaiming:

"Ah! good-morning, Jean. A very happy birthday, dearest," and bending, he kissed her fondly, while she returned his caress.

"Gunter told me that you did not get home until nearly four o'clock. You must be tired," she said.

"No, not very," he laughed. "I had a few hours' sleep in the train. I've just come down to spend the day with you, dearest. I must get back at midnight."

"It is really very good of you, dear," she replied. "You know how pleased we both are to have you at our side, aren't we, Enid?"

"Yes, mother, of course we are," declared the child, as her father bent to kiss her.

"And now, Jean, I've brought you down a little present, which I hope you will like. Men are all fools when they buy a present for a woman. But I've got this little trifle for you as a souvenir."

And placing his hand in the pocket of his dark, flannel jacket, he drew out a magnificent string of pearls—a gift worth, at the least, fifteen thousand pounds. Indeed, that was the price he had paid for them to a dealer in Hatton Garden.

And he had carried them loose in his pocket, leaving the dark green leather case lying upon the library table.

"Oh, how lovely!" Jean cried, in delight, as she saw them. Her eyes sparkled, for she had often wished for such a beautiful row. Pretty things delighted her, just as they delight a child. "It is good of you, dearest," she said, looking fondly into his face. "I never dreamed that I should have such a handsome present as that!"

"Let me put them on," he suggested.

Therefore she stood beside the little tea-table, and with Enid clinging to her gown, Lord Bracondale clasped the pearls around his wife's neck, and then bent to kiss her, a caress which she at once reciprocated, repeating her warm thanks for the magnificent gift.

They suited her well, and Miss Oliver at once went and obtained a small mirror so that her ladyship should see the effect for herself. Jean was not vain. She only liked to wear jewels because it pleased her husband. In the great safe in her dressing-room was stored an array of beautiful jewels—the Bracondale heirlooms. Some of the diamonds had been reset, and she wore them at various official functions. But she prized only those which her husband had given to her. In the Bracondale family jewels she took but little interest.

After all she was essentially modern and up-to-date. Her birth, her youthful experience, the bitterness of her first marriage, and her curious adventures had all combined to render her shrewd and far-seeing. She had kept abreast of the times, and that being so, she could, by her knowledge, often further her husband's interests.

It being her birthday, she invited Miss Oliver to take her coffee with them, and they were a merry quartette when they sat down to chat in the bright morning sunshine.

The scene was typically English—the long sweep of the park, the great elms dotted here and there, and behind the dark belt of firs the blue Channel sparkling in the morning sun.

"I think in the second week of September I may be able to get away from Downing Street," Bracondale said, as he sipped his cup of black coffee, for he seldom took anything else until his lunch, served at noon. Morning was the best time for brain work, he always declared, and mental work upon an empty stomach was always best.

"Shall we go to Saint Addresse?" suggested Jean. "The sea-bathing is always beneficial to Enid, and, as you know, the villa, though small, is awfully comfortable."

"We will go just where you like, dearest. I leave it for you to arrange," was his reply.

"I love the villa," she replied, "and Enid does, too."

"Very well, let us go," he said. "I'll make arrangements for us to leave in the second week in September."

Enid was delighted, and clapped her tiny hands with glee when Miss Oliver told her of her mother's decision, and then the governess took the child for a stroll around the rosery while husband and wife sat together chatting.

Bracondale sat with his wife's hand in his, looking into her eyes, and repeating his good wishes for many a happy return of that anniversary.

"I hope you are happy, Jean," he said at last. "I am trying to make you so."

"I am very happy—happier now than I have ever been before in all my life," she answered, looking affectionately into his face. "But do you know that sometimes," she added, slowly, in an altered voice, "sometimes I fear that this peace is too great, too sweet to last always. I am dreading lest something might occur to wreck this great happiness of mine."

He looked at her in surprise.

"Why do you dread that?" he asked.

"Because happiness is, alas! never lasting."

"Only ours."

"Ah!" she sighed, "let us hope so, dearest. Yet this strange presage of coming evil, this shadow which I so often seem to see, appears so real, so grim, and so threatening."

"I don't understand why you should entertain any fear," he exclaimed. "I love you, Jean; I shall always love you."

She was silent, and he saw that something troubled her. Truth to tell, the shadow of her past had once again arisen.

"Ah! But will you always love me as fondly as you now do?" she asked, rather dubiously.

"I shall, Jean. I swear it. I love no other woman but yourself, my dear, devoted wife."

"Many men have uttered those same words before. But they have lived to recall and regret them."

"That is true," he said. "Yet it is also true that I love you with all my heart and all my soul, and, further, that my love is so deep-rooted that it cannot be shaken."

"We can only hope," she said in a low voice, sighing again. "Though my happiness is so complete, I somehow cannot put this constant dread from me. It is a strange, mysterious feeling that something will one day happen to sweep away all my hopes and aspirations—that you and I might be parted."

"Impossible, darling!" he cried, starting to his feet; and standing behind her, he placed his arm tenderly around her neck. "What could ever happen that would part us?"

Then the thought flashed across his mind. Her past was enveloped in complete mystery, which, true to his word, he had never sought to probe.

"We never know what trials may be in store for us," she remarked. "We never know what misfortunes may befall us, or what misunderstandings may arise to destroy our mutual affection and part us."

"But surely you don't anticipate such a calamity?" he asked, looking into her handsome countenance, his eyes fixed upon hers.

"Well, I—I hardly anticipate it, yet I cannot get rid of this ever-increasing dread of the future which seems so constantly to obsess me."

"Ah, I think it may be your nerves, darling," he remarked. "You had a great strain placed upon you by the London season. All those entertainments of yours must have run you down. You must go to Monplaisir. The bracing air there will benefit you, no doubt. Here, in Devon, it is highly relaxing."

"No, it is not my nerves," she protested. "It is my natural intuition. Most women can scent impending danger."

He was inclined to laugh at her fears, and bent again to kiss her upon the cheek.

"Take no heed of such unpleasant forebodings," he exclaimed cheerily. "I, too, sometimes look upon the darker side of things, yet of late I've come to the conclusion that it is utterly useless to meet trouble half-way. Sufficient the day when misfortune falls."

"But surely we ought always to try and evade it?"

"If you are foredoomed to misfortune, it cannot be evaded," he declared.

"That is exactly my argument," she replied. "I feel that one day ere long a dark shadow, perhaps of suspicion, I know not what, will fall between us."

"And that we shall be parted!" he cried, starting. "You are certainly cheerful to-day." And he smiled.

"I ought to be, after your lovely present," she said, touching the pearls upon her neck with her white hand. "But I confess to you, dearest, I am not. I am too supremely happy, and for that reason alone I dread lest it may pass as all things in our life pass, and leave only bitter regrets and sad disappointments behind."

"You speak in enigmas, Jean," he said, bending earnestly to her again. "Tell me what really distresses you. Do you fear something real and tangible, or is it only some vague foreboding?"

"The latter," she responded. "I seem always to see a grim, dark shadow stretched before my path."

Bracondale remained silent in wonder for some time.

Then with words of comfort and reassurance, he again pressed his lips to hers, and urged her to enjoy her happiness to its full extent, and to let the future take care of itself.

"Have no care to-day, darling," he added. "It is your birthday, and I am with you."

"Ah, yes, you are here—you, my own dear husband!"

And raising her lips, she smiled happily, and kissed him of her own accord.

XX

CROOKED CONFIDENCES

About noon on the same day which Jean and her husband spent so happily together by the Devon sea, two men of about thirty-five met in the cosy little American bar of a well-known London hotel.

Both were wealthy Americans, smartly dressed in summer tweeds, and wore soft felt hats of American shape.

One, a tall, thin, hard-faced man, who had been drinking a cocktail and chatting with the barmaid while awaiting his friend, turned as the other entered, and in his pronounced American accent exclaimed:

"Halloa, boy! Thought you weren't coming. Say, you're late."

The other—dark, clean-shaven, with a broad brow, and rather good-looking—grasped his friend's hand and ordered a drink. Then, tossing it off at one gulp, he walked with his friend into the adjoining smoking-room, where they could be alone.

"What's up?" asked the newcomer, in a low, eager voice.

"Look here, Hoggan, my boy," exclaimed the taller of the two to the newcomer, "I'm glad you've come along. I 'phoned you to your hotel at half-past ten, but you were out. It seems there's trouble over that game of poker you played with those two boys in Knightsbridge last night. They've been to the police, so you'd better clear out at once."

"The police!" echoed the other, his dark brows knit. "Awkward, isn't it?"

"Very. You go, old chap. Get across the Channel as quick as ever you can, or I guess you'll have some unwelcome visitors. Don't go back to the hotel. Abandon your traps, and clear out right away."

Silas P. Hoggan, the man with the broad brow, had no desire to make further acquaintance with the police. As a cosmopolitan adventurer he had lived for the past six years a life of remarkable experiences in Vienna, Berlin, St. Petersburg, and Rome. He posed as a financier, and had matured many schemes for public companies in all the capitals—companies formed to exploit all sorts of enterprises, all of which, however, had placed money in his pocket.

Two years before he had been worth thirty thousand pounds, the proceeds of various crooked businesses. At that moment he had been in San Francisco, when, by an unlucky mischance, a scheme of his had failed, ingenious as it was, and now he found himself living in an expensive hotel in London, with scarcely sufficient to settle his hotel bill.

Since the day when he had stolen those notes from the coat pocket of his accomplice, and locked him in the trap so that the police should arrest him, and thus give him time to escape—for Silas P. Hoggan and Ralph Ansell were one and the same person—things had prospered with him, and he had cultivated an air of prosperous refinement, in order to move in the circle of high finance.

After his escape across the Seine, he had sought refuge in the house of a friend in the Montmartre, where he had dried the soddened bank-notes and turned them into cash. Then, after a week, he had taken the night *rapide* to Switzerland, and thence to Germany, where in Berlin he had entered upon financial undertakings in partnership with a "crook" from Chicago. Their first venture was the exploiting of a new motor tyre, out of which they made a huge profit, although the patent was afterwards found to be worthless. Then they moved to Russia, and successively to Austria, to Denmark, and then across to the States.

Losses, followed by gains, had compelled him of late to adopt a more certain mode of living, until now he found himself in London, staying at one of its best hotels—for like all his class he always patronised the best hotel and ate the best that money could buy—and earning a precarious living by finding "pigeons to pluck," namely, scraping up acquaintanceship with young men about town and playing with them games of chance.

As a card-sharper, Silas P. Hoggan was an expert. Among the fraternity "The American" was known as a clever crook, a man who was a past-master in the art of bluff.

Yet his friend's warning had thoroughly alarmed him.

The circumstance which had been recalled was certainly an ugly one.

He had found his victims there, in a swell bar, as he had often found them. About many of the London hotels and luxuriously appointed restaurants and fashionable meeting places are always to be seen young men of wealth and leisure who are easy prey to the swindler, the blackmailer, or the sharper—the vultures of society.

A chance acquaintanceship, the suggestion of an evening at cards, a visit to a theatre, with a bit of supper afterwards at an hotel, was, as might be expected, followed by a friendly game at the rooms of the elder of the two lads at Knightsbridge.

WILLIAM LE QUEUX

Hoggan left at three o'clock that morning with one hundred and two pounds in his pocket in cash and notes, and four acceptances of one hundred pounds each, drawn by the elder of the two victims.

Five hundred pounds for one evening's play was not a bad profit, yet Hoggan never dreamed that the London police were already upon his track.

What his friend had suggested was the best way out of the difficulty. As he had so often done before he must once again burn his boats and clear.

The outlook was far too risky. Yet he was filled with chagrin. In the circumstances, the acceptances were useless.

"I shall want money," he remarked.

"Well, boy, I guess I haven't any cash-money to spare just at the moment, as you know," replied his accomplice. "We've been hard hit lately. I'm sorry we came across on this side."

"Our luck's out," Hoggan declared despondently, as he selected a cigarette from his case and lit it. "What about little Lady Michelcoombe? She ought to be good for a bit more."

"I'll try, if you like, boy. But for Heaven's sake clear out of this infernal city, or you'll go to jail sure," urged Edward Patten, his friend.

"Where shall I go, Ted? What's your advice?"

"Get over to Calais or Ostend, or by the Hook into Holland. Then slip along to some quiet spot, and let me know where you are. Lie low until I send you some oof. You can go on for a week or so, can't you?"

"For a fortnight."

"Good. Meanwhile, I'll touch her ladyship for a bit more."

"Yes. She's a perfect little gold-mine, isn't she?"

"Quite. We've had about four thousand from her already, and we hope to get a bit more."

"You worked the game splendidly, Ted," Hoggan declared. "What fools some women are."

"And you acted the part of lover perfectly, too. That night when I caught you two together on the terrace at Monte Carlo—you remember? She was leaning over the balustrade, looking out upon the moonlit sea, and you were kissing her. Then I caught you at supper later, and found that you were staying at the hotel where she was staying. All very compromising for her, eh? When I called on her a week afterwards, and suggested that she could shut my mouth for a consideration, I saw in a moment that she was in deadly fear lest her husband should know.

But I was unaware that her husband had no idea that she had been to Monte, but believed her to be staying with her sister near Edinburgh."

"She's paid pretty dearly for flirting with me," remarked Silas P. Hoggan with a grin.

"Just as one or two others have, boy. Say, do you recollect that ugly old widow in Venice? Je-hu! what a face! And didn't we make her cough up, too—six thousand!"

"I'm rather sorry for the Michelcoombe woman," remarked Hoggan. "She's a decent little sort."

"Still believes in you, boy, and looks upon me as a skunk. She has no idea that you and I are in partnership," he laughed. "We'll get a thousand or two more out of her yet. Fortunately, she doesn't know the exact extent of my knowledge of her skittish indiscretions. Say, we struck lucky when we fell in with her, eh?"

Hoggan reflected. It was certainly a cruel trick to have played upon a woman. They had met casually in the Rooms at Monte Carlo, then he had contrived to chat with her, invited her to tea at a famous *café*, strolled with her, dined with her, and within a week had so fascinated her with his charming manner that she had fallen in love with him, the result being that Patten, who had watched the pair, suddenly came upon them, and afterwards demanded hush-money, which he divided with his friend.

Such instances of blackmail are much more frequent than are supposed. There is a class of low-down adventurer who haunts the gayer resorts of Europe, ever on the look-out for young married women who have been ordered abroad for the benefit of their health, and whose husbands, on account of their social, Parliamentary, or business duties, cannot accompany them.

Hunting in couples, they mark down a victim, and while one, giving himself the airs of wealth, and assuming a title, proceeds to flirt with the lady, the other carefully watches. Too often a woman at the gay watering-places of Europe finds the gaiety infectious and behaves indiscreetly; too often she flirts with the good-looking young stranger until, suddenly surprised in compromising circumstances, she realises that her husband must never know, and is filled with fear lest he may discover how she has allowed herself to be misled.

Then comes the blackmailer's chance. A hint that it would be better to pay than court exposure generally has the desired effect, with the result that the woman usually pawns what jewellery she possesses, and pays up.

Many an unfortunate woman, though perfectly innocent of having committed any wrong, has paid up, and even been driven to suicide rather than allow the seeds of suspicion to be sown in her husband's heart.

It was so in Lady Michelcoombe's case. She was a sweet little woman, daughter of a well-known earl, and married to Viscount Michelcoombe, a man of great wealth, with a house in Grosvenor Square and four country seats. Already the pair of adventurers had compelled her to pawn some of her jewels and hand them the proceeds. She was quite innocent of having committed any wrong, yet she dreaded lest her husband's suspicions might be excited, and had no desire that he should learn that she had deceived him by going to Monte Carlo instead of to her sister's. The real reason was that she liked the gaiety and sunshine of the place, while her husband strongly disapproved of it.

Certainly her clandestine visit had cost her dear.

"Well," exclaimed Hoggan, the perfect lover, "you'd better see her ladyship as soon as possible. Guess she's still in London, eh?"

"I'll ring up later on and ask the fat old butler. But you clear out right away, boy. There's no time to lose. Write to me at the *Poste Restante* in the Strand. Don't write here, the police may get hold of my mail."

"If her ladyship turns on you, I guess you'll have to look slick."

"Bah! No fear of that, sonny. We've got her right there."

"You can't ever be sure where a woman is concerned. She might suddenly throw discretion to the winds, and tell her husband all about it. Then you, too, would have to clear right away."

"Guess I should," replied Patten. "But I don't fear her. I mean to get another thousand out of her. Women who make fools of themselves have to pay for it."

"Well, I must say you engineered it wonderfully," declared Hoggan.

"And I'll do so again with a little luck," his friend declared. "Come and have another cocktail, and then shake the dust of this infernal city off your feet. Every time you have a drink things look different."

The two men passed into the inner room, where the bar was situated, and after a final Martini each, went out together into the handsome hall of the hotel.

"Wal, so long, old pal! Clear out right away," whispered Patten, as he shook his friend's hand.

And next moment Silas P. Hoggan passed across the courtyard and into the busy Strand, once more a fugitive from justice.

XXI

The Green Table

One afternoon a fortnight later Ralph Ansell, well dressed, and posing as usual as a wealthy American, who had lived for many years in France, stood at the window of his room in the expensive Palace Hotel at Trouville, gazing upon the sunny *plage*, with its boarded promenade placed on the wide stretch of yellow sand.

In the sunshine there were many bathers in remarkable costumes, enjoying a dip in the blue sea, while the crowd of promenaders in summer clothes passed up and down. The season was at its height, for it was the race week at Deauville, and all the pleasure world of Paris had flocked there.

Surely in the whole of gay Europe there is no brighter watering place than Trouville-sur-Mer during the race week, and certainly the played-out old Riviera, with the eternal Monte, is never so *chic*, nor are the extravagant *modes* ever so much in evidence, as at the Normandie at Deauville, or upon the boarded promenade which runs before those big, white hotels on the sands at Trouville.

Prices were, of course, prohibitive. The casino was at its gayest and brightest, and the well-known American bar, close to the last-named institution, Ansell patronised daily in order to scrape acquaintance with its chance customers.

Having been up playing cards the greater part of the night before, he had eaten his luncheon in bed, and had just risen and dressed.

He gazed out of his window down upon the sunny scene of seaside revelry, as a bitter smile played upon his lips.

"What infernal luck I had last night," he muttered, between his teeth. Then glancing at the dressing-table, his eyes fell upon the hotel bill, which had come up on the tray with his *déjeuner*. "Fourteen hundred and eighteen francs," he muttered, "and only those three louis to pay it with."

Those last three louis had been flung carelessly upon the table when he had undressed at six o'clock that morning.

He took them in his palm and looked at them.

"Not a word from Ted," he went on, with a sigh. "I wonder what can have happened. Has he got a bit more out of the Michelcoombe woman and cleared out? No," he added, "he's a white man. He'd never prove a blackguard like that."

Ralph Ansell had not recalled his own dastardly action when he robbed, deserted, and trapped his accomplice, Adolphe Carlier.

For a long time he remained silent as slowly he paced the small, well-furnished room, his hands thrust deep in his trousers pockets, his eyes fixed upon the carpet. His fertile, inventive brain was trying to devise some subtle means to obtain money. He was a genius regarding schemes, and he put them before his victims in such an inviting and attractive way that they found refusal impossible. For some of the wildest of schemes he had been successful in subscribing money—money which had enabled him to live well, to travel up and down Europe, and pose as a man of considerable means.

Railway concessions in the Balkans, the exploitation of oil in Roumania, of tin in Montenegro, and copper in Servia, had all been fruitful sources of income, and now when they had failed he had fallen back upon his skill at cards.

On the previous night, at a disreputable but luxuriant gaming-house situated only a few dozen paces from the hotel, he had met his match. His opponent was too wary, and he had lost very considerably. Indeed, all that remained to him were those three golden louis.

And with that slender capital he intended that night to retrieve his lost fortune. It is usually easy for the cheat to retrieve his fortune. So with a laugh he lit a fresh cigarette, put his three louis in his pocket, and muttered, "I wish to Heaven Ted would come over here. We might work something big. I'll wire him."

Then, examining himself in the glass, and settling his tie, he walked out at three o'clock in the afternoon, his first appearance that day.

Emerging from the lift into the hall, he passed through the low-built lounge, where a number of summer muslin-dressed idlers were chatting and laughing, and strode out upon the boards placed upon the golden sea-sands outside the hotel.

Trouville is unique. Other watering-places have a drive along the sea-front, but the gay little bathing "trou" has no sea-front. The hotels abut upon the actual sands, just as Arcachon abuts upon its shallow oyster-beds.

Ansell had not gone half-a-dozen yards along the *plage* before he met a young Englishman whose acquaintance he had made in a night *café* on the previous evening—a young cavalry officer, who greeted him merrily, believing him to be the well-known American financier. Even the men who are "British officers and gentlemen" in these days are prone to bow the knee to American dollars, the golden key which unlocks the door of the most exclusive English society. Only the old-fashioned squire of the country village, the old-fashioned English hunting gentleman, will despise the men who aspire to society because they can buy society's smiles

He walked with the young fellow as far as the casino. Ansell did not even know his name, and as he had already summed him up as living on his pay, with a load of debts behind, he did not trouble even to inquire. Only wealthy "mugs" interested him.

Entering the casino, they had a drink together, then smoked and chatted.

Ansell was half inclined to tell a tale and borrow a "fiver," but so clever was he that he feared lest the young fellow might speak of it in Trouville. Therefore he stood at the bar laughing merrily, as was his wont, and keeping a watchful eye upon any man who entered. He could fascinate other men by cheery good humour, his disregard for worry, his amusing optimism, and his brightness of conversation.

His training as a crook had surely been in a good school, yet there were times when, before his vision, arose the face of the true, honest girl whom he had married, and whom he had so cruelly treated. Sometimes, just as at that hour when he stood at the bar of the great gilded casino, laughing gaily, he would reflect upon his married life, and wonder where Jean was and how she fared.

The young Englishman, Baldwin by name, was spending the season at Trouville with his mother, who rented a pretty villa in the vicinity, and he, being on leave, was idling amid the mad gaiety of Paris-by-the-Sea.

He was much taken by the manners and airy talk of the rich American, whom he found much less vulgar than many he had met in London society. He made no ostentatious show, though it was whispered throughout Trouville that he was one of the wealthiest men in Wall Street. What would young Baldwin have thought if he had seen those three precious louis?

Until five o'clock Ansell chatted and smoked with him, all the time his brain busy to invent some fresh scheme to obtain funds. Then, punctually at five, he took leave of his friend, and entering a *fiacre*, drove along to Deauville, that fashionable village of smart villas, with its big, white casino and its quaintly built but extremely select Hotel Normandie.

At the latter he descended and, entering, passed through the big lounge where the elegant world and the more elegant half world were chattering and taking their tea after the races. He knew the big hotel well, and many men and women glanced up and remarked as he passed, for Silas P. Hoggan had already established a reputation.

Finding nobody to speak to, he took a seat in a corner, drank tea because it was the correct thing to do, smoked a cigarette, and became horribly bored.

Those who saw him reflected upon the great burden which huge wealth as his must be, little dreaming that, after all, he was but a blackmailer and an ingenious swindler.

Presently he looked in at the casino, where he found a French Baron whom he knew, and then, after a further hour in the *café*, he returned to his hotel in Trouville, where he dressed carefully and later on appeared at dinner.

Whenever funds were especially low, Ralph Ansell always made it a rule to order an expensive dinner. It preserved the illusion that he was wealthy. He was especially fond of Russian Bortch soup, and this having been ordered, it was served with great ceremony, a large piece of cream being placed in the centre of the rich, brown liquid.

The dinner he ate that night was assuredly hardly in keeping with the ugly fact that, within the next four days, if funds were not forthcoming, he would find himself outside the hotel without his newly-acquired luggage.

Truly his luck was clean out.

After dinner he sat outside the hotel for an hour, watching people pass up and down the *plage*. The evening was close, and the sand reflected back the hot rays of the sun absorbed during the day.

He was thinking. Only those three louis remained between him and starvation. He must get money somehow—by what means it mattered not, so long as he got it.

Suddenly, with a resolve, he rose and, passing along the *plage*, arrived at a large, white house overlooking the sea, where, on the second floor, he entered a luxuriously-furnished suite of rooms where roulette was in full swing.

Many smartly-dressed men and women were playing around the green table—some winning, some losing heavily.

The room, filled to overflowing, was almost suffocating, while, combined with the chatter of women and the lower voices of men, was the distinctive sound of the clink of gold as the croupier raked it in or paid it out.

To several acquaintances Ralph nodded merrily as he strolled through the room, until suddenly he came upon two men, wealthy he knew them to be, with whom he had played cards on the previous night.

"Ah, messieurs!" he cried, greeting them merrily. "Are you prepared to give me my revenge—eh?"

"Quite, m'sieur," was the reply of the elder of the men. "Shall it be in the next room? There is a table free."

"At your pleasure," was "The American's" reply. The man who had proved so shrewd on the previous night was absent, but the two other men were, he knew, somewhat inexperienced at cards.

They passed into the adjoining room and there sat down, a stranger joining them. Others were playing in the same room, including at least a couple of "crooks" well known to Ansell—one man an elegantly-dressed Italian and the other a Spaniard. The summer resorts of Europe prove the happy hunting-ground for the knights of industry.

The cards were dealt, and the game played.

At the first *coup* Ralph Ansell won three hundred francs, though he played fairly. Again and again he won. His luck had returned.

In half an hour he had before him a pile of notes and gold representing about three hundred pounds.

His face, however, was sphinx-like. Inveterate gambler that he was, he never allowed his countenance to betray his emotion. Inwardly, however, he was elated at his success, and when the stranger, a middle-aged Russian Baron, proposed to stake an amount equal to his winnings, he quickly welcomed the proposal.

In an instant he was on the alert. Now was the moment to perform one of his clever card-sharping tricks, the trick by which he had so often won big sums from the unsuspecting.

He placed two one-hundred franc notes aside in case he should lose; then the cards were dealt, and the game played.

Only at that moment did the "crook" realise what an astute player the stranger was.

He tried to cheat, and, though he performed the trick, nevertheless his opponent actually beat him.

He bit his lip in anger.

Then, pushing the money across to the Baron, he rose from the table and bade his companions good-night, though the sun was beginning to shine in between the drawn curtains of the stuffy room.

XXII

DISCLOSES A SCHEME

At noon next day, while Ansell was lying lazily in bed in the Palace Hotel reading the *Matin*, a page entered with a letter.

He tore it open, and found that it was dated from the railway buffet at Calais-Maritime, and read:

> DEAR RALPH,
>
> Impossible to send oof. Lady Michelcoombe squeezed dry. Husband knows. So lie low.
>
> TED

He crushed the letter in his hand with an imprecation. His mine of wealth had suddenly become exhausted.

From the address it was plain that Ted Patten was flying from England. Lord Michelcoombe had discovered the truth. Probably his wife had confessed, and explained how she had been trapped and money extracted from her. Well he knew that the penalty for his offence was twenty years' penal servitude.

It was all very well for Ted to advise him to "lie low," but that was impossible without ample funds. The "crook" who is big enough to effect a big *coup* can go into safe retirement for years if necessary. But to the man who is penniless that is impossible.

He rose and dressed even more carefully than usual. Afterwards he took his *déjeuner* in the big *salle-à-manger* and drank half a bottle of Krug with it. Like all men of his class, he was fastidious over his food and wines. The afternoon he spent idling in the casino, and that night he again visited the private gaming house with his two hundred francs, or eight pounds, in his pocket.

It proved a gay night, for there was a dance in progress. In the card-room, however, all was quiet, and there he again met the Russian, who, however, was playing with three other men, strangers to him.

After he had critically inspected the company, he at length accepted the invitation of a man he did not know to sit down to a friendly hand.

In those rooms he was believed to be the wealthy American, as he represented himself to be.

The men he found himself playing with were Frenchmen, and very soon, by dint of "working the trick," he succeeded in swindling them out of about fifty pounds.

Then suddenly his luck turned dead against him. In three *coups* he lost everything, except two coins he had kept in his pocket.

Again, with a gambler's belief in chance, he made another stake, one of five hundred francs.

The cards were dealt and played. Again he lost.

His brows knit, for he could not pay.

From his pocket he drew a silver case, and, taking out his card:

SILAS P. HOGGAN,
San Diego, Cal.

handed it to the man who had invited him to play, with a promise to let him have the money by noon next day.

In return he was given a card with the name: "PAUL FORESTIER, Château de Polivac, Rhone."

The men bowed to each other with exquisite politeness, and then Ralph Ansell went out upon the moonlit *plage* with only two pounds in his pocket, laughing bitterly at his continued run of ill-luck.

That night he took a long walk for miles beside the rocky coast of Calvados, through the fashionable villages of Beuzeval and Cabourg, meeting no one save two mounted gendarmes. The brilliant moon shone over the Channel, and the cool air was refreshing after the close, stuffy heat of the gaming-house.

As he walked, much of his adventurous past arose before him. He thought of Jean, and wondered where she was. Swallowed in the vortex of lower-class life of Paris—dead, probably.

And "The Eel"? He was still in prison, of course. Would they ever meet again? He sincerely hoped not.

As he walked, he tried to formulate some plan for the future. To remain further in Trouville was impossible. Besides, he would have once more to sacrifice his small belongings and leave the hotel without settling his account.

He was debating whether it would be wise to return to Paris. Would he, in his genteel garb, be recognised by some agent of the Sûreté as "The American"? There was danger. Was it wise to court it?

At a point of the road where it ran down upon the rocky beach, upon which the moonlit sea was lapping lazily, he paused, and sat upon the stump of a tree.

And there he reflected until the pink dawn spread, and upon the horizon he saw the early morning steamer crossing from Havre.

He was broke!

Perhaps Ted Patten had treated him just as he had treated Adolphe. That letter might, after all, be only a blind.

"He may have got money, and then written to frighten me," he muttered to himself. "Strange that he didn't give an address. But I know where I shall find him sooner or later. Harry's in Paris is his favourite place, or the American Bar at the Grand at Brussels. Oh, yes, I shall find him. First let me turn myself round."

Then, rising, he walked back to Trouville in the brilliant morning, and going up to his room, went to bed.

Whenever he found himself in an hotel with no money to pay the bill, he always feigned illness, and so awakened the sympathies of the management. In some cases he had lain ill for weeks, living on luxuries, and promising to settle for it all when he was able to get about.

He had done the trick at the Adlon, in Berlin, till found out, and again at the Waldorf-Astoria, in New York. This time he intended to "work the wheeze" on the Palace at Trouville, though he knew that he could not live there long, for the short season was nearly at an end, and in about three weeks the hotel would be closed.

But for a fortnight he remained in bed—or, at least, he was in bed whenever anyone came in. The doctor who was called prescribed for acute rheumatism, and the way in which the patient shammed pain was pathetic.

This enforced retirement was in one way irksome. Wrapped in his dressing-gown, he, after a week in bed, was sufficiently well to sit at the window and look down upon the gay crowd on the *plage* below, and sometimes he even found himself so well that he could appreciate a cigar.

The manager, of course, sympathised with his wealthy visitor, and often came up for an hour's chat, now that the busiest week of his season was over.

All the time Ansell's inventive brain was busy. He was devising a new scheme for money-making, and concocting an alluring prospectus of a venture into which he hoped one "mug," or even two, might put money, and thus form "the original syndicate," which in turn would supply him with funds.

He knew Constantinople, the city where the foreign "crook" and concession-hunter abounds. Among his unscrupulous friends was an under-official at the Yildiz Kiosk, with whom he had had previous dealings. Indeed, he had paid this official to fabricate and provide bogus concessions purporting to be given under the seal of the Grand Vizier of the Ottoman Empire. For one of these concessions—for mining in Asia Minor—he had paid one thousand pounds two years ago, and had sold it to a syndicate in St. Petersburg for ten thousand. When the purchasers came to claim their rights they found the document to be a forgery.

He was contemplating a similar *coup*. He had written to Youssof Effendi asking if he were still open for business, and had received a telegram answering in the affirmative. Therefore, after days of thought, he had at last decided upon obtaining a "concession" for the erection and working of a system of wireless telegraphy throughout the Turkish Empire, and opening coast stations for public service.

His ideas he sent in a registered letter to his accomplice in Constantinople, urging him to have the "concession" prepared in his name with all haste.

And now he was only waiting from day to day to receive the document by which he would be able to net from some unsuspecting persons a few thousand pounds.

True, the bogus documents concerning the mining concession had borne the actual seal of the Grand Vizier, but though an inquiry had been opened, nothing had been discovered. Corruption is so rife in Turkey that the Palace officials ever hang together, providing there is sufficient backsheesh passing. Ralph knew that, therefore he was always liberal. It paid him to be.

A few days before the date of the closing of the hotel a large, official envelope, registered and heavily sealed, was brought up to Mr. Hoggan's room by a page, and Ralph, opening it, found a formidable document in Turkish, which he was unable to read, bearing four signatures, with the big, embossed seal of the Grand Vizier of the Sultan.

With it was an official letter headed "Ministère des Affaires Étrangers, Sublime Porte," enclosing a translation of the document in French, and asking for an acknowledgment.

The imitation was, indeed, perfect. Ralph Ansell rubbed his hands with glee. In Berlin he could obtain at least ten thousand pounds for it, if he tried unsuspicious quarters.

But he wanted ready money to pay his hotel bill and to get to Germany.

An hour later, when the manager came up to pay his usual morning visit, he expressed regret that he had to close the hotel, and added:

"We have still quite a number of visitors. Among them we have Mr. Budden-Reynolds, of London. Do you happen to know him? They say he has made a huge fortune in speculation on the Stock Exchange."

"Budden-Reynolds!" exclaimed Ralph, opening his eyes wide. "I've heard of him, of course. A man who's in every wild-cat scheme afloat. By Jove! That's fortunate. I must see him."

The introduction was not difficult, and that same evening Mr. Budden-Reynolds, a stout, middle-aged, over-dressed man of rather Hebrew countenance, was ushered into the "sick" financier's room.

"Say, sir, I'm very pleased to meet you. I must apologise for not being able to come down to you, but I've had a stiff go of rheumatism. I heard you were in this hotel, and I guess I've got something which will interest you."

Then, when he had seated his visitor, he took from a drawer the formidable registered packet, and drew out the Turkish concession.

The speculator, whose name was well known in financial circles, took it, examined the seal and signatures curiously, and asked what it was.

"That," said Silas P. Hoggan, grandly, "is a concession from the Sultan of Turkey to establish wireless telegraph stations where I like, and to collect the revenue derived from them. Does it interest you, sir?"

Hoggan saw that the bait was a tempting one.

"Yes, a little," replied the speculator grandly.

"It's a splendid proposition! I'm half inclined to go with it straight to the Marconi Company, who will take it over gladly at once. But I feel that we shall do better with a private syndicate, who, in turn, will resell to the Telefunken, the Goldsmidt, or Marconi Company."

"I think you are wise," was the reply.

"There's a heap of money in it! Think of all the coast stations we can establish along the Levant, the Dardanelles, and the Black Sea, to say nothing of the inland public telegraph service. And this, as you will see by the French translation, gives us a perfectly free hand to do whatever we like, and charge the public what we like, providing we give a royalty of five per cent. to the State."

Then he handed Mr. Budden-Reynolds the letter from the Sublime Porte, together with the French translation.

The letter the speculator read through carefully, and then expressed a desire to participate in the venture.

Ansell's bluff was superb.

The two men talked over the matter, "The American" drawing an entrancing picture of the enormous sums which were bound to accrue on the enterprise until, before he left the room, Mr. Budden-Reynolds declared himself ready to put up three hundred and fifty pounds for preliminary expenses if, in exchange, he might become one of the original syndicate.

Upon a sheet of the hotel notepaper a draft agreement was at once drawn up, but not, however, until Ansell had raised many objections. He was not eager to accept the money, a fact which greatly impressed the victim.

An hour later, however, he took Mr. Budden-Reynolds' cheque, signed a receipt, and from that moment his recovery from his illness was extremely rapid.

Early next morning he handed in the cheque to a local bank for telegraphic clearance—which would occupy two days—and then set about packing.

On the second day, at three o'clock in the afternoon, he drew the money, paid his hotel bill with a condescending air, and prepared to depart for Constantinople, for, as he had explained to his victim, there were several minor points in the concession which were not clear, and which could only be settled by discussion on the spot.

Therefore he would go to Paris, and take the Orient Express direct to the Bosphorus.

He had been smoking with Budden-Reynolds from four till five, and then went out to the American bar for an *apéritif*.

When, however, he returned and ascended to his room to dress for dinner, he was suddenly startled by a loud knock on the door, and his friend Budden-Reynolds bustled in.

Facing "The American" suddenly, he said, purple with rage:

"Well, you're about the coolest and most clever thief I've ever met! Do you know that your confounded Turkish concession isn't worth the paper it's written upon?"

"What do you mean?" asked Ansell, with an air of injured innocence.

"I mean, sir," cried the speculator, "I mean that you are a thief and a swindler, and I now intend to call in the police and have you arrested for palming off upon me a bogus concession. As it happens, my son is in the British Consulate in Constantinople, and, having wired to him to investigate the facts, he has just sent me a reply to say that the Grand Vizier has no knowledge of any such concession, and that it has not been given by him. Indeed, the concession for wireless telegraphy in Turkey was given to the Marconi Company a year ago, and, further, they have already erected two coast-stations on the Black Sea."

Mr. Silas P. Hoggan, of San Diego, Cal., unscrupulous as he was, stood before his irate visitor absolutely nonplussed.

XXIII

The Falling Shadow

The country *château* of the Earl of Bracondale, though modestly named the Villa Monplaisir, stood on the road to Fécamp amid the pines, about half a mile from the sea, at St. Addresse, the new seaside suburb of Havre.

St. Addresse is, perhaps, not so fashionable as Etretat or Yport, being quieter and more restful, yet with excellent sea-bathing. Along the broad *plage* are numerous summer villas, with quaint gabled roofs and small pointed towers in the French style—houses occupied in the season mostly by wealthy Parisians.

Monplaisir, however, was the largest and most handsome residence in the neighbourhood; and to it, when the British statesman was in residence, came various French Ministers of State, and usually for a few days each year the President of the Republic was his lordship's guest.

It was a big, modern house, with wide verandahs on each floor, which gave extensive views of country and sea, a house with a high circular slated tower at one end, and many gables with black oaken beams. Around was a plantation of dark pines, protecting the house from the fierce, sweeping winter winds of the Channel, and pretty, sheltered flower-gardens, the whole enclosed with railings of white painted ironwork.

Over the doorway was a handsome semi-circular roof of glass, while from the west end of the house ran a large winter garden, full of palms and exotic flowers.

Before his marriage, Bracondale had been inclined to sell the place, for he went there so very little; but Jean, being French, expressed a wish that it should be kept, as she liked to have a *pied-à-terre* in her own land. At Montplaisir she always enjoyed herself immensely, and the bathing had always been to little Lady Enid of greatest benefit.

One morning towards the end of September Jean, in her white-embroidered muslin frock, the only trimming upon which was a single dark cerise rosette at the waist, and wearing a black velvet hat with long black osprey, stood leaning on the verandah chatting to Bracondale, who, in a well-worn yachting suit and a Panama hat, smoked a cigarette.

They were awaiting Enid and Miss Oliver, for they had arranged to take the child down to the sea, and already the car was at the door.

"How delightful it is here!" exclaimed Jean, glancing around at the garden, bright with flowers, at the blue, cloudless sky, and the glimpse of distant sea.

"Ah!" he laughed. "You always prefer this place to Bracondale—eh? It is but natural, because you are among your own people."

At that moment they both heard the noise of an approaching car, and next moment, as it swept round the drive past the verandah, a good-looking young man in heavy travelling coat, seated at the back of the car, raised his soft felt hat to them.

"Halloa!" exclaimed the Earl. "Here's Martin! Left Downing Street last night. More trouble, I suppose. Excuse me, dearest."

"Yes, but you'll come with us, won't you?"

"Certainly. But I must first see what despatches he has brought," was the reply. Then his lordship left his wife's side, passed along the verandah, and into the small study into which Captain Martin, one of His Majesty's Foreign Service Messengers, had been shown.

"Mornin', Martin!" exclaimed Bracondale, greeting him. "Nice passage over?"

"Yes, my lord," was the traveller's response. "It was raining hard, however, in Southampton. A bad day in London yesterday."

And then, unlocking the little, well-worn despatch-box which he carried, he took out half a dozen bulky packets, each of which bore formidable seals and was marked "On His Britannic Majesty's Service."

The Foreign Minister sighed. He saw that they represented hours of hard work. Selecting one of them, which he saw was from Charlton, he opened it, read it carefully, and placed it in his pocket. The others he put in a drawer and locked them up.

Then he scribbled his signature upon the receipt which Martin, the ever-constant traveller, presented to him, and the King's Messenger took it with a word of thanks.

"When do you go back?" he asked of the trusty messenger, the man who spent his days, year in and year out, speeding backwards and forwards across Europe, carrying instructions to the various Embassies.

"To-night, at midnight."

"Will you call here at eight for despatches?"

"Certainly."

"They'll be ready for you. I thought you were in Constantinople."

"Frewen went yesterday. He took my turn. I do the next journey—to Petersburg—on Friday," he added, speaking as though a journey to that Russian capital was only equal to that from Piccadilly to Richmond.

"Tell Sir Henry to send somebody else to Russia. I shall, I expect, want you constantly here for the next three weeks or so. And you have no objection, I suppose?"

"None," laughed Captain Martin, who for the past eight years had had but few short spells of leave. The life of a King's Messenger is, indeed, no sinecure, for constant journeys in the stuffy *wagonlits* of the European expresses try the most robust constitution. He was a cosmopolitan of cosmopolitans, and, before entering the Foreign Office, had held a commission in the Engineers. Easy-going, popular, and a man of deepest patriotism, he was known in every Embassy in Europe, and to every sleeping-car conductor on the express routes.

"And, by the way, on the mantelshelf of my room at Downing Street, Martin, you will find a small stereoscopic camera," added Lord Bracondale. "I wish you would bring it over next time you come."

"Certainly," Martin replied.

"Then, at eight o'clock to-night. You can leave your despatch-box here," his lordship said.

So Martin, a man of polished manners, placed his little box—a steel one, with a travelling-cover of dark green canvas—upon a side table, and, wishing the Earl good-morning, withdrew, returning to Havre in the hired car to shave, wash, and idle until his return to London.

Wherever Bracondale went, the problems of foreign policy followed him.

During the recess members of the House may leave the country and their cares and constituencies behind them, but to the Minister for Foreign Affairs, the despatches go daily by messenger or by wire, and wherever he may be, he must attend to them. International politics brook no delay.

Upon Bracondale's brow a shadow had fallen since he had scanned Charlton's letter. More trouble with Germany had arisen.

But he put on a forced smile when, a moment later, he rejoined Jean, who was now standing in readiness with Miss Oliver and little Enid, the latter looking very sweet in her tiny Dutch bonnet and a little Paris-made coat of black and white check and white shoes and socks.

In a few moments they were in the big, open car, and were quickly driven through the pines and out upon the sea-road until, when on the railed esplanade at St. Addresse, the car pulled up suddenly at some steps which led down to the sands.

Just before he did so his lordship, addressing Jean, said:

"I know you will excuse me staying with you this morning, dear, but I must attend to those despatches Martin has brought. And they will certainly take me till luncheon. So I will see you down to the beach and then go back. The car shall come for you at half past twelve."

"Oh, I'm so sorry," said Jean, regretfully. "But I know, dear, how worried you are. So I'll forgive you. I shall spend a quiet morning with a book, and Enid will enjoy herself."

Then the car stopped, he got out, helped Enid and Miss Oliver down, and then gave his hand to Jean, who, with her dark cloak thrown over her white dress, looked extremely dainty, and much younger than her years.

While the car waited for them, all four descended to the beach, where little Enid with her governess went forward, while Bracondale and his wife walked along to a secluded corner in the rocks, where it was Jean's habit to read while awaiting her little girl.

Then, after he had seen her comfortably settled in the shadow, for the sun was hot, he lit a cigarette and strolled back to where the car awaited him, absorbed in the international problem which had, according to Charlton, so suddenly arisen.

As he sat in the car and was whirled along the sea-front towards Monplaisir, he passed a clean-shaven, well-dressed man in a dark suit with carefully-ironed trousers, his handkerchief showing from his jacket pocket, patent leather boots, grey spats, and a light grey Tyrolese hat. The stranger gave him a curious, inquisitive glance as he passed, then, looking after him, muttered some words beneath his breath.

The idler stood and watched the car disappear in the dust along the wide, straight road, and then he walked to the steps over which Jean had passed and followed in her footsteps.

As a matter of fact, this was not the first occasion upon which the stranger had watched her ladyship.

On the previous day he had been passing along a street in Havre when a big red car had passed, and in it was her ladyship with little Lady Enid.

In a second, on looking up suddenly, he had recognised her.

But she had not seen him. At the moment she had been bending towards the child, buttoning up her coat.

　　　　　　　WILLIAM LE QUEUX

The stranger, who had only the day previous arrived in Havre, and was awaiting a steamer to America, turned upon his heel and, chancing to meet a postman face to face, pointed out the car and asked in French whose it was.

The veteran, for he wore his medal, glanced at the car and replied:

"Ah! That is the automobile of the English lord. That is the Countess of Bracondale, his wife."

"Do they live here?"

"At the Villa Monplaisir, m'sieur, out on the road to Fécamp."

"Are they rich?" he asked unconcernedly.

"Oh, yes; Lord Bracondale is the English Minister for Foreign Affairs."

"Bracondale!" echoed the stranger, recognising the name for the first time. "And that is his wife?"

"Yes."

"And the child?"

"His daughter."

"Is Lady Bracondale often here, in Havre?" he inquired eagerly.

"Not often. Perhaps once a week in the season. She comes shopping," replied the grizzled old man, hitching up his box containing his letters.

"Look here, my friend," exclaimed the stranger. "Tell me something more about that lady." And he slipped a two-franc piece into the man's hand.

"Ah! I fear I know but little—only what people say, m'sieur."

"What do they say?"

"That Madame the Countess, who is French, is a most devoted wife, although she is such a great lady—one of the greatest ladies in England, I believe. I have heard that they have half-a-dozen houses, and are enormously wealthy."

"Rich—eh?" remarked the inquirer, and his keen, dark eyes sparkled. "You know nothing more?"

"No, m'sieur. But I daresay there are people out at St. Addresse who know much more than I do."

"*Bien. Bon jour*," said the stranger, and he passed on, eager to make other and more diligent inquiries.

And the stranger, whose name was "Silas P. Hoggan, of San Diego, Cal.," was the same man who had watched the Earl of Bracondale depart in his car, and who now descended to the beach, following in the footsteps of the Countess.

XXIV

THE BLOW

With easy, leisurely gait, the man in the grey hat strode along the sands towards the rocks behind which the Countess and the governess had disappeared.

Upon his mobile lips played an evil, triumphant smile, in his keen eyes a sharp, sinister look as he went forward, his hands thrust carelessly into his jacket pocket.

His eyes were set searchingly upon the grey rocks before him, when suddenly he saw in the distance Miss Oliver and little Enid walking together. Therefore he knew that Lady Bracondale was alone.

"What luck!" he murmured. "I wonder how she'll take it? To think that I should have been lying low in Trouville yonder all that time while she was living here. I've got ten louis, and a ticket for New York, but if you are cute, Ralph Ansell," he said, addressing himself, "you won't want to use that ticket."

He chuckled and smiled.

"The Countess of Bracondale!" he muttered. "I wonder what lie she told the Earl? Perhaps she's changed—become unscrupulous—since we last met. I wonder?"

And then, reaching the rocks, he walked as noiselessly as he could to the spot where he had located that she must be.

He had made no error, for as he rounded a great limestone boulder, worn smooth by the action of the fierce winter waves, he saw her seated in the shadow, her sunshade cast aside, reading an English novel in ignorance of any person being present.

It was very quiet and peaceful there, the only sound being the low lapping of the blue, tranquil water, clear as crystal in the morning light. She was engrossed in her book, for it was a new one by her favourite author, while he, standing motionless, watched her and saw that, though she had grown slightly older, she was full of girlish charm. She was quietly but beautifully dressed—different indeed to the black gown and print apron of those Paris days.

He saw that upon the breast of her white embroidered gown she wore a beautiful brooch in the shape of a coronet, and on her finger a ring with one single but very valuable pearl. He was a connoisseur of such things. At last, after watching her for several minutes, he knit his brows, and, putting forward his hard, determined chin, exclaimed in English:

"Well, Jean!"

Startled, she looked up. Next second she stared at him open-mouthed. The light died out of her face, leaving it ashen grey, and her book fell from her hand.

"Yes, it's me—Ralph Ansell, your husband!"

"You!" she gasped, her big, frightened eyes staring at him. "I—I—The papers said you were dead—that—that—"

"I know," he laughed. "The police think that Ralph Ansell is dead. So he is. I am Mr. Hoggan, from California."

"Hoggan!" she echoed, looking about her in dismay.

"Yes—and you? You seem to have prospered, Jean."

She was silent. What could she say?

Through her mind rushed a flood of confused memories. Sight of his familiar face filled her with fear. The haunting past came back to her in all its evil hideousness—the past which she had put behind her for ever now arose in all its cruel reality and naked bitterness.

And worse. She had preserved a guilty silence towards Bracondale!

Her husband, the man to whom she was legally bound, stood before her!

She only glared at him with blank, despairing, haunted eyes.

"Well—speak! Tell me who and what you are."

The word "what" cut deeply into her.

He saw her shrink and tremble at the word. And he grinned, a hard, remorseless grin. The corners of his mouth drew down in triumph.

"It seems long ago since we last met, doesn't it?" he remarked, in a hard voice. "You left me because I was poor."

"Not because you were poor, Ralph," she managed to reply; "but because you would have struck me if Adolphe had not held you back."

"Adolphe!" he cried in disgust. "The swine is still in prison, I suppose. He was a fool to be trapped like that. I ran to the river—the safest place when one is cornered. The police thought I was drowned, but, on the contrary, I swam and got away. Since then I've had a most pleasant time, I assure you. Ralph Ansell did die when he threw himself into the Seine."

She looked at him with a strange expression.

"True; but his deeds still remain."

"Deeds—what do you mean?"

"I mean this!" she cried, starting to her feet and facing him determinedly. "I mean that you—Ralph Ansell, my husband—killed Richard Harborne!"

His face altered in a moment, yet his self-possession was perfect.

He smiled, and replied, with perfect unconcern:

"Oh! And pray upon what grounds do you accuse me of such a thing? Harborne—oh, yes, I recollect the case. It was when we were in England."

"Richard Harborne was a member of the British Secret Service, and the authorities know that he died by your hand," was her slow reply. "It is known that you acted as the cats'-paw—that it was you who tampered with the aeroplane which fell and killed poor Lieutenant Barclay before our eyes. Ah! Had I but known the truth at the time—at the time when I, in ignorance, stood by your side and loved you!"

"Then you love me no longer—eh, Jean?" he asked, facing her, his brows knit.

"How can I? How can I love a man who is a murderer?"

"Murderer!" he cried, in anger. "You must prove it! I'll compel you to prove it, or by gad! I'll—I'll strangle you!"

"The facts are already proved."

"How do you know?"

"From an official report which I have seen. It is now in my husband's possession—locked up in his safe."

"Your husband!" repeated Ansell, affecting ignorance of the truth.

"Yes," she said hoarsely. "I have married, believing that you were dead."

"And both pleased and relieved to think I was dead, without a doubt!" he laughed, with a sneer.

She said nothing.

At that instant when she had raised her eyes and met him face to face she knew that all her happiness had been shattered at a single blow—that the shadow of evil which she had so long dreaded had at last fallen to crush her.

No longer was she Countess of Bracondale, a happy wife and proud mother, but the wife of a man who was not only a notorious thief, but an assassin to boot.

Inwardly she breathed a prayer to Providence for assistance in that dark hour. Her deep religious convictions, her faith in God, supported her at that dark hour of her life, and she clasped her hands and held her breath.

The man grinned, so confident was he of his power over her.

"I believed you were dead, or I would not have married again," she said simply.

"Yes. You thought you had got rid of me, no doubt. But I think this precious husband of yours will have a rather rough half-hour when he knows how you've deceived him."

"I have told him no lie!"

"No? You told him nothing, I suppose. Silence is a lie sometimes."

"Yes. I have been silent regarding your crimes," she replied. "The affair is not forgotten, I assure you. And a word from me will sentence you to the punishment which all murderers well deserve."

"Good. Do it!" he laughed, with a shrug of his shoulders. "I wish you would. You would be rid of me then—the widow of a murderer!"

"You killed Richard Harborne because you were paid to do so—paid by a spy of Germany," she said, very slowly. "The report which my husband possesses tells the truth. The British Secret Service has spared no pains to elucidate the mystery of Harborne's death."

"Then they also know that I married you, I suppose? They know you are wife of the guilty man—eh?"

She bit her lip. That thought had not recently occurred to her. Long ago, when it had, she had quickly crushed it down, believing that Ralph was dead. But, on the contrary, he was there, standing before her, the grim vision of the long-buried past.

"Well," she asked suddenly, "what do you want with me now that you have found me?"

"Not much. I dare say you and I can come to terms."

"What terms? I don't understand?"

"You are my wife," he said. "Well, that is your secret—and mine. You want to close my mouth," he said roughly. "And of course you can do so—at a price."

"You want money in return for your silence?"

"Exactly, my dear girl. I am very sorry, but I have been a trifle unfortunate in my speculations of late. I'm a financier now."

She looked him straight in the face, her resolution rising. She hated that man whose hands were stained with the blood of Richard Harborne, who had been such a platonic friend to her.

"I wish you to understand, now and at once," she said, "that you will have nothing from me."

He smiled at her.

"Ah! I think you are just a little too hasty, my dear Jean," was his reply. "Remember you are my wife, and that fact you desire to keep a secret. Well, the secret is worth something, surely—even for the sake of your charming little girl."

"Yes," she said angrily. "You taunt me with my position—why? Because you want money—you, a thief and an assassin! No; you will have none. I will go to the police and have you arrested."

"Do, my dear girl. I wish you would do so, because then your true position as my wife will at once be plain. I shall not be Silas P. Hoggan, homeless and penniless, but Ralph Ansell, husband of the wealthy Countess of Bracondale. Say—what a sensation it would cause in the halfpenny papers, wouldn't it?"

Jean shuddered, and shrank back.

"And you would be arrested for the murder of Richard Harborne—you, the hired assassin of the Baron," she retorted. "Oh, yes, all is known, I assure you. Not a year ago I found the report among Lord Bracondale's papers, and read it—every word."

"And how does he like his private papers being peered into, I wonder?"

"Well, at least I now know the truth. You killed Mr. Harborne, and, further, it was you who tampered with Lieutenant Barclay's aeroplane. You can't deny it!"

"Why should I deny it? Harborne was your lover. You met him in secret at Mundesley on the previous afternoon. Therefore I killed two birds with one stone. A very alert secret agent was suppressed, and at the same time I was rid of a rival."

"He was not my lover!" she protested, her cheeks scarlet. "I loved you, and only you."

"Then why don't you love me now? Why not return and be a dutiful wife to me?"

"Return!" she gasped. "Never!"

"But I shall compel you. You married this man, Bracondale, under false pretences, and he has no right to you. I am your husband."

"That I cannot deny," she said, her hands twitching nervously. "But I read of your death in the papers, and believed it to be true," she added in despair.

"Well, you seem to have done extremely well for yourself. And you have been living in London all the time?"

"Mostly."

"I was in London very often. I have seen your name in the papers dozens of times as giving great official receptions and entertainments, yet I confess I never, for a moment, dreamed that the great Countess Bracondale and my wife, Jean, were one and the same person."

She shrank at the word "wife." That surely was the most evil day in all her life. She was wondering how best to end that painful interview—how to solve the tragic difficulty which had now arisen—how best to hide her dread secret from Bracondale.

"Well," she said at last, "though you married me, Ralph, you never had a spark of affection for me. Do you recollect the last night that I was beneath your roof—your confession that you were a thief, and how you raised your hand against me because I begged you not to run into danger. How—?"

"Enough!" he interrupted roughly. "The past is dead and gone. I was a fool then."

"But I remember it all too well, alas!" she said. "I remember how I loved you, and how full and bitter was my disillusionment."

"And what do you intend doing now?" he asked defiantly.

"Nothing," was her reply. Truth to tell, she was nonplussed. She saw no solution of the ghastly problem.

"But I want money," he declared, fiercely.

"I have none—only what my husband gives me."

"Husband! I'm your husband, remember. I tell you, Jean, I don't intend to starve. I may be well dressed, but that's only bluff. I've got only a few pounds in the world."

"I see," she said. "You intend to blackmail me. But I warn you that if those are your tactics, I shall simply tell Bracondale what I know concerning Richard Harborne."

"You will—will you!" he cried, fiercely, advancing towards her threateningly. "By Heaven, if you breathe a word about that, I—*I'll kill you!*"

And in his eyes shone a bright, murderous light—a light that she had seen there once before—on the night of her departure.

She recognised how determined he was, and drew back in fear.

Then, placing his hand in his jacket pocket, he drew forth a small leather wallet, much worn, and from it took a soiled, crumpled but carefully-preserved letter, which he opened and presented for her inspection.

"Do you recognise this?" he asked, with a sinister grin.

She drew back and held her breath.

"I'll read it," he said with a triumphant laugh. "I kept it as a souvenir. The man you call husband will no doubt be very pleased to see it." Then he read the words:

In spite of my love for you, Ralph, I cannot suffer longer. Certain hidden things in your life frighten me. Farewell. Forget me.

JEAN

For a few seconds she was silent. Her face was white as paper.

Then, with a sudden outburst, she gasped, in a low, terrified voice, and putting up her arms with a wild gesture:

"No, no! You must not show that to him. You won't, Ralph—for my sake, you won't. Will you?"

XXV

To Pay the Price

W ell?" asked Ansell, looking at his wife with a distinctly evil grin.

"Well?" she answered blankly, for want of something else to say.

"What will you give me for this letter?" he asked, carefully replacing it in his wallet and transferring it to his pocket with an air of supreme satisfaction.

"I have nothing to give, Ralph."

"But you can find something quite easily," he urged, with mock politeness. "Your ladyship must control a bit of cash-money. Remember, I've already made enquiries, and I know quite well that this man Bracondale is extremely wealthy. Surely he doesn't keep too tight a hold on the purse-strings!"

"I have already told you that I have no money except what Lord Bracondale gives me, and he often looks at my banker's pass-book. He would quickly ask me where the money had gone to."

"Bah! You are a woman, and a woman can easily make an excuse. He'll believe anything if he is really fond of you, as I suppose he must be. You wouldn't like him to have that letter—would you, now?"

"No. I've told you that," she replied, her pale, dry lips moving nervously.

"Then we shall have to discuss very seriously ways and means, and come to terms, my girl," was his rough rejoinder.

"But how can I make terms with you?"

"Quite easily—by getting money."

"I can't!" she cried.

"Well, I guess I'm not going to starve and see you living in luxury—a leader of London society. It isn't likely, now, is it?"

"No; knowing you as well as I do, I suppose it isn't likely."

"Ah! You do me an injustice, Jean," he said. "I only want just sufficient to get away from here—to America—and begin afresh a new life. I'll turn over a new leaf—believe me, I will. I want to, but I haven't the cash-money to do it. To be honest costs money."

"Yes," she sighed. "I suppose it does. And to be dishonest, alas! is always profitable in these days, when honour stands at a premium."

"Well, how much can you get for me?" he asked roughly.

"Nothing," she replied, holding out her hands in despair. "Where am I to get money from?"

"You know best, Jean. I don't. All I know is, I want money—and I mean to have it."

"But I tell you I can't get any," she protested.

"You'll have to. You don't want Bracondale to know the truth, do you?" he asked.

She shook her head. Her eyes were wild and haggard, her cheeks as pale as death.

"Well, look here," he said, again thrusting his hands in the pockets of his jacket. "Give me five thousand pounds, and you shall have your letter. I will be silent, and we will never meet again. I'll go back to America, and give my firm promise never to cross to Europe again."

"Five thousand pounds!" echoed the distracted woman. "Why, I can't get such a sum! You must surely know that."

"You will do so somehow—in order to save your honour."

"What is the use of discussing it?" she asked. "I tell you such a proposal is entirely out of the question."

"Very well. Then you must bear the consequences. If you won't pay me, perhaps Bracondale will."

"What!" she gasped. "You would go to my husband?"

"Husband!" he sneered. "I'm your husband, my girl. And I mean that either you or Bracondale shall pay. You thought yourself rid of me, but you were mistaken, you see," he added, with a hard laugh of triumph.

"I was misled by the newspapers," she said, simply, as she stood with her back against the grey rocks. "Had I not believed that you had lost your life in the Seine I should not have married Lord Bracondale."

"Deceived him, you mean, not married him," he said harshly. "Well, I haven't much time to wait. Besides, that governess of yours may come back. It won't be nice for that little girl to be taken from you, will it?" he said. "But when Bracondale knows, that's what will happen."

"Never. He is not cruel and inhuman, like you, Ralph!" she responded, bitterly.

"I'm merely asking for what is due to me. I find that another man has usurped my place, and I want my price."

"And that is—what?" she asked, after a few minutes' pause, looking him straight in the face.

"Five thousand, and this interesting letter is yours."

"Impossible!" she cried. "You might as well ask me for the crown of England."

"Look here," he said, putting out his hand towards her, but she shrank from his touch—the touch of a hand stained with the blood of Richard Harborne.

"No. I won't hurt you," he laughed, believing that she stood in fear of him. "I want nothing but the cash-money. I'll call at Monplaisir this evening for it. By Jove!" he added. "That's a nice, comfortable house of yours. You've been very happy there, both of you, I suppose—eh?"

"Yes," she sighed. His threat to call at the villa held her appalled. She saw no way to appease this man, who was now bent upon her ruin. The present, with all its happiness, had faded from her and the future was only a grey vista of grief and despair.

"You know quite well," he went on, "that when you tell me that you can't get money, I don't believe you. You surely aren't going to stand by and see your husband starve, are you? I've had cursed bad luck of late. A year ago I was rich, but to-day I'm broke again—utterly broke, and, moreover, the police are looking for me. That's why I want to get away to America—with your help."

"But don't I say I can't help you?" she protested. "Ah!" she exclaimed, a second later. "You can have my brooch—here it is," and she proceeded to take it from the breast of her white gown.

"Bah! What's the good of that to me?" he laughed. "No. Keep it— why, it isn't worth more than fifty pounds! You surely don't think I'm going to let you have your affectionate letter for that sum, do you?"

"I've got nothing else."

"But you have at home," he urged. "What other jewels have you got?"

"Nothing of great value here. The Bracondale jewels are at Bracondale," she replied slowly, after a few seconds' deliberation. "I have nothing much here, except—"

And she drew herself up short.

"Except what?" he asked sharply.

"Nothing."

"Oh, yes, you have," he said, in a hard voice. "Now tell me. What have you got of real value?"

"I tell you I have nothing."

"That's a lie," he declared. "You've got something you don't want to part with—something you value very much."

She was silent and stood there pale and trembling before him. He saw her hesitation, and knew that his allegation was the truth.

"Come, out with it! I mustn't stay here any longer. We shall be seen," he said. "What have you got?"

She bit her blanched lip.

"My pearls," she replied in a voice scarcely above a whisper.

"What pearls?"

"Matched pearls which my husband gave me for my birthday."

"Valuable—eh?"

"Yes," she sighed. "But you can't have them. I prize them very much."

"Greater than your own honour?" he asked, seriously.

"You shall never have them. What excuse could I make to Bracondale?"

"Leave that to me. Pearls are easier negotiated than diamonds. I can sell them at once. If they are the good goods I'll give you the letter in exchange for them. That's a bargain."

"They cost several thousands, I know."

"Good! Then we'll conclude the business to-night."

"No, no!" she protested. "What could I tell my husband?"

"I wish you wouldn't keep referring to him as husband, Jean, when he is not your husband."

"To the world he is. I am no longer Jean Ansell, remember," she protested.

"Well, we won't discuss that. Let's arrange how the exchange shall be made. Now, around your house is a verandah. You will accidentally leave the pearls on the table in one of the rooms at midnight, with the long window unfastened, and I'll look in and get them. You will be in the room, and we can make the exchange. Next day you will discover your loss and tell the police that burglars have visited you. By that time I shall be in Amsterdam. It's quite easy. Only keep your nerve, girl."

"But—"

"There are no 'buts.' We are going to carry this thing through."

She hesitated, thinking deeply. Then she openly defied him.

"I will not let you have those pearls. He gave them to me, and I won't arrange a mock burglary."

"You won't give them to me as price of your honour—eh? Then you're a bigger fool than I took you for. I dare say they won't fetch more than a thousand—perhaps not that. So it's a sporting offer I am making you."

"You can have anything except that."

"I don't want anything else. I want to do you a good turn by getting away from here—away from you for ever. I quite understand your feelings and sympathise with you, I assure you," he said, his manner changing slightly.

But she was obdurate. Therefore he at once altered his tactics and resorted again to his bullying methods. He was a low-down blackguard, although he was dressed as a gentleman and cultivated an air of refinement. Yet he was a prince among thieves and swindlers.

"All this is mere empty talk," he declared at last. "I tell you that if you refuse to do as I direct I shall call upon Bracondale this evening and ask for alms. Oh," he laughed, "it will be quite amusing to see his face when I show him your letter, for he no doubt believes in you. Are you prepared to face the music?"

And, pausing, he fixed his cruel, relentless eyes, beady and brilliant as those of a snake, upon his trembling victim.

She did not answer, though she now realised that he held her future in his remorseless hands. This man whom she had once loved with a strong, all-consuming passion, had risen to smite her and to ruin her.

"Will Bracondale be at home to-night?" he asked presently.

"No," she responded in a low whisper. "He will be at his club. He has arranged to play bridge with M. Polivin, the Minister of Commerce. You won't see him."

"Good. Then you will be alone—to meet me and take the letter in exchange for the pearls, which I shall take," he said, confidently. "I had a look around the house early this morning before anyone was about. It would be very easy to enter there—quite inviting, I assure you. I wonder you don't take precautions against intruders. I speak as an expert," and he laughed grimly.

But she made no response.

"I notice," he went on—"I notice that the room on the left of the front entrance is a small salon. It has a long window leading to the balcony. Leave that unlatched, and I will come there at midnight. If you are there, leave the light on. If there is danger then put it out. I shall know."

"But I can't—I won't."

"You will! You want that letter, and I will give it to you in exchange for the pearls! He will suspect nothing. A thief got in and stole them. That was all. He is rich, and will buy you another set. So why trouble further?"

"No—I—"

"Yes—ah, look! That woman is coming back with the child. I must clear. Remember, it is all arranged. At midnight to-night I'll bring you the letter. *Au revoir!*"

And next moment the evil shadow of her life disappeared around the corner of the rock and was gone.

XXVI

A Child's Question

At luncheon Jean met her husband, but so agitated was she that she scarce dare raise her eyes to his.

Before entering the dining-room where Bracondale awaited her she halted at the door, and with a strenuous effort calmed herself. Then she went forward with a forced smile upon her lips, though her cheeks were pale and she knew that her hand trembled.

His lordship had spent a strenuous morning with the papers Martin had brought from the Foreign Office. At least two of our Ambassadors to the Powers had asked for instructions, and their questions presented difficult and intricate problems which really ought to have gone before the Cabinet. But as there would not be another meeting just yet, everyone being away on vacation, it devolved upon Bracondale to decide the question of Britain's policy himself.

In the pretty, cosy room, outside which the striped sun-blinds were down, rendering it cool and pleasant after the midday heat on the beach, the Foreign Minister stood thoughtfully stroking his moustache.

"Well, Jean," he asked, "had a quiet morning, dear?"

"Yes, delightful," was her reply. "The heat is, however, rather oppressive."

"I'm awfully sorry I could not come down to fetch you, dear," he said; "but I've been dreadfully busy all the morning—lots of worries, as you know. I've only this moment risen from my table. There are more complications between France and Austria."

"Oh, I know how busy you are," she replied as she seated herself at the daintily set-out table, with its flowers, bright silver, and cut glass.

Their luncheons *tête-à-tête* were always pleasant, for on such occasions they sat at a small side-table, preferring it to the big centre-table when there were no guests.

"Did you see anyone you knew?" he asked, carelessly, for often Mme. Polivin, the rather stout wife of the Minister of Commerce, went to the sands with her children.

"Well, nobody particular," was her reply, with feigned unconcern. "Enid enjoyed herself immensely," she went on quickly. "She didn't bathe, so I told her to make a sand castle. She was delighted, especially when the water came in under the moat."

And then, as he seated himself opposite her, old Jenner entered with the *hors d'oeuvres*.

Jean was thankful that the room, shaded as it was, was in half darkness, so that her husband could not see how pale she was. Through the open windows came the scent of flowers borne upon the warm air, and the silence of the room was over everything.

He began to discuss their plans for the autumn.

"Trevor asks us to go a cruise in his yacht up the Adriatic in October," he said. "I had a letter from him this morning, dated from Stavanger. You remember what a good time we had with him when we went to Algiers and Tunis two years ago."

"I've never been to the Adriatic," she remarked.

"I went once, about nine years ago, with that financial fellow Pettigrew—the fellow who afterwards met with a fatal accident in a lift at the Grand in Paris. It was delightful. You would be interested in all the little places along the beautiful Dalmatian coast—Zara, where they make the maraschino; Sebenico, Pola, the Bay of Cattaro, and Ragusa, the old city of the Venetian Republic. Shall we accept?"

"It is awfully kind of your brother-in-law," she replied. "Yes, I'd love to go—if you could get away."

"I could come overland and join you at Venice or Trieste, and then we could put into Brindisi or Ancona for any urgent despatches. You see, there's no convenient rail on the Dalmatian side. Yes, I think I could manage it."

"Then accept by all means. I love the sea, as you know. Where do they sail from?"

"Marseilles. You will join the *Marama* there. She will then touch at Genoa, Naples, and go through the Straits of Messina, and I'll join you in the Adriatic."

"Helen is going, I suppose?" she remarked, referring to Trevor's wife. "Of course, and the two Henderson girls, and little Lady Runton. So we shall be a merry party."

Jean was delighted. In the excitement of the moment she forgot the dark cloud that had fallen upon her.

Yet next second she reflected, and wished that her departure upon that cruiser was immediate, in order that she could escape the man who had so suddenly and unexpectedly returned into her life.

"We shall go to Scotland after our return," he said. "Remember, we've got house parties on the eighth, seventeenth, and thirtieth of November."

"And Christmas at Bracondale," she said. "I love spending it there."

"Or perhaps on the Riviera? Why not? It is warmer," he suggested.

"It may be, but I really think that nowadays, with the change in the English climate, it is just as warm in Torquay at Christmas as at Nice."

"Yes," he replied with a smile. "Perhaps you are right, after all, Jean. If you want warmth and sunshine from December to April you must go to Egypt for it. People have begun to realise that it is often colder in Monte Carlo than in London. And yet it used not to be. I remember when I was a lad and went to Nice with the old governor each winter, we had real warm sunshine. Yes, the climate of the south of Europe has become colder, just as our English climate has become less severe in winter."

And he ate his lobster salad and drank a glass of Chablis, thoroughly enjoying it after the hard mental strain of the morning.

"I think I shall go for a run in the car this afternoon. I feel to want some fresh air. Will you come?" he asked.

"I think not, dear," was her reply. "I have a little headache—the sun, I think—so I shall rest."

"Very well. I'll have a drive alone."

"Let's see," she exclaimed; "didn't you say you were going out to-night?"

"Yes, dear, to Polivin's. There's a man-party this evening. You don't mind, do you? I promised him some time ago, and for political reasons I desire to be friendly. I shan't go till ten o'clock, and no doubt you will go to bed early."

"By all means go, dear," she said, very sweetly. "I—I had forgotten the day."

It was not often he left her alone of an evening when they were together during the recess. In the London season she was, as a political hostess, often compelled to go out alone, while he, too, had frequently to attend functions where it was impossible for her to be present. Sometimes, indeed, days and days passed and they only met at breakfast. Frequently, too, he was so engrossed in affairs of State that, though he was in the house, yet he was closeted hours and hours with Darnborough, with some high Foreign Office official, an ambassador, or a Cabinet Minister.

That big, sombre room of his in the dark, gloomy London mansion was indeed a room of political secrets, just as was his private room at the Foreign Office. If those walls could but speak, what strange tales they might tell—tales of clever juggling with the Powers, of ingenious counter-plots against conspiracies ever arising to disturb the European peace, plots concocted by Britain's enemies across the seas, and the evolution of master strokes of foreign policy.

"Are you quite sure you prefer not to go for a drive this afternoon?" he asked, looking across at her.

"No, really, dear. I don't feel at all fit. It is the excessive heat. It was awfully oppressive on the beach."

"Very well, dear. Rest then, and get right by the time I get in for tea."

She looked at him from beneath her half-closed lashes.

Why had he asked her whether she had met anyone she knew that morning? It was not a usual question of his.

Could he know anything? Had he been present and seen the meeting?

No, that was impossible. He had been at home all the morning. She had made enquiry of Jenner as she came in, so as to satisfy herself.

Yet there was a strange suspicion in his manner, she thought. It may have been her fancy, nevertheless he seemed unduly curious, and that question of his had set her wondering.

For some moments she ate her dessert in silence.

Before her arose all the horror of that amazing meeting. The words of the criminal who was her husband rang in her ears, cruel, brutal, and relentless. He had threatened to call there at the villa, and hand her letter to Bracondale, a threat which, she knew, he would carry out if she did not appease him and bow to his will.

She was to exchange those pearls, Bracondale's valued gift, for the silence of a blackmailer and assassin! Ah! the very thought of it drove her to desperation. Yet she was about to do it for Bracondale's sake; for the sake of little Enid, whom she so dearly loved.

Every word the brute had uttered had burned into her brain. Her temples throbbed as though her skull must burst. But she fought against the evil and against a collapse. She put on a brave front, and when Bracondale addressed her she laughed lightly as though she had not a single care in all the world.

The meal over, she took a scarlet carnation from the silver épergne between them, broke the stem and, bending, placed it in the lapel of his coat, receiving as reward a fond, sweet kiss, old Jenner having finally left the room.

"Now go and rest, dearest," his lordship said. "I have a few letters I will write before I go out."

And he was about to cross to the door when it suddenly opened, and little Enid in her white muslin dress danced into the room, rushing up to her mother's outstretched arms.

Bracondale caught the child and, taking her up, kissed her fondly.

Then, when he set her down again, she rushed to Jean, and in her childish voice asked:

"Mother, I was so afraid this morning when I saw you talking to that nasty man!"

"Nasty man!" echoed Jean, her heart standing still.

"Yes, mother. I ran across from Miss Oliver and was coming to you, but when I got round the rock I saw—oh, I saw a nasty man raising his hands, and talking. And you were so frightened—and so was I. So I ran back again. He was a nasty, bad man."

For a second a dead silence fell.

Then Jean, with a supreme effort, collected her thoughts and exercised all her self-control.

"What was that, Jean?" inquired Bracondale quickly.

"Oh, nothing. A man came along begging—rather a well-dressed man he seemed to be. And because I refused to give him anything he commenced to abuse me. But I soon sent him away."

"The child says you were afraid."

"Afraid!" she laughed, with a strange, hysterical little laugh. "If I had been I should have called for help. He was only some loafer or other who, finding me alone, thought he could get a franc, I suppose." And then, after a pause, she added, "I had a similar experience one day last year. The police really ought to keep the sands clear of such persons."

"What was he like? I'll tell the chief of police about it."

"Well, really, I didn't take very much notice," she replied. "I was reading, and looking up suddenly found him standing before me. I had no idea that Enid saw him. He asked me for money in a very rough manner. And naturally I declined, and told him that if he did not clear off I would shout for help. So—well, after a few more abusive words, he slunk away."

"He might have stolen your brooch," Bracondale remarked.

"He might, certainly," she said. "Not until after he had gone did I realise how helpless I had been."

"Yes, mother," exclaimed the little girl, "but you were frightened, weren't you? I thought he was going to hit you, for you put up your hands, and he clenched his fists and put his face right into yours. Oh! it did frighten me!"

"Didn't you tell Miss Oliver?" asked her father.

"No; but I will. I went digging, and forgot all about it."

"If I were you, Enid, I shouldn't tell Miss Oliver," her mother said, very quietly. "You were frightened for nothing. It was only a man who wanted money."

"But he was such a nasty man—he had a horrid face, and such big, big eyes!" declared the child, and then, turning, she danced away out of the room, leaving Bracondale facing Jean in silence.

XXVII

The Intruder

That afternoon Jean remained in her room in a fierce fever of anxiety, while Bracondale drove his car along the winding, shady road to Yvetot, and home by St. Valery-en-Caux, and the sea-road which commences at Fécamp.

Did he suspect? she wondered.

She could not help feeling mortified that the child should have made that unfortunate remark. She felt also that her excuse was a lame one. Did he really believe her story?

From the steel safe in her daintily-furnished room, with its silken upholstery in old rose, she took the big, square, velvet-lined case, and, opening it, gazed upon the string of splendid pearls. She took them out tenderly and, standing before the long cheval-glass, put them round her neck—for the last time.

As she examined herself in the mirror she sighed, her face hard, pale, and full of anxiety and distress.

Would Bracondale notice the change in her?

She put away the pearls, and, replacing the case in the safe, locked it.

Bates, her rather sour-faced maid, entered at the moment. She was a thin, angular person, very neat and prim, an excellent hairdresser, and a model of what a first-class maid should be.

"Why, you don't look well this afternoon, madam," she said, glancing at her inquiringly.

"No, Bates. It's the heat, I think. Will you bring me my smelling-salts?" she asked, as she sank into an arm-chair, a pretty figure in her pale-blue silk dressing-gown.

The maid brought the large, silver-topped bottle across from the dressing-table and handed it to her mistress, who, after sniffing it, dismissed her.

Then Jean sat for a full half-hour staring straight before her, looking down the long vista of her own tragic past.

At midnight that letter would be safe in her hand. She consoled herself with the thought that, by acceding to Ansell's demand, as she had done, she would rid herself of him for ever.

Her honour would be preserved, and Bracondale would never know. For the sake of her child, how could she confess to him?

He joined her in the *petit salon*, where she gave him tea, and then, till dinner, he retired into the study to complete the despatches for which Martin was to call and take to Downing Street.

At dinner she wore a pretty gown of cream lace, the waist and skirt being trimmed with broad, pale-blue satin ribbon, fashioned into big, flat bows; a Paris gown of the latest *mode*, which suited her admirably. It was rather high in the neck, and all the jewellery she wore was a single brooch.

He also looked smart in his well-cut dinner jacket, with a light grey waistcoat and black tie; and as they sat opposite each other they chatted merrily. She had composed herself, and was now bearing herself very bravely.

It was, however, a relief to her when, just as they had finished dessert, Jenner entered, saying:

"Captain Martin is in the study, m'lord."

"Oh, yes!" exclaimed the great statesman, rising at once. Then, turning to Jean, he said: "You'll excuse me, dearest, won't you? I must get Martin off. I've finished. Have you?"

"Yes, dear," was her reply. "You go. I'm just going to see Enid for a little while."

"After I've got Martin off I shall go along to Polivin's. I'm sorry to leave you this evening. But you won't mind, dear, will you?"

"Not at all," was her prompt reply. "I know it is a duty."

"I shall certainly not be back till one or two o'clock. They are a very late lot—the men who go there," he remarked.

"I shall go to bed, so don't hurry, dear."

"Good night, then," he said, crossing to her and bending till he touched her lips with his. Then he went along to the study, where the King's Messenger was waiting.

"Halloa, Martin!" exclaimed his lordship, cheerily. "You're up to time—you always are. You're a marvel of punctuality."

"I have to be, constantly catching trains, as I am," laughed the nonchalant traveller, as he unlocked his despatch-box and took the seven big sealed letters from the Foreign Secretary's hand.

Then he scribbled a receipt for them, packed them in a little steel box, and carefully locked it with the tiny key upon his chain. That box often contained secrets which, if divulged, would set Europe aflame.

"Don't forget my camera next time you come over," Bracondale urged.

"And tell Sir Henry that if Bartlett is back from Persia I would like him to run over and report to me."

"I won't forget," was Martin's reply; and then, with a word of farewell, he took up his precious despatch-box and left the room.

The evening was dark and oppressive, with black clouds threatening thunder. Those hours passed very slowly.

Jean tried to read, but was unable. Then she went to the big *salon* and, seating herself at the grand piano, played snatches of Grand Opera. But she was too anxious, too impatient for midnight to come and end all the suspense.

Miss Oliver joined her, as usual, about ten o'clock for half an hour's chat. But the presence of the governess irritated her, and she was glad when she retired. She wondered whether Enid had told her anything. The child's chatter had, indeed, been extremely unfortunate.

Eleven o'clock!

She sat in her boudoir trying to occupy her mind by writing a letter, but she could not. She had to go through the terrible ordeal of seeing that man again.

At one moment she felt impelled to confess all to Bracondale, yet at the next she thought of his honour, and of the child. No, at all hazards, at all costs, even if it cost her her life, she must preserve her secret.

For wealth or for position she cared nothing—only for Bracondale's love.

The little clock struck the quarter. It wanted fifteen minutes to midnight.

With knit brows she rose quickly. The whole household had now retired; all was silence, and she was alone. Outside Ralph was no doubt watching for the light in the little *salon*.

She ascended the thickly-carpeted stairs noiselessly, and from the safe in her room took the square morocco box. Then, assuring herself that no servant could be watching, she carried it down to the little *salon* and, switching on the light, placed the box upon a small Louis Quinze table in the centre of the room.

It was a prettily-furnished apartment, with genuine old Louis Quinze furniture. In a corner was a large palm, and upon a side-table a great vase of fresh flowers. The gilt furniture shone beneath the bright light, and the whole had an effect of artistic brilliancy and daintiness.

She crossed to the drawn curtains of daffodil plush and, placing her hand within, undid the latch of the long window which led out upon the balcony and pushed it open slightly. Then, recrossing the room, she stood near the door, waiting.

There was still time before he was due to enter there and give her the letter in return for the pearls.

Of what use was it to wait there? So she switched off the light in case Bracondale should return and wonder, and passed into the adjoining room What if Bracondale came back before the exchange were effected?

She stood holding her breath, listening in eager anxiety.

Suddenly the telephone-bell rang in the study, and in order that Jenner might not hear it and descend to answer it, she hurried to the instrument herself.

It was a call from the British Embassy in Paris. One of the secretaries spoke to her, asking whether his Excellency the Ambassador might speak to his lordship upon an important matter.

"Lord Bracondale is not in. I am Lady Bracondale," she replied.

"When do you expect Lord Bracondale back?" the voice inquired.

"Soon after twelve. Will you ring up again? Tell Sir Charles that I will at once tell my husband when he returns," she said, and then rang off.

Meanwhile a dark figure, which had stealthily crept along the road, entered the gate and stole noiselessly over the grass to the verandah.

The man had been watching the house for an hour past, and, as though with sudden resolution, he made up his mind to enter.

At first he seemed fearful of discovery. Indeed, for a full half-hour had he lurked motionless beneath a tree, waiting, and, though there was complete silence in that still, oppressive night, yet he appeared to hesitate.

All the rooms on the ground floor were in darkness save for the study, the curtains of which were only half-closed. Therefore, as he approached the house, he saw Lady Bracondale alone, speaking into the telephone.

Suddenly, with an agile movement, he scaled the verandah, and a few seconds later, without making a sound, he stood before the window against the entrance porch—the window of the little *salon* which Jean had indicated where the pearls would be. His movements betrayed that he was an expert at moving without making a sound.

Bending, the dark figure, still moving stealthily, crept up to the long window upon which there suddenly flashed a small zone of white light from an electric pocket-lamp, revealing the fact that, though the heavy curtain was drawn, the window was ajar.

For a few seconds the man listened. Then, having reassured himself that there was no one in the room, he slowly pushed back the curtain and peered into the darkness.

Suddenly he heard a footstep and, dropping the curtain instantly, stood in the darkness, quite motionless.

Somebody entered the room, switched on the light, crossed to the centre of the apartment, stood there for a few seconds, and then, receding, switched off the light again and closed the door.

The intruder stood in the room behind the curtain without moving a muscle.

He could hear sounds of footsteps within the house.

He had closed the long glass door when he had entered, and now stood concealed behind the yellow plush curtain.

Suddenly he heard the piano being played—a song from "La Bohême." He stood listening, for he was always fond of music. As he halted there the sweet perfume of the flowers greeted his nostrils, and he murmured some low words beneath his breath.

His hand sought his jacket pocket, and when he withdrew it he had in his grasp a serviceable-looking revolver. He inhaled a long deep breath, for he was desperate.

At last he summoned courage, and again drew back the curtain very slowly. All was darkness within until he switched on his pocket-lamp and slowly examined the place.

The light fell upon the table whereon stood the jewel-case, and he walked straight to it and opened it.

The moment his eyes fell upon the magnificent string of pearls he stood for a second as though in hesitation.

Then swiftly he took them up, and with a glance at them thrust his prize into his jacket pocket.

It was the work of an instant.

He reclosed the lid. It snapped and startled him.

Next moment his light was switched off and he disappeared.

A second later, however, Jean turned the handle of the door, entered the room, and again switched on the light.

The place became flooded with electricity, and she stood a pale, erect figure, staring at the clock, which was just chiming the hour of midnight.

XXVIII

The Closed Box

Hardly had the sound of the silvery bells died away when a second figure scaled the balcony, and, seeing the light over the top of the curtain, as arranged, he placed his hand upon the long glass door and slowly opened it.

He drew aside the curtain slightly to ascertain if Jean were there awaiting him, and, seeing her, he entered boldly.

Ralph was dressed just as he had been in the morning, only he wore yellow lisle-thread gloves, so as to conceal his finger-prints, which, alas! were too well known to the police.

Husband and wife faced each other, in ignorance that an intruder stood concealed behind that curtain within two or three feet of them.

The intruder had fixed his eyes upon Jean, and stood staring at her as though fascinated by her amazing beauty.

"At last, Ralph!" she gasped. "I—I thought perhaps you would not come—that you would think the risk too great."

"Bah! What risk?" he asked. "Even if I were discovered, Bracondale could easily be satisfied that we are husband and wife."

She shrank back at those words.

"The child saw you with me this morning and told her father."

"Awkward. What did you say?"

"I made an excuse. One which, I hope, satisfied him."

"Trust you, Jean, for a good excuse," he laughed brutally.

Then, with a glance at the jewel-case on the table, he added: "But if I were you I'd be very wary. I suppose I did wrong in meeting you openly as I did. I ought to have been more circumspect. But, my girl, we need not have necessity to meet again, need we?"

"I hope not—for my sake," was her reply, as she turned her pale face to his.

"If you play the game, I shall also do the same. So you needn't fear. Only I must have an address where to write to you."

"No," she protested. "You must not write. It will be far too dangerous. And, besides, you made me a promise that if I gave you those," and she glanced at the table, "you would give me back my letter, and go away, never to see me again."

He regarded her in silence for a few moments, a sinister smile playing about his mobile lips. But he made no reply.

"Ah, Ralph," she went on, "I—I can't somehow trust you. When you have spent this money you will come back again. I know you will. Ah! you do not know all that this means to me."

"Well, doesn't it mean a lot to me—eh?"

"But I am a woman."

"You have money, while I'm without a sou. You surely can't blame me for getting a bit to go on with!" he exclaimed. "Is anybody about?"

"No. Bracondale has not yet returned, and all the servants are in bed."

"By Jove! This is a pretty house of yours, Jean!" he remarked, gazing around. He had not removed his hat. "You ought to consider yourself deuced lucky. While I've been having all my ups and downs, you've been living the life of a lady. When I saw you in your car at Havre I couldn't believe it. But to see you again really did my eyesight good."

"And benefited your pocket," she added bitterly.

He grinned. His nonchalant air irritated her. He was just the same as he had been in those days of their poverty, even though he now wore the clothes of a gentleman.

"Well," he said at last, "I've been thinking things over this evening. You can't expect me, Jean, to accept a lump payment for my silence, can you? If you had a respectable sum which you could hand over so that my wants would, in future, be provided for, it would be different. I—"

"Your wants!" she interrupted in anger. "What are your wants? Money—money—money always! Ah, Ralph! I know you. You brought me to ruin once, and you will do so again. I know it!"

"Not unless you are a fool!" he replied roughly. "You want your letter back—which is only natural. For it you give me your pearls. It is not a gift. I take them. I find the window unlatched, and come in and help myself. To-morrow you will raise a hue and cry—but not before noon, as I shall then be nearing old Uncle Karl, in Amsterdam. Bracondale will be furious, the *Sûreté* will fuss and be busy, and you will be in picturesque tears over your loss. Bracondale will tell you not to worry, and promptly make you another present—perhaps a better one—and then all will be well."

"But you said you would leave Europe," she replied anxiously.

"So I shall."

"But—" and she hesitated.

"Ah! I see you don't trust me."

"I trusted you—once—Ralph. Do you recollect how brutally you treated me—eh?" she asked, in deep reproach.

"I recollect that, because of you, I quarrelled with Adolphe. He loved you, and now he's in prison, and serve him right, the idiot!"

The concealed intruder was watching them between the wall and the curtain, yet hardly daring to breathe for fear of discovery. He had the pearls in his pocket, and as the glass door was closed he was unable to reopen it and escape, lest he should reveal himself.

He heard Ansell's words, and understood the situation. If the lid of the jewel-case were raised the thief would be discovered, and the alarm given.

Those were moments of breathless peril.

"Adolphe protected me from your violence," she replied, simply. "He was my friend, but he did not love me, because I loved you—only you!"

"And you care for me no longer?"

"The fire of my love for you burned itself out on that tragic night," she replied.

"How very poetic," he sneered. "Is it your habit to talk to Bracondale like that?"

She bit her lip. Mention of Bracondale's name caused a flood of great bitterness to overwhelm her.

"I did not expect, when you came here, that you would insult me in addition to blackmailing me."

"Blackmail, you call it—eh?"

"What else is it?"

"A simple purchase, my girl. I have a letter, and you wish to buy it. The transaction is surely a fair one! Besides, if you do not wish to buy my silence, it is quite immaterial to me. I shall soon find another purchaser in Bracondale."

"He won't believe you."

"He has only to have a search made of the marriage register. Perhaps you don't remember the date. I do."

"And I, worse luck! Ah, how grossly you deceived me!" she exclaimed bitterly. "I thought I married a gentleman, only, alas! to discover that I had a notorious thief as husband."

"You expected too much. You thought you had become a lady, and were disappointed when you found that you were not. Yes—I suppose

WILLIAM LE QUEUX

when I told you the truth, it must have been a bit of a jag for you. That fool, Adolphe, wanted me to keep the truth from you. But what was the use?"

"Yes," she sighed. "You were at least frank—perhaps the only occasion upon which you ever told me the truth."

"The truth is generally unwelcome," he laughed. "Lies are always pleasant."

"To the liar."

"I'm afraid you'll have, in future, to lie to Bracondale."

"I shall use my own discretion," she responded. "Perhaps I shall confess."

"And if so, what then?"

"I shall tell him that you entered here and stole my pearls."

"How very generous that would be," he laughed angrily. "And I wonder what Bracondale would think of you if you endeavoured to send your own husband to prison—eh?"

"Ah, you will drive me to desperation!" she cried, her dark eyes glaring at him angrily. "Give me the letter and go—go! Bracondale may be back now—at any moment!"

"I assure you I fear neither Bracondale nor you—nor even the result of your confession. And I feel quite loath to-night to leave you; you look so extremely charming in that pretty gown."

"Don't be foolish. At least have some consideration for me—for my future."

"It is my own future I am thinking of," he declared harshly. "Your future is assured, so long as you play the game with Bracondale. If you act indiscreetly, and give way to silly moods, then you will only have yourself to blame for your ruin. Besides," he added, with his lip curling slightly, "you have the child to consider. What's her name?"

"Her name is of no matter to you," was Jean's hot response. "She is mine, not yours."

"I'm rather glad of that," he responded. "But I don't think this is really a fit opportunity to waste time in mutual recrimination."

"No. Go, I tell you. If you remain longer, it will be dangerous—dangerous for us both."

He looked at the clock, and then his gaze wandered to the closed jewel-case upon the Louis Quinze table. The small room, closed as it was, was filled with the perfume of the great bunch of flowers in the long Chinese vase—a perfume that seemed almost overpowering.

"But I tell you I see no danger," was his careless reply, for it seemed his object to taunt her. He had already hinted at a continued tax upon her resources if she desired him to keep his lips sealed, and she, on her part, realising his true character, clearly foresaw that all her efforts could have but one result. To satisfy his demands would be impossible.

A shadow had fallen upon her eventful life, one that would never again be lifted.

"Will you have no pity for me?" she implored. "Have you come here with the express intent of goading me to madness?"

"No—simply in order to have a straight talk with you—a chat between husband and wife."

"Well, we have had it. Take the pearls and go. Get clear away before you are discovered. Bracondale may now be back at any moment," she added in fear of his sudden return.

"I'm in no great hurry, I assure you," was his reply, as he seated himself upon the arm of a chair.

"Give me the letter, Ralph. Do—if you please."

He laughed in her face, his hands stuck in his jacket pockets, as was his habit.

She looked around her with an expression of terror and despair. She listened, for she fancied she heard a footstep.

They both listened, but no other sound could be distinguished.

"A false alarm," remarked the man. Then, suddenly rising from where he was seated, he placed his hand in his breast pocket, and, drawing out his wallet, took therefrom the well-worn letter.

"Well," he said reluctantly, "here you are. I suppose you'd better have it. And now you can't say but what I'm not generous—can you?"

Jean almost snatched the precious note from his fingers, glanced at it to reassure herself that she was not being tricked, and then, striking a match which she took from a side-table, she applied it to one corner of the farewell letter, and held it till only a black piece of crackling tinder remained.

"Now you are satisfied, I hope," he remarked in a harsh voice.

"Yes. Take the pearls. Take the box, and go," she urged quickly, placing her hand upon his arm to emphasise her words, and pushing him across to the table where stood the big morocco case.

"All right," he laughed. "Let's look at these wonderful pearls of yours. I wonder how much they are worth?"

He halted at the table, fingering the spring-fastening of the case, and at last raised the lid.

It was empty!

"You vixen! You infernal woman!" he cried, turning upon her, white with anger, and with clenched fists. "You've played a slick trick on me—you've had me—and now—by gad! I—I'll have my revenge!"

XXIX

Deadly Peril

Ralph Ansell made a sudden dash at his wife, gripping her by the throat with his gloved hands.

She staggered to the table, and he bent her backwards across it. His evil face was distorted by a look of murderous hatred, his big eyes started from their sockets in his wild frenzy of anger.

"Where are those pearls?" he demanded. "Speak! Give them to me at once, or, by Heaven, I'll strangle you!"

"I—I don't know," she managed to gasp. "They were in there. I—I—I thought they were there."

"You liar! You got the letter and burned it, well knowing that the jewels were not in the box! Where are they?" he demanded, tightening his grip upon her throat and shaking her roughly. "Speak, woman—speak! Tell me where they are!"

Jean struggled frantically to free herself from his murderous grip. He was throttling her.

"I—I don't know—where—they are!" she protested, with great difficulty.

"You do! You've kept them!" he hissed between his teeth, for he was in a fury of fierce anger at having been so deceived. "It's no use lying. I mean to have them, or go straight to this man Bracondale."

"I'm telling the truth!" protested the unhappy woman. "They were there half an hour ago. I put them there."

"Bah! Don't tell me that! They could not have gone without hands. No, you've worked a real slick trick! And I was fool enough to trust you! Come, hand them over at once—if you don't want Bracondale to know," and he again forced her farther back over the table. "He'll be here in a minute. What a nice scene for him—eh? Come, where are those pearls?"

"I've told you I don't know. It's the truth, Ralph, I swear it!" she cried, in wild despair. "Somebody must have stolen them!"

"You liar!" he cried, his face white with evil passion. "Do you dare to tell me that? Do you think I'm a fool to believe such a story? Stolen! Of course they're not stolen. You've hidden them. Yes," he added, "you've been devilish clever to get that letter out of me, and burn it before my eyes—haven't you—eh? But you shall pay for it!" he cried, between his teeth, as his strong hands compressed her throat until she went scarlet and her wild, glaring eyes started from her head.

She tried to cry out—tried to shriek and raise an alarm, for she knew her life was in danger. But she could utter no sound beyond a low gurgle.

"You refuse to give me the pearls—eh?" he said, his dark brows knit, and murder in his piercing eyes. "You think to trick me—your husband! By gad! You shall pay for this! Tell me where they are. This is your last moment. You shall die—die—curse you!" And his grip tightened upon her thin, white throat—the grip of a murderer.

Jean, unable to move, unable to cry out, felt herself fainting, when next second she was startled by a sharp pistol shot.

"Ah!" gasped her assailant, releasing his hold instantly and clapping his right hand to his back.

The shot had been fired from behind.

"Ah!" cried the wounded man in wild despair. "I—why, I—"

Then he reeled completely round and fell backward upon the carpet—inert—dead!

At the same instant Jean, staggered by the suddenness of it all, was confronted by a ragged, unkempt, hatless man in a striped jacket some sizes too big for him. Around his neck was a dirty scarf in lieu of a collar, and his dark hair was curly and ruffled.

She saw the man emerge from the curtain, and started back in increased alarm.

"Madame!" cried the newcomer, "it is me! Don't you know me?"

She stood rooted to the spot.

"Adolphe!" she gasped, staring at him.

"Yes, madame. I came here, not knowing that this was your *château*," he explained, in a low whisper. "I found the window open just before that man arrived. I came in and took your pearls. Here they are!"

And he drew them from the pocket of his shabby jacket and handed them back to her.

"Where—where did you come from? You have saved my life," she faltered in blank amazement.

"I came out of prison nine months ago," was his reply. "They brought me to Paris, but I could find no work, so I tramped to Havre, hoping to get a job at the docks, or to work my passage to New York. But all to no avail, so I—I had, alas! to return to my old profession. And the first house I enter I find, to my dismay, is yours!"

"You heard us talking?" she asked quickly.

"I heard everything—and I understood everything," was the quick reply. "That man," he went on, "robbed me and gave me deliberately into the hands of the police. I swore to be avenged, and I have killed him—as he deserves. He was an assassin, and I am his executioner!"

"But the servants will be alarmed by the shot!" she gasped suddenly. "There is no time to lose. You must want money. I shall send you some to the *Poste Restante* in Havre—to-morrow. Now go—or you may be discovered."

"But how will you explain?" he asked hurriedly. "Ah, madame, through those long, dreary years at Devil's Island I have thought of you, and wondered—and wondered what had become of you. I am so glad to know that you are rich and happy, as you assuredly deserve."

She sighed, for a flood of memories came over her.

"Yes, Adolphe, I am greatly indebted to you. Twice you have saved me from that man's violence. Ah, I shall not forget."

"But, madame, think of yourself! If he comes—if the servants come—how can you explain his body in your room? Let me think!"

Already Jean fancied she heard sounds of someone moving in the house, and of subdued and frightened voices.

Yes, the servants had been alarmed, and were searching from room to room! Not an instant was to be lost.

"I have an idea!" exclaimed "The Eel." "Here, take this, madame," and he held out his revolver to her with both hands.

But she shrank back.

"Take it—take it, I beg of you," he implored.

She obeyed, moving like one in a dream.

Swiftly he took up the pearls and, bending, placed them in the dead man's pocket. Then, having done this, he said:

"Your explanation is quite a simple one. You came in here unexpectedly, and found the man—a perfect stranger to you, and a burglar, evidently, from the fact that he wore gloves—taking your pearls from their case. You demanded them back, but he turned upon you with a revolver. There was a struggle for the weapon. You twisted his hand back, and in the fight it went off. And he fell dead. Keep cool. That is your story."

"But I—"

"That is the only story, madame," he said firmly. "It is a lie, I admit—but a white lie—the only explanation you can give, if you would still preserve your secret."

Footsteps sounded out in the hall, and therefore there was not a second to waste.

The thief grasped her thin, white hand and, bending devotedly, kissed it.

"Adieu, madame. May Heaven assist and preserve you in future!" he whispered, and next moment he had disappeared behind the curtain and dropped over the verandah.

XXX

The White Lie

For a few seconds Jean stood motionless, staring at the lifeless body of her husband, who lay with face upturned, the evil eyes closed, the hands listless by his sides.

His head was towards the window, close to a small gilt settee, his feet towards the door.

She stood with her eyes full of horror, fixed upon the white, dead face.

In that dread moment a veritable lifetime of despair swept through her fevered brain.

The servants, with hushed, terrified voices, were searching the rooms on the ground floor. She could hear Miss Oliver speaking.

Their footsteps sounded on the big, tiled hall outside the door. What if Adolphe were captured leaving the premises?

She held her breath. All her self-possession was required now, for she also recognised Bracondale's voice. He had returned!

Was silence judicious in those circumstances? She decided it was not. Therefore she gave vent to a loud scream—a scream which told them where she was.

In a moment they all burst into the room—Bracondale in his evening clothes, Miss Oliver in her dressing-gown, and the two footmen, who had hastily dressed, one of them without his coat.

The servants, seeing a man lying upon the carpet, halted upon the threshold, but Bracondale dashed forward to his wife, who stood with her hands to her brow in frantic terror. She was, he saw, on the verge of fainting. Therefore he took her in his arms and hastily inquired what had occurred.

"He's dead—I believe!" gasped one of the footmen, in French.

"Jean! What has happened?" Bracondale demanded, in amazement. "Tell me, dearest."

But she was too agitated to speak. She only clung to him and, burying her face upon his shoulder, sobbed hysterically, while Miss Oliver rushed away for a smelling-bottle.

"Who is this man?" Bracondale asked in a hard voice. "What is the matter? The servants heard a shot just after I came in. They came to me in the study—but I had heard nothing."

She raised her wild eyes to his, and then glanced round the pretty apartment. Her gaze fell upon Ralph Ansell's dead face, and she shuddered and shrank back. Her mouth was twitching. She was hysterical, and could say nothing.

"Tell me, Jean. What does all this mean?" asked Bracondale, very quietly, considering the circumstances.

"Ah! no dear!" she cried. "Don't ask me—don't ask me! I—I killed him!"

"Killed him!" echoed her husband blankly. "What do you mean? You are not yourself, dearest."

She looked at the servants meaningly.

"Will you leave us alone?" Bracondale said, turning to them just as Miss Oliver returned with the bottle of smelling-salts.

They all left the room, including the governess, husband and wife being left with the dead man.

"Tell me, darling, what has occurred?" asked Bracondale in a soft, sympathetic voice, endeavouring to calm her.

For a long time she refused to answer. She could not bring herself to speak a lie to him, not even a white lie! The night had been so full of horror and tragedy that she was beside herself. She wondered whether it were not, after all, a horrible dream.

Yet no! It was true. Ralph Ansell was dead. He had carried his secret with him to the grave, and she was free—free! She was really Lady Bracondale, the mother of Bracondale's child!

She had been at the point of confessing. But no. Bracondale must know nothing.

"You killed this man, Jean?" her husband was saying in a low, intense voice. "Why?"

"I—I—he attacked me, and I—"

She did not conclude her sentence.

"Why, your neck is all black and blue!" Bracondale said, noticing it for the first time.

"He tried to strangle me, then he intended to shoot me," she said hysterically. "We struggled—and—and it—it went off!"

"But who is he?"

"How can I tell?" she asked frantically. "I came in here unexpectedly, and saw him with my pearls in his hand. I—I demanded them back, but he refused. I threatened to shout and alarm the servants, but he sprang upon me and tried to strangle me!"

Bracondale, for the first time, noticed that the morocco jewel-case stood open on the table.

"He must have got them from your bedroom!" he exclaimed; and then, his quick eye catching sight of the tinder of the burnt letter in the fender of the stove, he bent, picked it up, and remarked·

"He seems to have also burnt something. I wonder what it was?"

His lordship crossed the carpet and stood looking upon the dead face.

"Who is he? Do you know, Jean?" he inquired in a serious, intense tone.

"I—I have no idea."

"The police will establish his identity, no doubt. I will telephone for them," he said. "But where are the pearls now?"

"In his pocket, I expect," she said.

Bracondale bent and hastily felt the outside of one of the dead man's pockets. But they were not there.

He felt the other, and, discovering them, drew out the beautiful string, and replaced it in its box.

"An expert thief, I should say, from his dress," remarked Bracondale. "He wears gloves, too—just as all modern burglars do."

"He nearly strangled me," Jean declared weakly.

"It was fortunate that the revolver went off during the struggle, or he might have killed you, dearest. Ah! you are a brave girl. The papers will, no doubt, be full of this!"

"Ah! no!" she implored. "Do not let us have any publicity. I—I hate to think that I have killed a man—even though he be an armed burglar."

"But the law permits you to take life in self-defence, therefore do not trouble yourself over it. He would, no doubt, have killed you with little compunction, rather than forego carrying away his prize."

"Yes—but—"

"No," urged her husband kindly. "Do not let us discuss it further. Come with me to your room. I will telephone to the police in Havre, and leave the rest to them. Come, dearest, you have had a terrible experience, and you must rest quietly now—and recover."

He linked his arms in hers tenderly, and conducted her slowly from the presence of that white, dead countenance she knew, alas! too well.

After taking her to her room and leaving her in the hands of Bates, her maid, he descended, and from the study telephoned to the Chef de la Sûreté at Havre.

Then, receiving a reply that three agents of police would at once be dispatched on cycles, he went upstairs to where she was seated in a big arm-chair, pale and trembling, still suffering from the shock.

It was only when they were again alone, and he took her in his strong arms, kissed her fondly upon the lips, and softly reassured her, that she could summon courage to speak.

"You do love me, Jack?" she asked with intense, eager eyes. "You do really love me? Tell me."

"Why, of course I do, dearest," he declared. "Why do you ask? Have you not seen that I love you?"

"I—I—yes, I know. But I thought perhaps you—"

She hesitated. She was wondering if he suspected anything. But no. She was free! Adolphe, ever sympathetic and ever faithful to her interests, had saved her. Yet, poor fellow, he was only a thief!

She swallowed the big lump that arose in her throat, and then, throwing her long, white arms wildly about her husband's neck, she kissed him with a fierce, intense passion, bursting into tears—tears of joy.

True, she had told a white lie, but in the circumstances, could you, my reader, blame her?

THE END

A Note About the Author

William Le Queux (1864–1927) was an Anglo-French journalist, novelist, and radio broadcaster. Born in London to a French father and English mother, Le Queux studied art in Paris and embarked on a walking tour of Europe before finding work as a reporter for various French newspapers. Towards the end of the 1880s, he returned to London where he edited *Gossip* and *Piccadilly* before being hired as a reporter for *The Globe* in 1891. After several unhappy years, he left journalism to pursue his creative interests. Le Queux made a name for himself as a leading writer of popular fiction with such espionage thrillers as *The Great War in England in 1897* (1894) and *The Invasion of 1910* (1906). In addition to his writing, Le Queux was a notable pioneer of early aviation and radio communication, interests he maintained while publishing around 150 novels over his decades long career.

A Note from the Publisher

Spanning many genres, from non-fiction essays to literature classics to children's books and lyric poetry, Mint Edition books showcase the master works of our time in a modern new package. The text is freshly typeset, is clean and easy to read, and features a new note about the author in each volume. Many books also include exclusive new introductory material. Every book boasts a striking new cover, which makes it as appropriate for collecting as it is for gift giving. Mint Edition books are only printed when a reader orders them, so natural resources are not wasted. We're proud that our books are never manufactured in excess and exist only in the exact quantity they need to be read and enjoyed.

bookfinity™

Discover more of your favorite classics with Bookfinity™.

- Track your reading with custom book lists.
- Get great book recommendations for your personalized Reader Type.
- Add reviews for your favorite books.
- AND MUCH MORE!

Visit **bookfinity.com** and take the fun Reader Type quiz to get started.

Enjoy our classic and modern companion pairings!

Classic & Modern